EVIL CORRUPTION ZEN & MARIO'S HAPPILY EVER AFTER

By

Zaneta Cannon Robinson

Copyright © 2023 – Zaneta Cannon Robinson

All rights reserved. This book or any portion thereof may not be reproduced or used in any manner whatsoever without the express written permission of the publisher except for the use of brief quotations in a book review.

ACKNOWLEGMENTS

I would like to thank all my readers and family for their continuous support. My writing journey has been amazing . I have experienced so much with a pen and a pad ; I had no idea my mind could expand so courageously , I love to hear feedback from my readers , I get great pleasure from conversing with someone who has read my stories . This book is the 2nd novel to Corruption of a Woman's Mind . Please  take time to read them both ,
from Z.Z. THAT AUTHOR

About the Author

Zaneta Cannon Robinson better known as Z.Z. was born in Greenville South Carolina on February 16th. Along beside her Author title she is an entrepreneur, mother, wife, and grandmother. She works with artistic adults and does charity events and teaches praise dance. She loves spending time with her family, holidays especially. This is Zaneta's fifth publish book, she has gained the name Z.Z. that Author from her fans. Zaneta recently became a grandmother for the second time to a healthy baby boy, Zacchai Ralph Cannon who she loves to cuddle and spoil. Zaneta has a great liking for, cooking, writing, dancing, traveling, casino gambling, party planning, and making gift baskets. She is well rounded and full of life and excitement, Zaneta loves to meet people and fellowship, she's the life of any party. Zaneta will continue to strive for excellence and bring her fans more urban thrillers.

TABLE OF CONTENTS

CHAPTER 1 1
   THE AFTERMATH 1
CHAPTER 2 7
   I DON'T TRUST EM" 7
CHAPTER 3 16
   DON'T PLAY WITH US 16
CHAPTER 4 24
   WE ALL COCKY 24
CHAPTER 5 29
   DEAL GONE BAD 29
CHAPTER 6 34
   MONEY IS THE MOTIVE 34
CHAPTER 7 42
   JAMAICAN SOIL 42
CHAPTER 8 50
   YOU SHOULD BE ASHAMED 50
CHAPTER 9 57
   IT'S JUST BUSINESS 57
CHAPTER 10 65
   THEY STARTED IT 65
CHAPTER 11 78
   WE'RE BACK 78
CHAPTER 12 84
   MAKING ENEMIES 84
CHAPTER 13 98
   SWITCHING SIDES 98
CHAPTER 14 107
   CREATING BEEF 107
CHAPTER 15 116

BEING GULLIBLE	116
CHAPTER 16	125
THE JAMAICAN MONSTER	125
CHAPTER 17	136
ARE YOU SERIOUS?	136
CHAPTER 18	144
FUGITIVE ACTION	144
CHAPTER 19	153
KIDNAPPED	153
CHAPTER 20	162
MIND GAMES	162
CHAPTER 21	170
HOUSTON BOUND	170
CHAPTER 22	182
NO REMORSE	182
CHAPTER 23	190
THE BRAWL	190
CHAPTER 24	199
YOU'RE COMING WITH US	199
CHAPTER 25	207
DON'T GET TOO COMFORTABLE	207
CHAPTER 26	218
HANDLED	218
CHAPTER 27	231
YOU'VE CROSSED THE WRONG ONE	231
CHAPTER 28	240
ZEN'S & MARIO'S HAPPILY EVER AFTER	240

CHAPTER 1

THE AFTERMATH

Mario was released from prison, and he and Zen reunited as a married couple. Zen secretly saw Mario while he was incarcerated. She never went through with the divorce and hid that from her family and friends. Zen's divorce party was a front. She only participated in the party to satisfy others, and that was also a chance for her to vent and bash Mario. Zen was fed up, but never had any intentions to divorce Mario. Divorce is what her friends strongly forced her way. Zen felt a small bit of shame because she and Mario went through so much behind his habitual infidelity. Mario was excessive with errors and disrespect towards his marriage. Zen finally took some ownership of her faults in their marriage; she was no angel. She, too, was heavy with the nightlife and indulged with a nigga or two. Zen displayed a team of side niggas, that knew how to stay in their lane.

Zen used and abused niggas for some good head and deep penetration. Zen tried her hardest to get serious about another nigga, but no one was built like Mario. From the money to the sex, Zen came up short fucking with other niggas. Zen would say: *I rather deal with the devil I know than the devil I don't know!* Zen and Mario were back together in full swing of things. They did lots of damage control, and the two love birds saved their sour marriage by journaling with one another and multiple sessions of marriage counseling. Zen and Mario prayed daily for God to strengthen their marriage and put the fire back into their hearts. The bulk of the turbulence came from letting outsiders into their business. The couple was blinded by the time and effort people put into sabotaging their happiness. Mario and Zen vowed to create their own fame by starting over and killing the past that destroyed their happiness. They both lived a wild and sinful life, tearing each other down tremendously. Tick for tack was the game they played. Much infidelity, drugs, and lies were also a constant play in their lives.

Fighting became a norm in the neighborhood for the two. How they made it together, no one knew. No one understood Zen and Mario. They were the strangest couple, but their love was so real. Whenever they were good, it was awesome, but baby, when it was bad, it was holy hell for whoever was around. Cookie and Lucious from Empire were the off-screen Zen and Mario. The bounce-back was the greatest. Zen and Mario found love again. This time they were on their grown-up shit, and it showed. Zen and Mario buried their past and focused on money and family. Life is too short for the bull shit; they were going to make the rest of their life the best of their life. Zen knew her associates, and ain't shit friends had experienced way more drama than she and Mario. If Zen wanted to get trifling, she could air out loads of dirty laundry and create some ugly situations. Low budget and leach is the best way to describe most of the men Zen's associates fucked with. Not justifying Mario's wrong, but he was a saint compared to most men. He always provided and never left Zen in a financial crisis.

Zen and Mario owned several rental properties in the upstate of South Carolina. Flipping housing became a newfound hustle for the two. Mario hired a few Jamaicans,

Al and Face, as contractors to demo and rehab most of the properties. Al and Face became very attached to Mario. The two men road Mario's coat tail a little too close for Zen's liking. They never took payment from Mario for the labor they completed on the properties. While Al and Face worked on the properties, they were secretly moving the weight of marijuana from different property locations. They dug holes throughout the yards and buried large amounts of marijuana underground. A Home Depot utility van would come to deliver material every hour, but that was only a deco. The driver picked up the weed product and dropped it off to the buyer. Uber Eats, and Door Dash drivers were also on their payroll moving weed products. The routine was the same. Al and Face were making beau coups of money. Face's brother Heavy lived in Jamaica but kept Al and Face with re-up on the weed. That expanded their clientele, and business was booming for the two.

"Bae, what's the deal with them, Bob Marley look a-likes not taking payment for the construction work they've completed?" Zen asked Mario.

"Chill out, love. They're just doing a kind act that was Mario's defense."

"Well, I don't trust them bamboo-smoking mutha fuckas. I'm going to have my girl Ashley have them both checked out. I sense evil spirits when they're around," Zen spoke with a serious tone.

"No need for you to start your vigilante shit Zen. Let them live bae their good men." Mario continued to advocate for Al and Face, but by Zen's facial expression, he knew she wasn't feeling it.

Zen was still a gun-slanging bad bitch that niggas and bitches feared. Her alliance with Victor Lee and Pound Puppy would forever have her shielded. Zen and her crew split up because Zen found out that mutha fuckas wasn't solid as they portrayed to be. Zen is an 'I don't give a fuck' type of bitch. She continued to excel in life and eighty-sixed her once-sister squad. Zen was unbothered by being blocked on social media. She gave zero fucks about who didn't like her or talked about her. God removed those people from her life for a reason. Conversations were being held that Zen couldn't participate in to defend herself. Mutha fuckas always play the victim and sugarcoat the idiotic reason for falling out with Zen. Zen became tired of overplaying her loyalty, so she said fuck it and focused on money and her family. The love was one-sided and not genuine from the gate. The negative energy was just too damn much, so she cut ties with most of the squad, even her brother ZA. ZA was so grimy he robbed and shot Toulip three times in the head, leaving him for dead. Everybody knew how Zen got down when it came to Toulip.

Toulip hit a lousy luck patch, and shit continued to storm on him. One year ago, Toulip lost his daughter Nadaja, in a tragic accident that devastated the entire family. That alone made Toulip off balance and on edge. Toulip's mental state was holding on by a thread. The state trumped some bogus charges on Toulip, which added more chaos to his life, landing him a five-year bid in a level two state prison. With the help of his baby mama and family, Toulip did a tremendous bounce back. Toulip held on to the love of his daughter Nadaja. She is his angel, a true testimony of a daddy's girl. Nadaja did not play about her dad; she was his twin, and their connection was perfect. Nadaja will always be remembered and loved. Flamin Hot Cheetos was the name Toulip gave her because she would fight and blaze heads like her big cousin Zen. Money and family remained Zen's motive, and that's what she did best, take care of her family and make money.

Zen decided to scoop Lady J and Sundae to give them the rundown about the Jamaicans. First, Zen filled them in on T-Baby's love fling. T-Baby was in Houston, Texas visiting her daughter and riding a young Texas bull. "Y'all, our girl has fallen in love with a local Houston rapper. That's why her ass hasn't returned home yet. T-Baby is loving that Texas dick she's receiving from her rapper boy toy. Zen explained that they talk on the phone about how his freak level is a ten. T-Baby feels like Stella because she got her groove back."

"She is all chipper and shit, loving her life on the other side of the map. The saying must be true. Everything is bigger in Texas," Sundae added as they shared a laugh.

"Ok bitch, you know those Jamaicans are crazy as hell. You need to have facts before you approach these niggas," Sundae said while popping her bubble gum. "I have a big hunch that they are trying to get my husband caught up in some shit. Mario is on probation, and I refuse to let my husband get trapped. Mario is being too damn nice; his kindness is being played for his weakness." Zen continued to elaborate. "So, what the fuck we gone do lil girl?" Lady J asked Zen.

"If these dread heads are making any left-handed moves, then we must apply pressure," Zen responded. The ladies rode around for hours, smoking and choking. They executed a plan to place hidden cameras on the properties that Al and Face were not scheduled to be at until next week. Zen was adamant that she would find something fishy.

Zen ended the day early with her girls. Zen did not want Mario to get suspicious. Mario monitored Zen's every move. If Zen farted at two o'clock, Mario knew about it. He had eyes everywhere. Mario greeted Zen at the door with a wet kiss. "Did you miss me, daddy?" Zen asked as she grabbed Mario's dick.

"Yes, I did, sweetness. I saw you and your combat soldiers looking for trouble earlier today," Mario said sarcastically

"No, babe, we just enjoyed a girl's day, we smoked all your weed, did a few TikTok's, and posted about our businesses on social media. Besides, we have retired from that life unless a mutha fucka crosses the line. Husband, you worry too damn much," Zen said as she playfully hit Mario.

"No, Zen, it's not that I just know my wife, you'll pull a hell Mary quick," Mario said, laughing. Zen unbuckled her husband's jeans and rubbed his dick until she felt that stretch. She then dropped to her knees, forcing all her saliva to the front of her mouth. Zen widened her mouth gap and began sucking his dick, taking it deep down her throat. Giving her husband what he liked was better than retail therapy for her. Being that Mario was about to start policing her daily activities. Zen knew how to shut him up with a dose of her knock-out medicine.

CHAPTER 2

I DON'T TRUST EM"

Zen and Mario were dropping off blueprints at their Pickle Tower property to Al and Face. It's called Pickle Tower because the condos are being built like towers with pickle green siding. The property has become a major attraction to the public. People enjoy seeing the green tower come together. Zen decided to keep it fun and display pickle shape shrub trees throughout the property. Mario named the street Green Avenue, and the property is in Greenville. What a story for the press and tourists, Zen and Mario often laughed about it. When Zen and Mario stepped on the property, Al held a female from behind, rubbing her ass and blowing on her neck. "Here's the rest of the prints Mario and I designed for the property, Zen said as she passed the prints to Al."

"Looks like y'all need something to do anyway. This is a mutha fuckan work sight, not Motel 6," Zen said with attitude. Al dismissed his lady friend, and after the lady turned around to walk off, Zen went ape shit. "Oh, hell nah, I know damn well you don't have this dirty face bitch on my property." It was Nicolette Childress, a thot that would not go away. Mario once participated in a fuck fling with the bitch, causing Zen to beat her ass more times than she has seen a doctor. "I'm sorry, Ms Zen. It will not happen again," Al said as he pushed the hell out of Nicolette, causing her to stumble and fall." Zen kicked her on the side of her face and was getting ready to shame her badly when Mario grabbed her, telling her to chill out. "I know you're not taking up for this whore, Mario. Zen was boiling. So, that's why you continue to campaign for these niggas. You're providing them with more than work, pussy is included in the deal, too, huh,?" Zen screamed out.

"I have nothing to do with that. I don't want you out here fighting and risk going to jail," Mario said. He was so disappointed in Al because he knew how much Zen hated Nicolette. "I met her on Plenty of Fish, and I knew she was a thot. I just needed her to show my man wiggle a lil pleasure; no disrespect to you Ms Zen. I sincerely apologize, and it will not happen again," Al spoke. Face managed to sneak his fuck buddy out the sliding doors without being seen. Face was in the back of one of the laundry rooms fucking this fat bitch, Stella Rammings. When Stella heard Zen's voice, she did not want any trouble with Zen. Stella knew Zen and her crew portrayed a deadly reputation, and she wanted no part in anything that involved them. Face covered his mouth because he couldn't stop laughing at Stella running her chunky ass out of the laundry room. Stella Barely made it through the sliding doors. Her clothing was getting snagged as she ran. Zen and Mario drove off and headed home for lunch with Star. Mario went into overdrive, explaining to Zen that that was a coincidence and he had no play in that move. When they made it to the stop sign, Stella was on the sidewalk, bent over, out of breath, half-dressed, and looking fat and hungry. That broke the silence with Zen. She, too, laughed at that horrible sight. Mario was making throw-up faces that caused Zen to laugh even harder.

Zen was now more eager to catch Al and Face in the act. She knew some sheisty shit was up with them. The next day Zen went by the Pickle Tower to view the camera. After Zen's thorough investigation, her intuitions about Al and Face were correct. She discovered they were not only hiding Marijuana, but they were using the property for prostitution and selling the Marijuana. She noticed Nicolette so many times on camera she lost count. Nicolette was coming after hours with a blanket, meeting men for sex. Marijuana was hidden underground throughout the property, inside orange Home Depot paint buckets. Pink flags were stapled to wooden stakes down in the ground for landmarks. Zen evaluated the other six properties; the same activities were on the camera footage with more traffic flow and double the weed activity. More pink flags were throughout the properties, meaning more weed was buried.

Zen took the information to Mario, and he looked dumbfounded. "Nigga get out your feelings. I told you these niggas were up to no good. They don't give two fucks about us," Zen stated angrily.

"I'm going to fuck them rope head niggas up," Mario said as he strapped up his pistols. Zen followed his lead as they headed for their jeep. They were on their way to Al and Face's condo when Zen was hit with a clever idea. "Hey, bae, why don't we rent a U-Haul, dig up all their weed, then place it in a secure location until the time is right? We can smoke good and push that shit in the streets since Murry and Bruce are always in the hood impersonating cops. I have the perfect job for them," Zen said, smiling. Murry and Bruce were Mario's go-to men for assignments like this. On the way to the U-Haul store, Zen and Mario went over the specifics of the plan. While en route, they picked up some local crackheads to help dig up the buckets. After they were finished digging, the overnight landscapers planted grass and trees where there was once dirt.

Early the next morning, Al and Face hit the property on Flowers Lane. As they were about to get down with their usual routine, they noticed the lawn covered up with beautiful grass and trees. The overnight landscapers were still working on the back side of the property. The landscapers pulled an all-nighter finishing up the properties. Just when Al was about to speak, a uniformed police officer came from the side of the house. "Good morning, gentlemen. My name is Murry. My partner, Bruce, and I will secure this property for a while until things get back on track."

"What the fuck you mean back on track? Please fill us in," Al asked with a raised eyebrow.

"It's been some strange activities going on late at night on this property and a few others. We strongly believe prostitution and the distribution of drugs are being solicited on several properties throughout the area. Bruce co-signed right after introducing himself."

"Who the fuck did this landscaping, and why is all this grass here," a mad Face asked.

"Hold on, sir. I was informed that you two were contractors and would proceed with your assigned work. Why in the world are you so hostile about some damn grass? Murry asked with a mug on his face. You must pipe the attitude down; the owners will be here shortly."

"I don't give two fucks about no damn owners." Face was about to blow up. Al suddenly pulls him to the back of the townhomes. The two were scrambling, trying to make sense of what the fuck was going on. "Are we being punked, bro? There is no way the police are here, and all our shit is underground. This must be a bad dream?" a confused Al asked.

"This shit has that slut Nicolette's name all over it," Face said. He was so mad he was slurring his words. "I told you to dismiss that thirsty ass bitch," Face screamed at Al in a rage. Soon as Al and Face proceed to hurry off to check on the other properties, Zen and Mario pull up. Mario got out of the car, walked over to the men, extended his hand, and reached for a brotherly hug. Neither one of them returned the friendly gesture. "What's good, fellas? You seem a bit salty anything you need to say, Mario, said firmly?"

"We feel blindsided with all the overnight changes. It's going to be hard as fuck working around the police this. Feels like jail, bro," Al said with a frown.

"I feel like I just stepped into a hostile environment, by the mean mugs you niggas are showing. If either of you wants to leave, feel free to do so. My wife and I are the captains of this ship, so we do not owe either one of you any explanation on how we move. Quick question, do you fellas know anything about prostitution and drug selling on the properties you two are renovating for us." Mario asked, returning the same mugging face. "What the fuck? We look like pimps?" said Face.

"Yes, low-budget pimps to be exact, nigga you fucked ocean spray Stella fishy ass that speaks volumes on your character, Zen said as she walked off to tell the landscapers what to do next." Al and Face just stood there for minutes, not knowing what to do. "So, what you fellas gone do barbeque or mildew? There's work to be done," Mario asked while looking both men in the eye.

"Do your own damn work. You and your wife come around here getting jazzy out the mouth like we're some clown ass fuck boys. Nigga, you and that bitch got the game twisted," Al said loudly, then he screamed, "WE QUIT."

"Fuck you nigga, we were blessing your ass with free labor. Hat crabby wife of yours got you soft as fuck punk boy," Al added. Mario quickly grabbed his pistol, and with an open hand, he smacked the hell out of Al. Face forced Al to the car. They then burned rubber leaving the property. "That clown ass nigga will pay for that move he just made," said Al.

"You are so right, bro, but right now, let's find our drugs so we can set up shop somewhere else," Face explained. Al and Face paid a visit to the other properties hoping for different results, but luck wasn't on their side. The scenery was the same uniform police posted up on duty, and the grounds were perfectly manicured. Al and Face knew they must devise a plan, but they headed to find Nicolette.

Zen felt they were going after Nicolette, so she beat them to the punch. Only a few spots Nicolette would be that early in the morning. Nicolette was a regular at the retirement home. She cased the place to find old geriatrics to suck and fuck on. Her kids were familiar with her method. They would come through and get lunch money from the smelly old men. Zen pulls up behind the activity van shaking her head about the scenery of the elderly pushing walkers and rolling around in wheelchairs. The staff loaded the senior citizens on the van for the day program. Mr Willy was damn near eighty years old, but he loved young pussy. Mr Willy would instruct the tricks to call him big dick Willy. There were no boundaries when

Nicolette and her colleagues were on a trick mission. They would call him King Kong or Papa Smurf and even blow bubbles up his ass on check day. Willy was very generous with his money when it came to purchasing pussy. He neglected to buy his daily essentials. Willy's lack of cleanliness left him and his apartment smelling like the unknown. Nicolette was immune to the smell because her trifling ass was not clean or fresh herself. Nicolette only cared about popping pills and sniffing cocaine and whatever else the street life had to offer. Zen noticed Mr Willy loading up on the van. She went straight to his room, knowing Nicolette would be there sleeping. Nicolette was snuggled in a worn, dirty blanket on top of Willy's pissy bed. She was resting like a queen covered in filth. She was tired from the whore hopping she had done the night before. Mario did not like that Zen dragged him along. He hated being around Nicolette with Zen because when he made poor decisions, Mario used Nicolette for the mouth tricks she was so famous for. He was so embarrassed he went there with her. Looking at her now is a total shame. Zen walked straight into the room with Mario in tow. "Wake your bitch ass up. Zen screamed while pouring a hot King Cobra beer on Nicolette's back." Nicolette raised with her eyes squinting tightly.

"Zen, what the fuck, I haven't seen Mario?" Nicolette said, confused.
"Bitch don't flatter yourself. I got business with you, so get your trick ass off that pissy mattress and let's talk." Zen stood over Nicolette, looking at her with disgust.

"Ok, what is it?" Nicolette asked.

"Before you start to lie, just know I have you on tape. What the fuck is going on at my rental properties with you, Al and Face?"

"I would hook them up with some buyers from the club. I was the middle person when the young cats hustling on Jones Street wanted to cop some weed. Al would let me turn a few tricks; in return, I would bring a few girls by every so often to entertain him and Face. I swear on my MAMA, I never knew those were your properties," Nicolette said, looking pitiful.

"Maybe so, but this is what you are going to do. Take your nasty ass a bath first, then meet me at this address. Bring an overnight bag because you're staying for a few days," said Zen.

"Hell, nah Zen, I got shit to do. I can't be fooling with you on no crazy shit, plus I have kids."

"Bitch you are gone. Do what the fuck I say. You're not worried about them, damn kids. Your Mama been on babysitting duty since you popped out your first one at twelve. Besides, you owe me. You wobbled on my husband's dick without permission. Don't make me have a flashback. I might fuck around and beat your ass and your kid's ass too."

"Please leave my kids out of this," Nicolette pleaded.

"Shut the fuck up; it won't hurt them badass dirt devils to get their ass whooped. When Al and Face find out their drugs are gone, who the fuck do you think they're coming for. A hideout will do you some good right now."

"OH MY GOSH, I don't know nothing about no missing drugs. How the hell do I get mixed up in this shit," Nicolette cried.

"Because you're the neighborhood thot, and that's your motive, and you were the only one helping them move the weight, so that makes you a major liability right now," Zen said with attitude. Mario stayed by the front door the entire time. Nicolette had no idea he was there.

CHAPTER 3

DON'T PLAY WITH US

Al and Face were on a manhunt looking for Nicolette. Weighing out all options like real bounty hunters. They continued to run into dead ends. No one has seen or heard from Nicolette. "A bro, somebody has to pay for this shit. There's no way we can take a major hit like this," Al said to Face.

"Damn right, I believe some jack boys were watching us. It makes no sense for Nicolette or any of her coke-sniffing bitches to be behind this. We have been dealing with them for too long. Besides, none of them knew our shit was underground," Face said angrily. "Over two hundred pounds of quality weed don't just vanish from underground. This shit was thought out and executed well. Just think about it, bro, we leave one night, and the next morning, we arrive right after sunrise to discover the grounds fully covered and manicured. Nicolette can't make a major play like that." Face sounded convincing to Al.

"Well, that leaves only one window open, and that's Mario and his bitch," Al sounded off. Al and Face started conjuring up a plan and went to recruit some reinforcement.

Nicolette was unhappy about giving up her daily activities to be held hostage. She was in a rage but would not dare go against Zen. So, she wore a smile and kept her comments to herself. Nicolette, hate she fell victim to

Mario. She was mesmerized by his cool boy persona. Mario's swag had her intoxicated. Nicolette once had a deep infatuation with Mario. She loved to suck his dick and felt like a queen whenever she did. Nicolette was so fucked up in the head about Mario she would pay other niggas to fuck her and let her scream out Mario's name. The performance she put on was exclusive. Niggas were lined up at the club door with an eight-ball of White Girl, waiting on Nicolette to exit so that they could play the role of Mario. After all the abuse Zen has brought upon Nicolette, she hated she ever laid eyes on Mario. Nicolette endured all those ass kicking's for nothing in return but a throat shower.

Zen housed Nicolette at one of her high-efficiency apartments on the west side of town. Nicolette was allowed two cigarettes and a glass of wine outside under the tree, only at nightfall. Zen maintained a Strick no-smoking policy, which Nicolette hated because she was a pack-a-day smoker.

"Zen, why the hell are we wasting time with Nicolette and treating this bitch like royalty? I'm confused," Mario asked.

"It's not going to take long for Al and Face to start looking for the person responsible for taking their weed. Their first stop will be to find Nicolette, them mutha fukars will kill her thinking it was her who wronged them."

"What the fuck that got to do with us housing this bitch, Zen?" inquired Mario.

"Let me finish, damn. Well, you know everybody, and their Mamas knows I hate Nicolette. The bitch has me on no trespassing and has a restraining order on me. I have humiliated and beat her ass and drugged her shamelessly out of several clubs. I have taken an evil attraction to the bitch, all because she fucked my husband and the whole world knows it. So, if she comes up dead, who the fuck the police and her people going to blame?"

"First of all, don't be throwing sneaky shots at me. That was a long time ago. And nobody told you and your gang of misfits to go around tormenting her."

"Fuck. What you're talking about, that's the price you pay when you fuck with a married man. Now shut the fuck up before I think you're defending her and smack your ass." Mario just shook his head at his evil wife because one more word was about to have him on the couch. Ashley and Zen were still down like four flats. Ashley had a tracker on Al and Face's vehicle. Zen was keeping up with their whereabouts.

Ashley placed a call to Zen. "Sis, their car just drove up to Pickle Tower," Ashley stated loudly through the phone.

"Copy that. Make sure the cameras are in position. Mario and I are headed that way."

Face jumped out of the car and immediately went up to Murry and Bruce. Face shot them both in the kneecap, asking questions about the weed. "Man, we don't know shit about no fucking weed, you pussy, Bruce said while sharp pains ran through his knee." Face shot him again in his other knee. "Oh, shit Bruce screamed out in agony. Man, please don't shoot me again. I promise we don't know anything about no weed," Bruce begged. Al was returning from the utility house with shovels when he snatched Murry up by the shirt and forced him to help dig. Murry did not exchange a word; he limped over to the designated area and did what he was told. The grounds were still soft, so the digging was going fast. After thirty minutes, the duo knew someone had confiscated their weed for sure. Al threw the shovels down and shot Bruce and Murry twice, killing them instantly. Face kicked both bodies into the hole that Al and Murry had just dug. The duo took time to shove dirt on top of the bodies giving Murry and Bruce an early burial. Once they were finished, Al and Face bolted back to the car and sped off, leaving tire marks. The men were unaware that Zen's secret camera had recorded the shooting.

Al and Face were long gone by the time Zen and Mario drove up. Ashley was shocked by what she viewed on camera she forwarded the footage to Zen and Mario. Before Zen walked over to the crime scene, she alerted Ashley to send the cleanup crew ASAP to dig up and burn the bodies. "These punk niggas wanna go to war, I see," Mario said directly to Zen.

"Hell, yeah, and war is what they're going to get. You know they are going to suit up for us next and were going to be mutha fuckan ready. Don't freeze up, lover boy, its show time," Zen said as she popped the extended clip in her pistol.

Zen marinated a crew of girls, which would burn the city down. After the original crew went sour, Zen knew she needed to have tryouts for her bad bitches only club. Lady J, Nena, Sundae, and T-Baby were her A-1s. The five of them were able to feed off one another. Sundae, Nena, and Lady J often played the backfield and only got dirty when the whistle was blown. You still had to force shit out of T-Baby, but she was always down to ride. The new crew would take the old crew along to handle missions when a sharpshooter was needed for a play. No matter the distance, the old heads were iconic with any firearm. Razia Parks, known as Raz was the smallest female but deadly. Raz tallied a massive body count and would kill you for wiping your mouth wrong at the dinner table. Raz's face would look like a Dalmatian dog if she wore tear drops representing her body count. Raz was down with Zen back in the day, completing assignments. Raz retired from the military, and she has a major crush on Pound Puppy.

Milly Mill was a Latino stud who loved trouble. Milly Mill was a professional wrestler in Mexico. She was tied up in her family's cartel business, where she was forced to kill on command. Milly Mill is wanted for murder in Mexico, so she headed for the border, dropping her government name, Alberta Noraiz. She now goes by Milly Mill, after her favorite rapper Meek Mill. Last on the docket is Bleu Davenport. She's a sophisticated top model. The only difference is her runways are deadly. Bleu is a beautiful black woman. Her parents are both Nigerian, so her skin is darkened toned. If it wasn't for her perfectly white teeth, Bleu could not be seen at night. Bleu was very confident with her skin color. Bleu displayed a coke bottle shape, wearing high heels, she stood 6'2. Bleu was a high-maintenance killer. She would fuck your brains out, then smile on top of you while your bussin a nut and put a bullet right between your eyes.

 When these ladies join a round table meeting, some mayhem is about to go down, no questions asked. Zen handed picked this crew using her special training from Victor Lee. There was no mission these ladies could not handle. Zen passed the torch to the newbies to take over the famous business she and the old crew started. Advocating deadly force for married women who want revenge on their cheating husband or the husband's sidepiece. Women worldwide continued to pay top dollar for the ladies to eliminate the shame and the prey at hand.

Zen instructed everyone to meet at her and Mario's pool house. Mario did not have an alliance of eight, but his two main niggas, White Boy and Kash, need no introduction. They were thorough as fuck.

As usual, Zen turned the meeting into a family cookout and seafood boil. It wouldn't be Zen if she's not entertaining with her delicious foods and drinks. "Grab your plates and drinks; we must get straight to business. It's crunch time, Zen said loudly, making her way to the front of the pool house." Zen pulled out pictures and taped them to the wall. "Alden Thompson is known to the streets as Al or Jamaican Al." Zen pointed to the picture on the right. "Fabian Badrick is known to the streets as Face. These two hot head Jamaicans will be coming full force with deadly intentions for Mario and me. Those tongue-tied mutha fuckas roll in packs, so we must walk light, so we don't step into one of their booby traps." Zen continued with her detailed tutorial. Mario added his spin and concerns and stressed the seriousness of the situation.

Just when the crew solidified a plan, shots came from all angles. Everyone ducked for cover. Mario and his homie, Kash brought the game Call of Duty to life. They pushed everyone inside the pool shower area and began crawling like combat soldiers to the front of the pool house. Kash started firing back rounds from an A-K 47. Mario was popping off with an assault rifle. Milly Mill and Bleu were Glocked up and popping hollow point bullets. After three long minutes of chaos, the shots came to a cease. Two of the men that played a part in the attack must have been on foot patrol because Kash blew one of their shoulders clean off. The other perpetrator tried to redeem himself and get up and run. He was quickly beaten with the back of Mario's rifle. Mario then placed the barrel of the rifle down perp number one throat. "I'm not going to go back and forth with you are beg for any information. You have one chance to tell me what I want to know. Where are Al and Face?" The dude manages to grab his dick and mumbles out fuck you. Mario and Kash pumped them both full of rounds. Their bodies were jerking up inches off the ground from the lethal shots. "This was clearly a suicide mission; them niggas knew what would happen to these cats if they were left behind," Mario said with his rifle still drawn. Sundae and lady J was late as usual. Soon as they drove up to the pool house, a car full of dread heads rode by shooting. Sundae instantly started following the car, bussin shots back at the Jamaican shooters. Sundae and Lady J splattered the two men hanging out of the back seat shooting. One of the men flipped out the window when the deadly shot hit him in the head from Sundae's Glock forty. He was then run over by Sundae's expedition. His head was flattened like a pancake. That left the driver and passenger to get away.

Sundae wanted to continue the chase, but a group of bikers were riding the bike trail, and she didn't want to risk any innocent lives. Zen and Raz made it out the back and discussed their play. Raz took a wood-cutting axe and chopped both dead perps' heads off. Mario then released his rifle, and he and Kash instantly vomited gruesomely all over the place. "Bag these heads up and deliver them to Al's American auntie that lives on the southside. Attach a just because of card and balloon," Zen instructed Ramo Mario's do boy.

"What the fuck, bro? They're bagging heads like groceries," Kash said, wiping his mouth with the back of his hand, looking crazy at Mario. "Yeah, fam, these ladies or cut from a different cloth," Mario said with a grin, thinking about when he found out his wife was a natural-born killer.

"Aint no soccer moms around this bitch," Kash said as he shook his head.

CHAPTER 4

WE ALL COCKY

The rivalry between Zen and the Jamaicans became more intense. Both sides were on the hide from one another. Within weeks two of Zen and Mario's properties were partially burnt down. Mario's do boy Ramo was caught slipping. Al and Face captured him leaving a nursing home and visiting his mom. After some brutal torture, they finally took Ramo out of his misery. A Mack ten was shoved up his ass and unloaded, and Ramo was fish bait by the time they were done. Al and Face hand-delivered what was left of Ramo's body to the Pickle Tower. No one would have known it was Ramo if it weren't for the clothing. Ramo has twin boys thirteen years of age. The crew had no time to grieve. They needed to stay on top of their game and outwit Al and Face.

Zen secretly reached out to Pound Puppy, Victor Lee's right-hand man. Since the death of Victor Lee, Pound Puppy took over running the streets of Greenville. Pound Puppy was a street king. With the blow of a whistle, he could make shit magically happen. Pound Puppy has always been the muscle for the crew. Making sure they remained safe on their assignments and keeping them off the radar from the Feds and jack boys. Pound Puppy eliminated several niggas for planning to viciously attack Zen and her crew. Pound Puppy never bothered telling Zen or the Crew because he secretly kept eyes on them, no matter where they were. No one was able to speak salty about Zen without it getting back to Pound Puppy. The situation with the Jamaicans slipped by him because it was more of Mario's beef than Zen's. "Look, Zen. This is a situation for the big boys. I need you to fall back. Raz, Milly Mill, and Bleu as well. Focus on rebuilding the properties that were sabotaged. I have a team of contractors that will have both properties up and running in a few months. Don't worry. They're not Jamaicans, Pound Puppy added jokingly."

Zen felt the need to protect Nicolette's kids and mom. Al and Face were on a rampage and would not hesitate to kill them. Nicolette was happy to have company and was glad Zen showed compassion for her and her family. Nicolette was afraid to address Zen. She felt nervous, and her body would clam up whenever Zen was around. "Zen, can I talk to you for a second?" Nicolette asked, shaking like a leaf.

"What is it slut? I'm in a hurry. I brought your yaps to you. What more do you want?" Zen asked, full of attitude and a lethal facial expression.

"Al and Face hang out in Brook Town apartments. Two sisters, Davia and Tara, live on the bottom level, known as the basement. That is where people score drugs, have parties and have much sexual activity. The entire bottom level is shut off, and no other tenants can enter that level. A fat dike bitch name Boonie will be at the top-level patrolling and policing the traffic. Anytime Al and Face are on the premises, Boonie will be on post. She is the only person they are comfortable with because she keeps shit running smoothly." When Nicolette finished talking, she just walked away, not wanting to face Zen any longer. Zen rolled her eyes and walked off but was thankful for the information. Zen calls Pound Puppy to deliver the information she just learned from Nicolette. Pound Puppy put his best men on the job, casing the apartments and taking notes on frequent movement and activities. Another group of men were at the entrance focusing on the traffic flow in that area. Soon as Boonie arrived on the post they were instructed to move in full force.

A little after midnight Pound Puppy and his men receives the information they have been yearning for. Al and Face were spotted with two freak bitches heading down to the basement. Pound Puppy instructed his men there was no need to move fast because those freaks were thirsty to juggle some balls and suck some dicks. The two-man crew expanded to thirty. Pound Puppy decided to call in all his heavy hitters to avoid any fuck ups. The army of men surrounded the complex ready for war. A few men were stationed on the next street and in the alleyway. Tang, one of Pound Puppies' vets, walked beside Boonie and injected her with a lethal dose of anaesthesia.

Boonie never saw it coming. Tang covered her up with a blanket, giving a head signalling for the men to move. The men bombarded the basement laying everybody face down on the floor. Al and Face were dragged out by their dreads with a hard dick. The two-half dead-looking freaks were tag teaming sucking on Al and Face dicks, when they were violently interrupted. This ambush was unexpected for Al and Face. "Y'all mutha fuckan Americans portray to be so damn tough. In reality, you niggas are cunts, Al said as he was being drugged outside." Tang smacked Jim, one of his men, upside his head, for allowing Al to keep popping off at the mouth.

Jim caught on quickly, he pistol-whipped Al until he began leaking blood. Face was forced on the opposite side; he was not happy about being taken against his will. Face suddenly gained the strength of Hercules; Face instantly strategized his next play. The two men that were dragging Face were no match for him. Face gained momentum and began to throw a few uppercuts and strongarm the gun from one of the men. Face moved quickly and effortlessly. Once Face retrieved the gun, he fired shots at the two men blowing their brains out. Face started shooting his way out of the complex. Face made it a few streets over and spotted two more men. The men became bored with their job and decided to bring excitement to their posts. Stan and Dean had a homosexual encounter. Stan was on his knees sucking Dean's dick and playing in his ass hole. Stan's rifle was laying on the sidewalk unguarded. Face crept over to the rifle and quickly swooped it up. Face immediately blasts off rounds of shots killing Stan and Dean right in the middle of their hanky-panky. "Fucking queers, y'all niggas fucked up my session," Face mumbled in a low tone. The other men came running, not knowing where the shots came from. Face dipped back behind the tree twigs to camouflage himself. That gave him the upper hand on the men because they could not see him. After a few seconds Face said fuck it and began spraying the rifle, shooting everything moving his way. Once there was no more movement, Face ran fast to safety.

Al, on the other hand, was getting beat down. Pound Puppy contacts Zen to meet him at their secret location. Zen and Mario arrived in riot gear, feeling like Bonnie and Clyde. Al was on his knees with his hands tied over his head. He was beaten badly. Pound Puppy explained that Face managed to get away. He elaborated on how many of his men were killed. "Damn, Pupp, I never meant for this to go down. I told you we had it, fam," Zen said, saddened.

"No problem, Zen. I'm going to protect you, rather you like it or not. All my men knew the tremendous danger they faced when they signed up to my squad."

"I know, fam, I just hate when shit happens on our side of the fence. Ya, feel me," Zen spoke softly.

"Whatever play you decide to deliver to this fuck nigga, I am down," Pound Puppy said while pointing at Al.

"Put his ass in the Lion's Den, and we will let him call his partner in a few days. I will hit them with a major ultimatum. Either return to Jamaica with the stipulation of never coming back to the States. Or I can show the police the footage of them killing two of my husband's men," Zen explained. The Lion's Den was a six by twelve cement shed out in the middle of nowhere, filled with hundreds of non-poisonous snakes.

Nicolette begins to make a fuss about not being able to move freely. Nicolette was craving cocaine and dick; she was missing her street life and all the bullshit that came with it. Being with her eight yaps day after day was too much like motherhood for her. That was the most time she had ever spent with her kids. Sadly, it was not by her choice. Nicolette coached her mom on how to tell Zen she needed to let them leave. Maggie was firm and stood up to Zen. Zen did not hesitate. She put Nicolette, her mom, and the kids off her property. Zen made them walk home. With eight kids in tow, it would take every bit of two hours. Zen faced bigger issues; she was not about to bother with Nicolette breaking down ass any longer than she needed to.

CHAPTER 5

DEAL GONE BAD

Zen, Mario and Pound Puppy met up at the lion's den. When they pulled Al out, he was covered with over a thousand snake bites over his body. Al was swollen so bad he looked like he weighed four hundred pounds. Zen bent down to look Al in his eyes. "I knew you and your nappy-headed partner were up to no good from the gate. My husband is the one who campaigned for you nasty hair fuck boys." Zen pulled the video clip from her jacket and placed it in Al's face. "This is the video of you two pussies killing some off-duty cops. So, looks like you fellas need to kick rocks back to your homeland. Do not return to the States, or I will give this video to the police. Two Jamaicans doing a life sentence in America is deadly. Zen explained, remaining calm.

Mario handed Al his phone and instructed him to call Face. Al hesitated for a few seconds. "Fuck that. Throw his ass back in the Lion's Den and let him die. Why the fuck are we negotiating with these faggots anyway?" Mario sounded off.

"Because we can't keep looking over our shoulders, we're done with that life, remember," Zen said softly.

"I can't tell Zen; you and your misfits are chopping off heads and gun slagging like crazy. I'm not stupid; I know about the secret gun shops with the high-tech artillery and other combat devices. I know men across the world are still losing their lives for cheating. You, ladies, are a mutha fuckan Mob within yourselves. Y'all will never stop, so let's just kill these punks and get it over with," Mario said loudly.

"Zen is right, Mario; we are not above the law. The FEDS come looking for Zen every time shit gets hectic in the streets. These fuck boys have an army of Jamaican thugs ready for war. So, it is best if we cop deuces and casually end this beef," Pound Puppy said, sounding like the God Father.

"I feel you, Pupp, but we can't trust these niggas. They can say anything," Mario responded and threw his hands up.

"That's a chance we must take fam and be ready for war if they fold," Pound Puppy said as he walked back to his car. Al made the call to Face; Al's lips were so swollen he was having trouble speaking. "What the fuck have they done to you, Al. I'm going to kill them mutha fuckas," Face said repeatedly. Al slowly explained the leverage Zen had over them. Al told Face there was no way he could do hard time in the States for killing two cops. Al and Face did not know Murry and Bruce were not real cops. Face got quiet as he let the information soak in. Zen snatched the phone from Al. "Ok, lover boy, what is it going to be? We don't have time to keep playing footsy with you Shabba Ranks-looking mutha fuckas," Zen spat. "I never liked your fat ass anyway; I wish I could choke you with my dick and sprinkle my pubic hair down your throat," Face said aggressively. Mario grabbed the phone from Zen. "Only dick my wife will be choking on is mine, nigga. So, since you want to be swift with your lips about my wife, I will make your boy pay since I can't get to you right now."

"No, please, Mario. Please don't hurt him. He already sounds fucked up. I'm sorry, I really am," Face pleaded.

"I will text you an address. You need to meet us there tomorrow at noon. When you arrive, you will strip down naked and walk down the end of the parking lot and enter a green Chevy Impala," Mario explained.

"What the fuck is this a joke? Face asked, looking puzzled. "Nah nigga I'm taking all precautions just in case your bitch ass wanna try some slick shit. You got away once and bodied a few good men, but you can bet them sour-ass dreadlocks it won't happen again. Once you are in the car, you will later meet up with Al. Then you two will be taken to the airport, where you will go back to Jamaica for good," Mario Explained.

Milly Mill scheduled a meeting with a few well-established British women about an assignment. These women were rich and lived a glamorous lifestyle. They had everything a woman could ever desire, but like most women, their husbands cheated on them. In the profile the ladies provided Milly Mill with, the husbands were cheating with the nanny, soccer coach, and random whores, and one of the men was cheating with a British police officer. A few ladies wanted their husbands humiliated.

In contrast, the other ladies wanted the million-dollar package. Dead was the only way these ladies saw fit to handle their situation. No sparing, no negotiating, get in and out was the direct order. The lady leading the pack of women her name is Chunchi. Chunchi's husband is sleeping with the British police officer, and she wants the officer humiliated to the highest degree. Milly Mill could not join the ladies on this assignment due to her trouble in

Mexico. It would not be wise for her to Travel. All the ladies were more than qualified for the job. This assignment will be a smacking three million dollars. Once Milly Mill presents these numbers to the ladies, she's sure they will suit up and be down to catch the flight.

The next morning Zen and Mario were up handling the arrangements to send Al and Face away on their journey. At exactly eleven-thirty, they headed to the location to meet Face. Pound Puppy and one of his men were already at the location with Al in tow. Two of Pound Puppies men would also ride on the plane with Al and Face. Mario did not want any flaws with returning them to their country. When Face arrived, he spotted the green Chevy Impala. Face also noticed a group of men, and Mario and Zen huddled up around a black van. Face exits the car and immediately puts his hands up in surrender form. Face slowly started walking towards the green Chevy. Mario fires a series of gunshots on the ground, inches away from Face's feet and legs. "Mutha fucka, I told you to strip down naked ain't nothing changed nigga," Mario screamed at Face. Face quickly undressed and then continued his walk with his hands up. Face was steps away from the car when he was manhandled and thrown violently against the car. Pound Puppy placed him in handcuffs and locked them extra tight, cutting off his circulation. "GAWD DAMN! You pussy mutha fuckas trying to play hardball I see. Loosen up these fuckan cuffs," Face said with a mean mug.

"Get your lil pee-wee ass dick in the fuckan car," Zen added. Zen noticed a few gold teeth inside Face's mouth, something she had never noticed before. She quickly shook it off, thinking it was a grill and maybe he wanted to return home with gold mouth bling. "So y'all sending us back to Jamaica after you faggots strong-armed us for our weed. That's some straight-up bullshit. You Americans are weak as fuck. If you were about that life, my partner and I would be dead right now. Kill me, you cowards," Face screamed. Face began to show resistance, acting as if he wanted to be killed. "I told y'all let's kill these pussies, at least this one. If not, it's going to be trouble for us," Mario said as a plea to Zen and Pound Puppy. "Do it, you scaredy cats, kill me already. All you punks know how to do is beat a mutha fucka. Y'all bitch niggas are a group of first-grade remedial thugs. None of you bastards has the heart to kill. Every one of you fuck wads are toilet tissue soft," Face screamed out.

Face was riled up, purposely pushing their buttons. "Zen, you must trim some fat and make your husband a cunt sandwich. I'm sure the cornball will eat it up," Face laughed loudly. Face spit out the car window, trying to land it on Zen. Pound Puppy and Mario both gave Face two shots to the dome. As Face fell out of Zen's car, she spat on his lifeless body. "Who's the cunt now, bitch?" Zen said as she dialed Ashley to send the clean-up crew to their location?" Zen and Mario sent Al back to Jamaica somehow. They felt that was best. Al would just be traveling alone. No Face, no case.

CHAPTER 6

MONEY IS THE MOTIVE

Chunchi contacted Milly Mill around the clock, waiting for confirmation about the assignment. The ladies were meeting up at the round table to discuss the specifics. Everyone arrived, and Milly Mill started the meeting by passing out assignments and an itinerary. The ladies immediately started looking them over. The down payment amount and completion payment amount was added as well. The assignment was huge for the ladies. They haven't been on a mission like this since Victor Lee. This assignment will take place in London, England. "As you can see, the numbers on this assignment are very friendly," Zen stated with a smile. "After this assignment, we will be set financially, so there's no need to risk our life any further. Sundae, Lady J, Nena, T-Baby, and I are supposed to be in retirement already, but we must take one for the team when something big comes along. Milly Mill will stay back with Ashley, help with the tracking, and hold down the fort while the rest of us handle the business. I need you ladies to ensure your passports are current and ready for takeoff next Friday. This is not our first rodeo, so let's continue to move in silence and stay professional. I will be missing in action for a few days because it will take some serious convincing for my husband to agree with me leaving the country," Zen continued to discuss the plans. All the ladies engaged in conversation as they studied their itinerary.

Zen made plans with Mario for the entire week. She was cooking his favorite meals and giving him sex around the clock. Mario felt something was up, but he didn't speak about it because he enjoyed his wife's attention. Zen was always a hard ass, so when she was at her best, Mario was not about to spoil that. "Hey babe, I love the steak dinner you cooked, but I'm feeling greedy." Mario suggested, " Let's get some king crab legs from the new restaurant Crackin Crabs by the mall."

"I'll go get it for you. Just stay in bed naked. And when I return, I'm going to put my mouth on your joystick," Zen said seductively.

"Never mind, you don't have to go," Mario begged with a hard dick.
"Nah, babe, I got you when I get back," Zen said, kissing Mario passionately before leaving.

Zen left the house and headed to the restaurant. After Zen made a few turns, she noticed a white Dodge Journey following her. Zen knew it was an amateur because the driver continuously drove closely behind her, frequently stopping on the brakes. Zen outsmarted the driver. She stalled at a red light. She was camouflaged behind her dark window tints, so there was no way the driver could see any movement. Zen eased her way to the passenger side; she slightly opened the door drooping to the ground, and began to crawl like a combat soldier. When Zen reaches the driver's side of the Dodge Journey, she snatches the door open and points her gun directly in the older lady's face. "Why the fuck are you following me bitch?" Zen screamed out.

"Please don't shoot me, Ms. Zen. I need your help." It was Maggie Nicolette's mom with her oldest three kids in the back seat.

"I don't know why the fuck you would need my help, but a little advice for the future. You can't just go around following people. You need to be careful how you approach me. I usually shoot first and ask questions later. But I see the good Lord was on your side tonight. Zen sounded off," Zen instructed Maggie to pull over to the Old Navy, which was a block away. Zen pulls her car into the parking lot next to Maggie. Zen exits her car, anxious to know what was on her mind. "Ms. Zen, you can put your gun away now. My old ass is not a threat," Maggie stated nervously.

"I can't be too sure. By you following me, that raises a red flag, and your daughter and I are not play pals," Zen responded.

"My daughter looks up to you for some strange reason. I know about all the fights and torture you have done to her. Nicolette is scared shitless of you, and right now, I see that as a good thing," Maggie begins to explain.

"Ma'am, no disrespect, but you are not making any damn sense to me. I mean, I hear you talking but ain't shit clicking," Zen said, looking confused.

"Let me finish, please," Maggie stated softly. "My daughter is caught up in these streets, hooked on cocaine and Roxi pills, and that alone has sentenced her to live a life of street crime. Nicolette has recently let this pimp take over her life. She is shamelessly selling her body. Her face is rough and tough full of dirt. You can't see her light completion from all the built-up dirt. This low-life pimp nigga Stone is beating her brains out and forcing her to do only God knows what. Nicolette will not listen to me, but she will do whatever you say with no questions asked. Her kids and I need her, Ms. Zen. I went to the doctor and received a bad report. I was diagnosed with lung Cancer. I will be starting chemo treatment in a few weeks." Maggie began to cry hysterically. Zen even became teary-eyed herself from the tragic story. Nicolette's seventeen-year-old daughter Allison exited the car and hugged her grandma. "Ms. Zen, I know the story with you and my mom, and I don't blame you for how you feel about her. But if you got to beat her ass again and make her come home and take care of us and my grandma, then so be it, Allison spat while holding her grandma tightly."

"Here is my card. Give me a call in a few days, and I will hand deliver your mom to you and your grandma. Ms. Maggie, you must stop worrying about Nicolette and take care of yourself. You can beat this demon that has formed up against you. FUCK CANCER!! You got this," Zen spoke as she gave Maggie a long comforting hug." A hug she knew Maggie wished was from her daughter, but it felt good to Maggie to hear some encouraging words. Maggie held on to Zen extra tight. The loving embrace gave her motivation. Zen had a tender spot for the situation because she lost her mom to COPD, and Mario lost his mom to Cancer. Zen sit in the parking lot for over an hour crying, thinking about her mom. Zen became furious with Nicolette on a different level. Zen could not believe Nicolette wasn't able to love her mother and show her affection, but she chose a different route acting dumb and stupid. Zen would give anything to see her mom again.

Mario began to panic when he realized the length of time Zen was gone. After she did not answer her phone, he quickly got dressed. Mario turned on his tracker to Zen's car and went straight to her location. As he reached the location, he rushed to Zen's car and opened the car door, "What happened, bae? Why are you just sitting here?" Mario asked nervously. Zen immediately reached for a hug, holding Mario so tight. "Ok, Zen, you're scaring me. What's wrong? Please talk to me," Zen explained to Mario what had just happened and was only feeling down because of the news Maggie had delivered to her. Hurtful wounds resurfaced; Zen was caught up in her feelings about her mom. "Zen, this is not your battle. I feel sorry for her mom, but if Stone is pimping out, Nicolette..." Zen blankly stared at Mario. "Dammit, Zen, I know that look. We have enough on our plate right now. Let that shit go," Mario spoke.

"My girls and I got this. You can sit back and twiddle your thumbs. While you at it, hop out and go get yourself some tampons 'cause you acting like a lil SAP right now," Zen sounded off.

"Hell, nah, Zen. Now you trying to play me like I'm a pussy. Don't do that. You know damn well if you make a move, I'm behind you. I feel like this is none of our damn business. My heart is saddened by Ms. Maggie's news as well, but you're still grieving and emotional over the loss of your mom, so you can't play superwoman based on your emotions," Mario said as he reached for Zen's hand.

"Are you mad at me, Mario?" Zen asked with a sad look.

"No, I love your ass to the moon and back, but you're a fucking hand full," Mario said as he gave his wife a kiss.

The next day Pound Puppy drove out to Zen and Mario's pool house. Zen was there doing some minor renovations. "Oh, Lord. What brings you my way, Pupp? I can tell by your look you're about to get in my ass about something," Zen said quickly, then poured them a drink of Crown.

"I don't know if you thought I was playing when I said I always have eyes on you. I know you have a husband, and that's his job to protect you. That's why I owe him the right to handle you on this end as well. Pound Puppy looked at Zen with a side eye."

"Talk to me, Pupp. What's good, fam," a confused Zen asked.

"I know you are planning to leave on a mission to London in a few days. I also know I can't change your mind but do know this, and one of my men will be tagging alone. And once I tell Mario, I know he will also be coming. We will catch a separate flight from you and the crew, we will stay in a different hotel, but on the same strip," Pound Puppy continued to explain. Zen was about to say something When Pound Puppy put his finger to his lips for her to hush. "It's non-negotiable," Pound Puppy said as he turned up his glass of Crown.

Zen sent out a forwarded text to the crew that she needed them at the pool house ASAP. The ladies were clueless about the sudden urgency. The ladies were there in less than twenty minutes. The entire squad was strapped and geared up for war. "Glad to see when I sound the alarm, you ladies waste no time responding. But it's not that type of action right now. All of you know Pound Puppy is my family. He and Victor Lee trained me. Pound Puppy is overprotected when it comes to me. Living this thug misses life. But somebody in this crew is reporting my every move to him, and I want to know who the fuck it is. I am not mad about it; I just would like to know what is up with that. Please speak now," Zen spoke in a chill tone. Raz stood up and cleared her throat.

"Pupp and I are secretly in a love fling. I have mentioned some of our moves to him on different occasions. I didn't feel like I was snitching because he's a big part of our team. I beg you, Zen. Please don't let this break our trust. I will never talk outside of our alliance, and that's on my life," Raz pleaded her case, waiting patiently for Zen's response.

"Raz, you're a real live bad bitch, and for Pupp to trust you on that level ain't no love lost, fam. Believe me, if you are in his personal space, he knows your whole life story and your Mama's credit score, too," Zen said with a laugh. The other ladies chimed in, and Raz hugged Zen apologizing for being dickmatized. "I can't be mad because he's going to find out from your pillow talking or from another source," Zen spat. Zen and Raz dapped each other up and continued laughing with the ladies.

Zen later pulled Milly Mill to the side and explained what she needed her to handle while the rest of the crew were going to be away in London. "We will snatch Nicolette's ass up the night before we leave. I will put her in a secure location with around-the-clock nurse care. Nicolette will get daily doses of detox medication to help with her withdrawals. Your job is keeping her in line and not letting her leave. Keep the bitch hydrated with Gatorade and make the slut eat some fucking food. The bitch is little as fuck. My girl Kelly Hill is a certified nurse who used to care for my mom. Kelly will choke her ass out if it comes down to it. I was thinking about recruiting Kelly at one time. But she loves the lesbian lifestyle too much for me. Not judging her, but that will throw her off her game, so I decided against it. Bitches worse than niggas, Kelly stayed into altercations with her studs."

"So, she a fem lesbian. Ain't shit in the rules about me can't fuck her, is it?" Milly Mill asked with a devilish smile. Zen shook her head, knowing Milly Mill was going to try some nasty shit now that she had Kelly's profile.

CHAPTER 7

JAMAICAN SOIL

Zen received confirmation that Al had made it to Jamaica. Once the plane landed, Al was given a sweat suit to wear because he rode the entire plane ride naked. Al exited the plane and moved far away from Kool Breeze and Big Mike, who worked for Pound Puppy. The men were instructed to make sure Al made it off the plane then they were to head straight back to the States. Kool Breeze suddenly received the case of the bubble guts during the plane's landing. He was clamping his ass cheeks together in desperate need of a restroom. Kool Breeze reframed from using the small toilet on the plane. He knew he needed room to maneuver, so he hurried to use the airport restroom. "Nigga you better make that shit quick; you know how Pupp gets when we don't stick to the schedule," Big Mike thundered.

Al was desperately trying to find a phone to use. Al was suddenly grabbed forcefully and pulled beside Starbucks and a water fountain. Al started swinging punches, ready for a fight. "Al, Al, it's me nigga." Al took a terrifying look and realized it was Face.

"What the fuck, bro? Is that you? I thought them fuck niggas killed you," Al said, looking confused.

"That's what they thought too, bro, but you know your boy is a genius. That fuck nigga Gus was on the docket to be killed. Heavy sent the order confirming Gus had to die. So, you know us Jamaicans with long dreads look alike. And we damn sure sound alike. I gave Gus some overnight lessons on how to do and move. I made him a promise that I would take care of his family. His mom and dad are sickly, and he has ten bambinos running around. Gus knew he had to die either way, so that was good enough for him. Gus went heavy with the insults, and you know, once he mentioned Zen's fat prissy ass Mario and Pound Puppy was going to step," Face explained.

"Hell yeah, I'm sure they offed that nigga quick," Al added. Face continued telling Al the specifics giving him a brotherly hug in between. Al was shocked but happy to know his boy was alive. "So, what's the move, bro? You know damn well shit about to get real in the Ville for them pussies," Al said.

"We may be banned from the States, but we got some hungry mutha fuckan Jamaicans who live to kill," Face said with certainty.

"Two of Pound Puppies men rode here on the plane with me, they should still be around. Their flight does not leave back out until 6:15, and it's only 5:20 now," Al said ready for revenge.

"Hot damn, step one of the eliminations plain just fell in our lap, let's go get em, bro," Face said as he rushed through the airport, following behind Al.

Minutes later, Al spots Kool Breeze coming out of the bathroom. Kool Breeze was feeling light as a feather rubbing his belly. Al and Face did a quick huddle to quarterback the next play. Face stepped behind Kool Breeze, and Al stepped in front of him. Face put his revolver pistol in Kool Breeze's back and dared him to scream. Face instructed Kool Breeze to keep walking and play it cool. "If you make any faulty moves, I will kill you inside this airport," Face sounded off. Kool Breeze was beating himself up for taking that shit. Kool Breeze knew he fucked up, and shit was about to get ugly for him. They made it to the parking lot. Waiting inside the van was Face, older brother Heavy, and Al's cousin Glo. Soon as everyone was loaded in the van, Heavy knocked Kool Breeze out cold with a left hook. Heavy was a three-hundred-pound tar baby greasy nigga. Heavy's hands were big as boxing gloves. Glo drove off, and they headed to Downtown Kingston, one of the roughest and toughest parts of Jamaica.

The plane was getting ready to board, and Kool Breeze was nowhere in sight. Big Mike displayed a worried look on his face. Big Mike did not want to call Pound Puppy with this news. Big Mike knew he was getting his ass on that plane with or without Kool Breeze. Big Mike felt something was wrong. He had a nervous feeling creeping through his body. Big Mike boarded the plane and sat in between a group of nuns. Big Mike was no punk, but he could sense trouble a mile away. It was something he was blessed with. Big Mike knew he would be fighting a losing battle if he stayed and looked for Kool Breeze. No need for them both to be jammed up were Big Mike's thoughts. Big Mike sent Pound Puppy a detailed text explaining the situation with Kool Breeze. *"I searched the airport high and low. I checked all the restrooms from end-to-end multiple times. I asked around a few people that were on our flight, but no one had seen him. The Airport only has a hand full of people roaming around, so if he is here, I would have spotted him by now. I am on my way back to the States. We can further handle this when I return."* Pound Puppy texted back.

"Be careful, fam, watch your surroundings. I'm on it."

Pound Puppy forwarded the text from Big Mike to Zen. Zen texted back Ashley's address so Pound Puppy could meet her there. Zen grabbed her purse and called Ashley on the way to her garage, giving her the specifics of what she needed her to handle. When they arrived at Ashley's garage, the airport footage was already across the screen. Ashley enlarged the screen to get a better view of the footage, starting from when the plane landed. The footage shows Kool Breeze going into the restroom. Then Al is spotted being grabbed by a man. Seconds later, they discovered that the man was Face. "OMG, what the fuck Pupp. You see this shit?" Zen yells out. "It can't be Mario, and I let loose on that nigga," Pound Puppy said, scratching his head.

"That dirty mutha fuckar, I kept looking at that nigga that night. I noticed the nigga had gold fronts in his mouth, but I shook it off. I thought Face was sporting a grill, trying to stunt. We have been deceived Pupp; we were so riled up off emotions we slipped badly. They fuck wads out slicked the slicksters," Zen spoke loudly.

"Damn, who the fuck did we Kill then, Pound Puppy?" asked out loud.

"Ashley, cross reference all Jamaicans living here in Greenville associated with Al and Face," Zen instructed.

"Ok, sis, I'm on it." While Ashley was handling that, Zen and Pound Puppy continued to watch the footage. They saw the whole scenario play out from beginning to end. Ashley even played it in slow motion. "Here are twelve names and photos of Jamaicans dealing with Al and Face closely. This guy here raises a red flag. His name is Gus Reynolds. His family has been looking for him for the past few days. He damn sure can pass for Face," Ashley sounded off.

"Bingo, that's him. He and Face look identical," Zen screamed. Pound Puppy went to Gus' Facebook page, and that was Gus who they killed. "Kool Breeze will not be returning; they niggas will torture him, then kill him. Al and Face will not chance coming back to the States because we have them scared about going to jail for killing Murry and Bruce. But they will be gunning for us, so we must stay ready," Pound Puppy stated while trying to strategize a countermove.

Zen sent Mario a text going over the Face situation. Mario knew Zen was upset, and so was he. "No need to get off our grind Zen. We have handled much worse. When the time comes, we will go hard to correct our fuck up. Just come home, bae, so you can relax. You're putting too much thought into this shit. I got us covered, I promise you that." Mario had some skeletons in his closet, and he would let them out real soon. When the enemy came fucking with him and his family, it was going to be World War III made over.

Mario and Zen went to their favorite rooftop restaurant in downtown Greenville. Mario called ahead to place their order. Chef Peter knew all their favorite foods because they were regulars. They were served a complete surf and turf meal with all the fixings. A bottle of Crown was being chilled on ice. Zen hugged Mario tight, kissing him passionately. She then sat on his lap and began feeding him his food. "I know about London no need to butter me up."

"Huh?" Zen replied dumbfounded.

"You heard me, Tubbie." Tubbie was a nickname that Mario called Zen that she grew to love.

"So, you're not mad?" Zen asked as she continued to feed her husband.

"A little, but you already know," replied Mario.

"Yeah, I know, you are coming too, and it's NON-NEGOTIABLE. What else is new?" Zen said sarcastically.

"Now that we got that out the way, go eat your dinner so I can take your Tubbie ass back to the pool house and make you scream my name."

"Waiter, we need to go boxes please," Zen screamed so loud the other guest turned to look her way. "The fuck y'all looking at, my husband finna get in these guts. WAITER, CHOP CHOP, PLEASE. IM IN A HURRY." Zen waved her hand, rushing the young waiter. Mario laughed while they waited on the to-go boxes.

Al, Face, Glo, and Heavy arrived in Downtown Kingston. Downtown Kingston was the lowest of the low. Any and everything went down there. Police were down with whatever fuckery the criminals were on. Nothing was hidden. You could commit a crime in broad daylight and not gain any consequences. This was a neighborhood where you had a slim chance of survival if you were the enemy. The strip was packed with locals trying to make a hustle for a few dollars. Heavy flashed JMD currency in the face of some street thugs. That is what Jamaicans call their money. The men jumped up and down as if they were on a trampoline. "I need you guys to take this man and drag his ass up and down the strip. I want him beaten badly. If any of the sweet tarts wanna get some but love, let them dig his ass out. I want to see so much blood that I can fill up my bathtub. And if the job is done right, there will be more JMD waiting on you. Heavy sounded off while taking a swig from a bottle of cheap liquor." Face then handed Glo a video camera so she could follow them and catch the excitement.

"When the time is right, we will solidify a crew that will not be afraid to get down and dirty," Heavy sounded off.

"No doubt, bro. I know some money-hungry killers over in Tivoli Gardens that will wreak havoc in the States on Mario," Face added.

"That may be true, but Zen and her crew must be our focal point. They bitches are lethal. They have an itch for this life. At this point, We need to switch gears. They fuck wads are going to expect us to retaliate, but we will shake shit up if we send in some females. I can guarantee you any roughneck Jamaicans entering the States is about to catch hell. The law and every street nigga are looking for us by now. A group of females will slip right in unnoticed," Al continued with the details. Al was around Zen and her crew enough while he was captured to figure out their way of thinking. "It's settled then. Let's recruit the baddest bitches walking in Jamaica," Face said with assurance.

"We don't need them, bad, bro. We need them deadly. Zen will not know what hit her loudmouth juicy pussy fine ass," Al said smiling.

"Damn nigga you in love with the enemy?" Heavy asked. "Nah, she just makes my dick hard, taking control, how she does," Al responded.

"Sounds like you been backdooring Mario," Face said jokingly.

"Man, y'all niggas can't tell me if the opportunity presented itself, you wouldn't fuck Zen," Al responded.

"Nigga you're tripping, but hell yeah, I'll buss a nut all on that ass, Heavy said, laughing."

"You two love birds, stop thinking with your dicks, and let's get down to business," Face said, fully confused about why Zen was the topic of their discussion.

"But anyway, it will be best for us to lay low for now, get this play solidified, and most of all, get back to the grind. That was a major loss we took, but them Americans will pay, and that's on Jesus' toes," Heavy said with much attitude. Al and Face agreed while the three men sealed the deal with their long brotherly two-minute handshake.

CHAPTER 8

YOU SHOULD BE ASHAMED

It was the night before the crew took off to London. Milly Mill, Zen, and Bleu went on a search for Nicolette. They finally caught up with her at an assisted living home for men on the Southside of town. Nicolette loved to manipulate old men with her worn-out pussy. Nicolette would make rounds on the first and the fifth tenth of each month. Nicolette knew when Social Security and retirement checks were issued. Nicolette was skipping while exiting the building. She earned well over two hundred bucks performing sexual acts on senior men. She was about to enter a cab when she was snatched up from behind by Bleu. Nicolette was thrown in the back of Zen's Excursion. "Oh, hell nah, not this shit again," Nicolette said loudly.

"HELP, HELP, HELP. " Nicolette screamed. She began to resist and tried to exit the vehicle.

"Look bitch we don't want to hurt you, but we will, so shut the fuck up and listen to what the fuck is about to go down," Bleu spoke, being as nice as she could.

"Zen, please. What have I done to you? THIS IS BULLSHIT. Leave me the fuck alone, damn it." Nicolette continued to weep. She wiggled and moved back and forth, totally frustrated. She cursed in a low tone complaining the entire ride.

Nurse Kelly was there waiting at the apartment with all the supplies she needed to get Nicolette off the dope. After they were inside, Nicolette was placed in a chair where she was about to be hosed down. "Your mom is sick, bitch, and it's time for you to step the fuck up for her and your kids. I don't give two fucks about your smelly ass, but your mom came to me for help, and I will not let her down. I personally want to smack your ugly ass for not appreciating the fact that your mom is alive. Especially one as good as Maggie. Your family needs your grimy ass right now. Maggie has been caring for your eight bambinos, working and paying bills while you're out sucking and fucking for BOOGER SUGA bags. No matter how much you pout, no matter what you say, this is where the fuck you will remain until nurse Kelly gives you your walking papers. And if you think I'm hell fuck with my girl Milly Mill and she will have you hating life," Zen spoke firmly and clearly, making sure Nicolette understood. But she jumped up out of the chair, trying to run. Milly Mill was in motion to grab her, but Kelly two-pieced her in the face and gave her a double dose of Thorazine. Milly Mill licked her lips and looked Kelly over sexually, remembering her and Zen's conversation about her.

The crew met at the bowling alley to unwind before catching the long sixteen-hour flight to London. Pound Puppy invited his boy Big Mike to tag along. They were joining up with Mario, Kash, and Justin, better known as White Boy. White Boy and Mario have been friends since grade school. The two were so much alike it was scary. The guy's flight was three hours behind the ladies. They didn't want to enter the country together in case they were being watched. Mario and Pound Puppy knew Zen and the ladies could go to war with the best of them, but they did not have them travel to London without backup. While bowling and throwing around some shots, the ladies conjured up a plan for how they were going to stick and move and which mark to take out first.

The ladies were up at three am loading their luggage into the sprinter. The ride to the airport was long and boring. The ladies struggled to stay fully awake. The ladies arrived at the airport and began to board the plane. "What the hell is wrong with Bleu?" Raz asked out loud. Everyone turned around, and Bleu was in a panic with a face full of sweat. "Oh, shit, she's afraid to fly," Sundae thundered. Lady J and Nena gathered some paper towels, and Zen handed Bleu a bottle of water. "Damn, sis, I need you to calm down and focus. Just breathe in and out slowly. Take this half of the Xanax pill, and you will start calming down shortly. This was going to be a long flight, so I had to take a half too for me to be brave. I got you, fam. Just relax," Zen coached Bleu. Bleu shook her head. Yes. She took a few deep breaths and closed her eyes tightly. "Who would have thought Bleu would be scared to fly? A Top Model certified killa, that's tough as nails. This is one for the book's sis," Raz said jokingly.

"To be honest, we all have something we're afraid of. With my understanding, you get a bit jittery and claustrophobic when Pupp rams that dick up your ass. Freak tip number one. Rub some KY Jelly between your ass next time. The dick will glide right in. You're guaranteed to ease up on the screams. You can thank me later," Zen said, laughing. Raz didn't think that was funny.

When the ladies woke up, an hour remained before they landed. The guys were also on their flight and would be landing hours behind them. While exiting the plane, the ladies were all stiff as a board. "I know this is a business trip, but google me a fucking bar. I need about three double shots," said Bleu.

"Sis, I was worried about you, girl," Zen said, hugging Bleu.
"I'm back, sis. I promise," Bleu responded.

The ladies arrived at their hotel, Morgan Palace, and proceeded to check in. The hotel was breathtaking. They planned to jump right into the action, but the jet lag was no joke, so they unpacked their luggage and made their way to the hot tub and pool for some relaxation and, of course, some Margarita. Zen sent a confirmation to Chunchi that they had arrived safely. Chunchi wanted to meet with Zen, but Zen declined. Chunchi felt the need to get involved. She wanted to vent and add specifics to the already ordered. Zen instructed her where to wire the rest of the down payment. And that she would contact her only if she needed any further information. Zen never mixed business with pleasure, and she never met or talked with the clients.

The ladies finished off the day just chilling and site seeing. London was a spectacular country, and they were continuously snapping pictures of the beautiful monuments and other attractions. The ladies used that free time to grab a few gifts and shop on the main strip. Mario gave the thumbs-up emoji to Zen, indicating they had arrived safely. The guys stayed at the Swift hotel, three hotels down from the Morgan Palace.

The guys walked into their hotel with their swag on ten. They were bum-rushed by some groupies. "Damn, they have thots in London," White Boy asked loudly?

"Thots are everywhere. They don't die. They multiply," Kash responded. The thirsty women continued to flirt with the guys as they checked in. The woman was damn near masturbating in the lobby, lusting seductively after the guys. The guys looked like they were celebrities to the woman. London women had a thing for successful black men. "These whores wanna fuck something. They got the right one because I will put dick in their ear if they want it," Kash blurted out, while being overwhelmed by the thirst of the ladies.

The following day the ladies headed out to get started on their first assignment. Zen decided they would do Chunchi's order first because she was about to lose her mind. The female Police officer doing her husband made Chunchi's blood boil. Uma Shaw was her name. She could pass for a man. Uma was identical to the Russian Ivan Drago from the movie Rocky IV. Chunchi's husband, Macky Gilliard, was an old-school black player. A Britain pimp was what Macky strived to be. Uma was not his only love fling. She was just the only one Chunchi learned about. Zen will not share that information with Chunchi because that is not what she's paying for.

Lady J and Nena went to case the police station watching Uma's every move. Macky met Uma for lunch at a Bodega shop opposite town from the police station. The two were hugging and kissing in public like two horny teens. Sundae zoomed her camera in close, retrieving their continuous flirtatious behavior. Moments later, another white woman with a police uniform joined Uma and Macky. The woman shared the same characteristics as Uma. You would strongly believe she was male if it wasn't for her tits. The mystery woman joined right in with the flirtatious behavior. The three of them engaged in a steamy kiss right at the table of the Bodega. It was clear that Macky was into stud women. The trio finally ate lunch and swiftly returned back to work. Zen and Raz went to Uma's apartment to set up camera surveillance. Ashley maneuvered into the alarm system placing Uma's home alarm to not be armed for thirty minutes. That was enough time to distribute cameras throughout the house.

The ladies took on four assignments, and the bait was set for the first one. Bernstein Brown known as BB, has been dealing with infidelity with her husband Martin for decades with the same two women. Teola Doles, his mistress, accrued more authority with Martin than BB. Teola controlled Martin completely. He allowed her to disrespect his wife. Martin never put up a fight to protect his wife. For some strange reason, Martin would not divorce BB. Martin paid all the bills and kept BB living a glamorous lifestyle, but his time was devoted to Teola.

Teola and Martin were participating in an open relationship causing BB total humiliation. Teola purposely sabotages Martin's and BB'S marriage by aggressively targeting Martin. Cindy Jacobs was Teola's lesbian fling. Cindy was introduced to Teola's and Martin's relationship to keep things promiscuous and spicy. The three of them indulged in a sexual playground, and other females and males would sometimes get invited to play as well. Teola's job required her to travel two weeks out of the month. Teola did not want Martin to be with his wife while she was away. So, Cindy was being used as a sex slave to satisfy Martin and spy on him when she was away at work. Teola did whatever it took to keep Martin from being with his wife, Teola made sure he did not show BB an ounce of love. Martins' sexual desires were being handled, so Teola's method worked.

BB was fed up. Her request was to confront Teola and Martin at the same time. BB wanted to lay down some new demands and take control of her marriage. BB wanted them both to suffer. She desperately wanted a few rounds with Teola. BB's days of being nice were over. She was out for blood, and Zen and the crew were going to help her get it.

CHAPTER 9

IT'S JUST BUSINESS

Pound Puppy and Big Mike went downstairs to their hotel to eat lunch. Some of the same groupies from before surrounded them on the elevator. "We are flattered with the love and attention you ladies are showing us while we are visitors to your lovely country. But please, we are not celebrities. We are here to relax. So, give us our space. GEESH," Pound Puppy said to the groupies nice as possible. The groupies smiled and waved hello, poking out their chests, trying to deliver a sexy image for Pound Puppy and Big Mike to look at. Mario, Kash, and White Boy later joined them. They experienced the same issues with a different set of groupies when they were walking through the hotel lobby. "These fucking British women are some freaks; American men must be a hot commodity in this country," said Mario.

"Hell yeah, they are. But we must keep these thirst buckets in check before hurricane Zen, and her demon seeds find out," Pound Puppy responded.

"Y'all can chill, fam. Let me handle the mob squad if its dick they want, I will fuck em all," White Boy said, being serious.

"Apparently, you don't know my wife. She will fuck me up for you using your dick. So, chill your ass out nigga," Mario sounded off.

Back at Uma's apartment Macky and the mystery cop Fatima were all winding down with some soft music and drinks. Uma was cooking dinner while Macky and Fatima entertained each other with some foreplay. Uma shortly joined in. The lovers begin having wild and unusual sex throughout Uma's apartment. The women were taking the lead, placing their fingers inside Macky's butt. He was enjoying the feeling and moving his hips with pleasure. Fatima fucked Macky and Uma with a large size dildo. Uma then pleasured Macky and Fatima the same way. They continued for hours until the fire alarm sounded off. Uma let the steaks burn in the oven, and the apartment was covered with smoke. The fire department and the police both came to answer the alarm. Following protocol, the fire chief needed them to exit the apartment. While standing outside half-dressed, they were spotted by a colleague of theirs. "Hey, are you guys' alright?" Tameka asked, looking confused.

"Yes, we're good," Fatima answered.

"I didn't know you and Fatima were roommates," Tameka said as she looked them over.

"We're not. We just have game nights sometimes after a long shift," Uma said, irritated.

"What game were y'all playing, strip poker?" Tameka asked as she laughed.

"Clearly, there is no harm done here, are you done?" Uma asked the fire chief.

"Yes, ma'am. Officer Shaw, you're all clear to enter," Chief Sanders replied.

Zen and Bleu were following Teola. After hours of running errands, Teola made it home and was greeted by her three pit bulls, Rain, Sleet, and Snow. "Bitch, you know I don't do dogs. How the fuck we're going to get her with them fucking killers running free?" Zen asked in a panic. Everyone knew Zen was rough and tough until it came to a dog. Zen was terrified of dogs. "Calm your ass down. Now you're acting like me on the plane," Bleu said jokingly. "Our best play is to sit here and wait till she gets back in the car, then we make a move, cause them dogs do look vicious, sis," Bleu sounded off.

Sundae, Lady J, Nena, and Raz were seconds away from snatching up Martin. Martin was coming out of the pharmacy. When he entered his car, Sundae and Raz was inside. "Let's keep this simple. I need you to follow that car in front of you. If you scream or make a wrong move, I will off you," Raz explained to Martin while showing him her Glock.

"Do I make myself clear? Raz asked, wanting clarity. Martin shook his head yes repeatedly. Lady J drove to the Culture hotel an hour outside of town. When they arrived, Martin was instructed to walk every day, and the same rules apply.

Nena went inside first to swing by another room and get BB. Sundae and Raz walked into the room with Martin in the middle of them. Martin was pushed down into the corner of the floor. He hit his head hard against the air conditioner, busting his head open slightly. Martin wiped some blood from his head while looking at BB for help. The crew already prepped BB on how to handle Martin and Teola. "Hello, Mr. Brown. How's it going with you and your side piece?" BB asked.

"BB, what the fuck is this about? Let's talk about this in private. Who are these women, and how the fuck do you know them?" Martin asked while trying to cop a plea.

"When I wanted to talk, you refused, so I'm going to talk, and you will listen. You have been disrespecting me for years, running around like you're a single man. Teola has brainwashed you against me, but she can only do what you allow her to. I have been good to your trifling ass, stood around for over ten years, and let you shame me. All I ever wanted was love from you. My heart will not let me kill you, but I won't speak too soon. I will not let this heffa win against me. I will not just let Teola have you because I'm the one who married you. I'm the one who carries your last name, not her," BB continued with her venting process, sobbing and crying in between words. BB then let loose with her demands and stipulations. "First of all, you will no longer see Teola or Cindy. Your party with them sluts is over. Your nasty sorry ass will honor me as your wife instead you want to or not. You owe me that nigga. The only way out is death, mutha fuckar. This form is identical to a prenuptial agreement. You will be signing your finances and your properties over to me. Everything you own, including the house you purchased for your bitch will be mine. Since you have carried on for these years not knowing how to be a husband, I will help you out. You will work and come home and cater to me and do what the fuck I say. You will stay in the guest bedroom and live as a guest. This muscle-bound nigga right here is Nathan." BB signaled for Nathan to come in. Nathan was a tall black sexy piece of eye candy that BB had been dating for almost a year. Nathan cared for BB and relaxed her mind by satisfying her many needs that her husband neglected.

"Nathan and I will share the bedroom that used to belong to us."

"Bitch you're out of your fucking mind," Martin said as he attempted to get up off the floor. The ladies were all anxious to fuck him up, but they were letting BB vent because it was long over. But his luck just ran out. Sundae, and Raz jerked Martin up and slammed him into the wall face-first. Raz kneed him a few times in his back, then Sundae shot him three times in his calf with her twenty-two pistol. Raz turned Martin around to face her, clinching his face tightly. "You will do what the fuck she says, and then some. You're a cheating ass pussy with no morals. If you fail to comply, the next bullets will be to your chest and not with a twenty-two. You're going to live in the same house with your wife chained up while she fucks the life out of her new boo thang in your face. Nathan and BB will live off your money, and you will become the yard boy because that's the only place you will be allowed. You should have thought about how your wife could eventually get tired of your shit one day and flip the fuck out. My team and I hate it took her ten-plus years to get to this point because we would have been whipped back to reality," Raz said with disgust.

Zen received a text from Raz. "*Sis, where y'all at? We good on this end, oh boy, need medical attention, but he'll live?*"

"*This bitch has three CUJO-looking pits, so we went another route. Send a text from Martins phone giving Teola the address, and we will follow her ass straight there,*" Zen replied.

"Already done," Raz texted.

Teola rushed out of the house with a smile on her face. Raz sent her a text so sweet, portraying she was Martin.

Teola was lusting about being with her man. Teola was speeding down the highway. Zen and Bleu were right behind her, talking on the phone to BB, giving her a tutorial on how to handle this bitch. Zen also instructed BB to call a contractor and install a wire fence inside her guest bedroom. Inside the fence will be a doggie bed and ink pens and pads so Martin can write apology letters to BB. Teola cut her time in half, making it to the hotel in thirty minutes. Teola exits her car and grabs her overnight bag from the trunk. She then proceeds to make her way to room 1734. Teola knocks on the door lightly.

"It's me, bae," Teola did not see Zen and Bleu behind her. BB opened the door, "Come on in, sidepiece," BB stated. Teola instantly turned around to leave but was punched repeatedly in the face by Zen. Bleu grabbed Zen. "Ok, sis. Imma let BB handle it. I just couldn't help myself," Zen said, frustrated because she wanted to fight Teola. BB started smacking Teola across the face with the ice pitcher. Teola dropped her bag and was ready to square off with BB. Zen could not hold it any longer. She and Sundae tag-teamed on Teola's head. Every time Teola would try to say something, she was punched or kicked in the mouth by one of the crew. Her lips were swollen like melons, her body was bruised, *and she was now sore and could barely move.* "BB, this is what you paid us to do. You keep your energy so you can give Nathan some of that kitty," Bleu spoke.

"All of you are going to jail," Teola manages to mumble out.
"Bitch shut the fuck up. You been fucking this woman man for years like you're Queen Sheba. How rude and disrespectful of you not to consider this woman's feelings. I bet you didn't know you would be getting your ass kicked

about Martin when you woke up this morning," Raz said while poking her finger in Teola's face." Teola began to cry loudly.

"We have no remorse, so you can save them tears. Nobody will hear you because we are the only ones on this floor," said Zen.

"You were on top of the world when you were fucking my husband, you sick bitch," BB said right before spitting in Teola's face. Sundae begins singing the famous Pokey Bear sidepiece anthem, and the rest of the ladies joined in. "I LEFT HOME BABY, TO BE WITH MY SIDE PIECE, MY SIDE PIECE, I LEFT HOME TO BE WITH SIDE PIECE." The ladies dragged the hook, making fun of Teola singing and dancing in front of her.

BB cleaned up Martin's leg only so he wouldn't raise any attention once they reached the lobby. BB and Nathan left the hotel. Martin was escorted back to the car by Sundae and Nena. Soon as the ladies receive confirmation that the fence is completed, Martin will later be dropped off to begin his life as a natural live caged dog. Teola was left in the room being filmed by several male prostitutes. "Since you like to fuck so much, these men are paid to serve you for two weeks with nothing but pure dick," Zen said before walking out of the room. Teola wanted to die, but the male prostitutes wasted no time. They stripped her down and fucked her bruised body, enjoying her screams.

Nicolette was getting fucked up by nurse Kelly. She was not cooperating with her recovery process. Milly Mill tried to step in, but Kelly was adamant about handling Nicolette herself. Milly Mill noticed Kelly looking at her, giving her the green light to shoot her shot when she saw fit. Milly

Mill checked on Maggie to ensure she was supplied with her medications. Milly Mill left money for gas and other house supplies as well. Maggie was sleeping, but Allison received the money. "Do you know when my mom will be back? Stone said he was going to hurt my grandma if my mom doesn't come to see him by Friday?" Allison asked Milly Mill.

"Don't worry about that. You just take care of your grandma and your sisters and call 911 if anybody comes over here making threats, then you call me ASAP," Milly Mill responded.

Zen wanted to check out the Swift hotel that Mario and the guys were staying at before they all retired to their hotel for the night. As the ladies walked into the hotel, they saw several British models and a massive group of females scattered over the place. They found the guys in the arcade room playing a game of pool. As Zen approached Mario for a hug, a groupie chick intercepted, grabbing Mario. "He's with me." Before Zen could blink her eyes, she boxed the frail-looking white girl until she could not stand. "Oh, hell nah." Raz and the rest of the crew were in rotation to snap. Mario tossed Zen over his shoulder as if she was a size two. When they were outside, Mario pleaded with Zen. "I know that bitch was wrong, but please, let's not make unnecessary attention while we're here. PLEASE, BAE, shake it off," Mario begged. Zen was so mad she walked off with her crew in tow.

"That's what the fuck I was afraid of," Pound Puppy said aloud while looking at White Boy.

CHAPTER 10

THEY STARTED IT

Zen and the ladies chilled at the hotel for the next few days. They wanted to be seen around the hotel as a tourist just in case they were being watched. They also made a few trips to the Swift hotel disguised as men. They witnessed firsthand how thirsty the British women were for black men. Pound Puppy was being attacked while at the breakfast buffet. Security was slack. They turned a blind eye to the possessive women. It was becoming a problem with the women disturbing the men while they were on vacation. "This hotel better gets this shit under control, or I will Bleu," co-signed by Zen and Raz.

Lady J and Nena went to check on Teola. She was still getting fucked every which way her body could bend. "I am so sorry. Can all of you please let me go? I will not violate or disrespect any other woman, I promise. Please, please, I'm begging."

"You weren't begging when you were fucking Martin and shaming his wife," Nena said as she shut the door. Word had gotten around about the woman in 1734. More men were dressed as businessmen to get a piece of that pie.

Uma was at her desk when she received a series of emails. The emails were of her Fatima and Macky doing their shenanigans. Fatima received the duplicate emails at her desk as well. Uma started receiving more emails about her masturbating and smoking marijuana inside her home.

Seconds later, the entire police station was receiving these emails. The chatter begins to surface at the station. Everyone was walking from room to room, discussing Uma and Fatima. Uma stormed out of the station in a rage. Fumes were added to the fire as soon as she spotted the sixty-inch plasma TV mounted to the support beam in front of the police station. Videos of her Fatima and Macky were playing on the screen. Sexual sounds were coming through the police station's intercom. Officers were running around trying to cut the volume, but it only became louder. Ashley hacked the system and was in complete control of the switch. A letter was left explaining who was responsible for this sudden adventure.

"My name is Macky Gillard. I have been extorted by two of your female officers for years. I was forced to participate in sexual activities with both officers. They used me and made me do shameful, disgusting acts. They both promised to fabricate bogus charges on my wife if I declined their request. I am coming forward with this information because these women have begun to have a fetish for young kids, and that's where I draw the line. Uma Shaw and Fatima Mash are sick individuals. They are sexual sadist women. It is clear they are on the wrong side of the law; this situation and others need immediate attention. Please help me help others because it is too late for me."

Uma and Fatima were fired on the spot and arrested for extortion and misuse of police authority. Macky was home begging Chunchi for forgiveness and doing everything he could to be in her good grace again.

Heavy and Face were out scouting for the most treacherous females Jamaica had to offer. Number one on the recruit list was Gucci. Gucci lived most of her life as a man. Recently, she began to dress in female clothes and fuck men, so her title went from stud to bi-sexual. She had a mouth full of fake gold teeth and a short fade cut. Gucci was a low-budget bounty hunter. That was her hustle. She was used by several of the street thugs to locate their prey. She enjoyed hurting people and would become excited when mischief came her way. Rainbow and Selena were next on the roster. Rainbow was a pretty and delicate female with a Hollywood figure. Rainbow has been under the knife so much she was banned from Dr. Moto, the Jamaican plastic surgeon. Niggas and bitches were blindsided by her beauty and her girly ways. Rainbow was a killer. She killed men for money to continue her surgery lifestyle. Rainbow put the crime into crime. Her arrest record was long as her bundle inches. Rainbow helped other people with their caseloads because she knew the law well. Selena was last on their list; she was a classy female that liked to fight cops. Selena's nickname was Mike Tyson because she bit a cop's earlobe off. She has shot two cops and was charged with first-degree murder on a cop. After three years of being locked up, she convinced this scary chick Ayonda to take the wrap for it. Ayonda was with her the night Selena shot the cop. Ayonda was being charged with accessory. Ayonda was getting bullied and beaten up so much that she confessed to the shooting to save her family and to get away from Selena.

Al was busy coming up with a game plan to get these ladies to the States and make shit happen for them.

Mario called Zen. He wanted to see his wife. "Hey, Tubbie, what's the status? Is everything going ok?" Mario asked.

"Yes, husband, we will be complete in a few days. The next two assignments will be quick. After that, we will need to move quickly back to the States. Ashley booked us all on the same flight, so you fellows are ready to move. Pass it along," Zen said to Mario.

"I was hoping to see you. Can you at least come give me a kiss and let me fill you up with some dick while we're in London? I wanna fuck my whore in a different area code," Mario said jokingly.

"No, sir, this is a business trip, no pleasure. We can have some phone sex like we used to do when you were locked up." Zen shot back, laughing.

"Damn, bae, I want you bad," Mario begged his wife.

"You just stay your ass away from them freak bitches. I'll text you later. Love ya."

Milly Mill was watching over Maggie's house when she saw two niggas knocking on the door like they were the Feds. Milly Mill stepped out of hiding and approached the men. "Why the fuck are you punk niggas knocking on Miss Maggie's door like that? She is asleep. Have some mutha fuckan respect. Her grandkids live here. And what do you pussies want anyway?" Milly Mill asked angrily.

"Who the fuck are you? I advise you to mind your fuckan business bitch." A short midget-looking bumpy face nigga screamed out at Milly Mill. She pulled out her nine-millimeter pistol and pointed at the nigga.

"I will shoot the pus out of them bumps on your face if you call me a bitch again." The nigga reached for his gun, and Milly Mill laid them both on the front porch. She called Ashley to get the cleanup crew to Maggie's house ASAP.

Milly Mill stopped Allison just in time from dialing 911. She and Allison moved quickly, getting everybody's things together. Allison made sure Maggie secured her medications and her crossword puzzles. Milly Mill was placing them in unit five at the Pickle Tower, with surveillance cameras and security. She knew Zen would not trip about that. All the kids were helpful. They were happy to be going to a place with an air conditioner and Wi-Fi.

The Swift hotel hosted a poker night monthly. British and poker-playing men worldwide would travel for a seat at this table. All guests at the hotel received a thousand dollars in complimentary chips. That was enough bait to get the guys moving. They all played poker and dominoes back home. This put a smile on the guys' faces. They were about to see who could hold em and fold em.

The guys walked in and were immediately greeted by the hostess. They were given a glass of champagne and escorted to their table. White Boy and Pound Puppy were at the first table, and Mario Big Mike and Kash were direct across from them. Pound Puppy ordered a bottle of Crown for each table, and they sipped and observed the other men at the tables until the game started. Six young loudmouths, attention-seeking thugs come in with an entourage. The groupies crowded around the thugs and were eating up the attention. The thugs made a ten-minute scene and did a fashion show walk through the hotel just to get to the poker table. "Who the fuck is these clowns?" White Boy asked with a whisper.

"Man, I don't know, but they need to take them hot ass fur coats off its ninety degrees outside," Pound Puppy responded. Mario did a small giggle to himself.

"You think something is funny, the pierced face nigga?" Doug asked Mario.

"Nah, I just suddenly had a flashback when my homeboy right her choked a man at the club last night," Mario responded, pointing at Big Mike.

"Well, it won't be any choking in here tonight, playboy." Another tatted nigga Vernon, responded. Pound Puppy sent Mario a quick text. *"Chill, bro. Let's enjoy the game."* The dealers came to the tables to start the games. The guys were intrigued by the experience. They displayed the poker vibe, with Cubin cigars and Crown straight up. Mario and Kash's poker chips begin to grow. The thugs were looking sad and getting frustrated because their game was off. They were losing quickly. The groupie chicks were walking around, showing attention to Mario, Kash, and White Boy. Doug called one of the chicks over to him for a back rub, and she declined. "We're too busy focusing on these handsome American men," the chick responded.

"Bitch, get your slow ass over here!" Doug screamed out.

"Go handle that. We're good over here." Pound Puppy addressed the chick.

"Who the fuck asked you?" Vernon sounded off. At that point, the guys knew shit was about to get ugly. Hours into the game, Mario became the big winner. Feeling a bit tipsy, Mario signaled for his crew to get ready to cash out. They were going to call it a night. "I know you American fuck boys are not trying to dine and dash out the game," Doug thundered.

"Don't know who the fuck you're calling a fuck boy, but if you're addressing my boys or me, you need to take the aggression down a notch," Mario sounded off, looking Doug and his entourage directly in the face. Corey, a big, fat sloppy Shrek look-alike, stood up with his green hair shedding all over the place as if he was infested with Manges. "You fellows are not going anywhere until we say you can leave," Doug spat with aggression.

"Nigga fuck all y'all British talking mutha fuckas we're about to leave this bitch, and if any of you feel froggy, then leap y'all ass this way," Kash said, full of rage. Mario and his boys stood up to walk away from the table. Vernon and Doug popped Big Mike over the head with a champagne bottle. From that moment on, all hell broke loose. Pound Puppy and Mario grabbed Vernon and Doug by the neck with one hand and forcefully punched them with the other hand. Big Mike recovered quickly when Pound Puppy threw Doug on the ground. Big Mike started whaling on Doug, showing no mercy. He was dropping elbows and doing other wrestling moves. Mario continued to punish Vernon, beating him senselessly. He wanted Vernon to remember this beating, so he put in work violently damaging him. White Boy and Kash were breaking limbs, two of the other thugs received dislocated shoulders, and one of their elbow bones was popped out of the socket. White Boy took the same broken bottle Doug hit Big Mike with and sliced one of the thugs in the face cutting his nose completely off. Pound Puppy stabbed his victim in the neck with the silver tongs in the ice bucket on the table. These thugs opened a can of whoop ass for themselves. Mario and Pound Puppy did not want to stop beating the thugs. They became excited with adrenaline. White Boy and Kash were pumped. They both took off their shirt, flexing their muscles, telling the thugs to bring them on. It was a royal rumble at the Swift hotel. A few of the groupies manage to get Mario's attention. "The police are minutes away, and one of the young boys' fathers is the chief. You fellows need to go NOW." Mario stopped in his tracks and gathered the others. They were headed out the front door when the Asian chick said, "No, this way, follow me." She took them out the side door, and they loaded up in her van. Mario called Zen, telling her what had just happened. "Ok, I'll get Ashley to book y'all another hotel on the other side of town. We will handle our last two assignments tonight and leave in the morning on another flight," Zen explained to Mario.

"The men come across some turbulence at their hotel," Zen explained to the ladies.

"Them mutha fuckan freaks again, let's get them whores," said Raz.

"Nah, this time it was some fucking street thugs. But we got to move tonight and move quickly because they fucked them niggas up bad," Zen said to her crew.

Ashley was sent the address of Nelson Walters and Phil Lawton. Their wives wanted them dead. Both wives were on a baking cruise in the Bahamas. Sara Walters and Linda Lawton knew their husbands would have their side piece over while they were away. Ashley cut the power off at Walter's home; moments later, Nelson came outside in his underwear, flipping the breaker box. Lady J was posted in the neighbor's tree, waiting for the perfect shot. The mistress stepped outside to join Nelson. Ten seconds later, Lady J fired the winning shot with an assault rifle, hitting Nelson in the back of his head. "Yep, I still got it, Lady J said as she climbed down the tree." The mistress, Sylvanna, dropped down, screaming next to her lover, shaking his body, hoping he would respond. Nelson was dead, and now Sylvanna must explain why she was at Sara's house with Sara's husband.

Other neighbors begin to surface, asking who Sylvanna is and where was Sara. The mistress Sylvanna tried to leave but was stopped by two older ladies that lived two houses down. "The police will need to talk to you. You can't just leave. Nelson is lying here dead, for God's sake," Miss Pattie screamed. Co-signed by Miss Eugena. "Your bitch ass playing wifey to this married man, up in Sara's home as you live here. You're a fucking home wrecker and should be punished." Miss Eugene tried to attack Sylvanna with a garden rake she grabbed from her yard to walk over.

The police were still investigating the brawl at the Swift hotel poker night. After they gathered the guy's poker chips, the groupies were helpful and let the police know that the young thugs orchestrated the entire fight. Ollie was friends with the Asian chick Juicy, that helped the guys getaway. Ollie contacted Juicy and told her she had their poker chips. Juicy asked the guys whether they wanted their items from the room. "Hell, nah, we're not going back there," Mario said, looking at Juicy sideways.

"Nah, if you guys would like your belongings, my girl can get in your room and retrieve your things," Juicy explained.

"How the hell she's going to get in? We have our keys right here," Pound Puppy said, jingling the keys. "Trust me. She can get in."

"Hell, yeah, if that's the case, I want my shit," said White Boy.
"So, since we're semi-friends right now, what do y'all females do at that hotel?" Kash asked.

"Let's just say we're investment brokers. We see many black American rappers or entertainers come through Swift, and we keep them from being homesick. We make a living entertaining the rich. When you guys stepped in, we automatically speculated a profile in our head that y'all were in the entertainment industry. My crew and I were told to back off because y'all were affiliated with some American females that were not to be fucked with." Juicy kept it real as she continued explaining to the guys

Milly Mill decided to visit Stone. She wanted to be real with the nigga to see if he had a heart or if he was going to choose to go to war with them. Walking into the bar, Stone was surrounded by two females looking half-dead. "I need a few minutes of your time, big pimping," Milly spoke, being relaxed. Stone looked Milly Mill up and down with his crooked eyes.

"You can speak," Stone replied.

"I'm not asking permission to speak nigga. I'm trying to address a situation with you. I'm not under your command, pimp," Milly Mill said with much attitude. Stone waved the woman away and stood up with a mug on his face thinking he was about to scare Milly Mill.

"My time is valuable. What's the urgency?" Stone asked.

"You're sending mutha fuckas to Nicolette's mom's house looking for her. Her mom and kids are innocent in this pimp shit you have going on with Nicolette. Her mom Maggie is sick with Cancer, and Nicolette has eight children that live in that house. All I'm asking is take your beef up with Nicolette when you see her on the street and leave her mom and kids out of it," Milly Mill spat.

"So, you wouldn't know what happened to my two cousins that went over there the other day. Somebody told me gunshots were fired, but my cousins never surfaced?" Did stone ask with a curious look?

"Nah, I don't know shit, so do we have an agreement or what nigga?" Milly Mill was now irritated.

"Imma eases up, but it's only because Pound Puppy asked, not because of you wanna-be a gangsta ass," Stone said with a deep voice, trying to show he was a boss. Milly Mill laughed; "I see you didn't step. She looked him in his crossed eyes as she walked off, flipping him the finger."

Phil was not home. He and his mistress were at a late-night movie. Ashley killed the power at home, and Zen and Sundae popped a window and went inside to wait on his arrival. Once they were in, Ashley resumed the power. Bleu, Lady J, Raz, and Nena were kept looking out from behind the parked cars on the opposite side of the street. Sundae and Zen set up what they needed in the laundry room. Now it was only a race against time when Phil was coming home. Zen sent a quick text to Mario. *'Last mission. Be at the airport in two hours.'* Mario sent the thumbs-up emoji in response.

Nena shined the flashlight twice, indicating a car pulling up in the driveway. "About damn time," Sundae spoke. The two lovers enter the house drunk as hell. How they made it home was a mystery. Berta Phil's mistress needed a shower to sober up a bit. Phil went to fix a snack and turn on the downstairs tv. "Hurry up, bae, so we can watch Water Boy," Phil slurred.

"Ok, love, I'll be quick," Berta yelled from the bathroom. Phil was on the couch rolling up a blunt and munching on a bag of hot Cheetos. Sundae struck him from behind in the head with a metal pot. Phil never saw it coming. Sundae and Zen carried him to the laundry room. They prepared a hanging rope from the top support beams. Phil was placed securely in the thick rope noose by his neck. He then was left to hang; eventually, all his air would expire from his body. The ladies typed up a suicide letter using the paper from Phil's office with his fingerprints.

"My name is Phil Lawton. I have been secretly cheating on my wife with Berta McCombs. I am so ashamed of myself for doing this to my lovely wife, Linda. Linda is the best thing to ever happen to me, and I have betrayed her and broken our vows. I have disrespected my wife, allowing another female to take her role. I can't continue with life knowing I have hurt my Linda. I have finally realized that my infidelity is wrong. Berta McCombs is entirely at fault. Berta has been manipulating me for years to sleep with her. Berta manipulated me into believing my wife did not love me because she often taught baking classes and spent her free time in the kitchen, not sucking my dick. I fell victim to letting Berta keep me away from my wife and commit adultery with her. I would like to apologize to my wife and kids for this embarrassment. By the time you read this letter, I will be dead. Linda, my sweet wife, I am deeply sorry I hurt you. And for Berta, I'll see you in hell bitch."

When Berta left out the bathroom, Sundae, Zen, and the pot were long gone. Berta slipped into her comfy sleepwear and then proceeded to the couch to join Phil. "Bae, where you at? I'm all done and clean for you," Berta yelled out. Berta noticed the weed on the floor, and the blunt was unrolled. She grabbed a few hot Cheetos from the bag, started the movie, and dozed off. When she woke up, the movie was about over. She walked through the house, calling Phil's name and checking the bedrooms. A worried looked came across Berta's face as she continued to look for Phil.

Walking fast by the laundry room, the hanging rope caught her eye. Berta turned around and went inside and discovered Phil was dead, dangling from the noose. Berta screamed and climbed the step ladder, trying desperately to get him down. She had no luck. Berta spotted the letter and began to read it. She was hysterical. By the end of the letter, she was shaking, and her screams became louder. She was not about to call the police, so she gathered her things and left the house. When she opened the door, the police were just about to knock on the door. "Ma'am is everything ok the neighbors heard screaming from inside?" the nice policewoman asked. After her partner noticed the confused and strange look on Berta's face, he went inside with his weapon in hand. The policeman was moving through the house cautiously. When he found the body, he immediately felt for a pulse. "We have a dead body. Call the medics!" he yelled out to his partner. The medics were called, and the police bagged the letter and further searched the house. "Ma'am, do you have any identification? You need to hang around. We have some questions for you," the policewoman explained.

CHAPTER 11

WE'RE BACK

Mario and the guys were dropped off at the airport by Ollie. Juicy later met them to deliver their belongings. Juicy played fair, and nothing was missing, just like Ollie told them. "There is nothing we can do with these poker chips. We're on our way back to the States. So, you two ladies can split them. That's our way of saying thank you. When the radar is turned down, y'all are not bad," Kash spat, co-signed by the rest of the guys.

"As I said before, we were warned to back up, and that was the only warning that was going to be given," Ollie said softly. Ollie and Juicy hurried back to their vehicles. They were avoiding the vicious female crew they had heard so much about. "Thanks, fellows. Be safe." It was all they said before they drove off.

Zen contacted Chunchi after her incident with the random white chick that grabbed up on Mario. Chunchi was familiar with the ladies and their thirst at the Swift Hotel. Chunchi let it be known that this crew of girls was heavy, and no one stood a chance against them.

Berta was not charged with Phil's death, but she had to be placed in a psychiatric hospital to undergo evaluation. Berta's body went numb after the tragic death of Phil. After the letter was explained to her, Berta was shocked by how Phil blamed her for his suicide. That caused Berta to have a nervous breakdown.

Zen and the ladies were moving fast, gathering their luggage from the hotel. They arrived at the airport just in time to board the plane. They confirmed their payment from Ashley, and London was now a memory.

They shared the stories of their London experience on the plane. The guys failed to mention Ollie and Juicy. Even thou it was innocent, they knew it would have been hell from Zen. The poor girls would have been found in the park with a duck stuck up their asses if Zen had any clue of them being around her husband.

The plane ride back was twenty-four hours. Somehow eight hours were added to this flight. Bleu was in a deep sleep the entire plane ride. Zen juiced her up with a double-dose concoction of lean syrup. Zen took a swig herself feeling no pain. Zen was being extra flirtatious with her husband thirty thousand feet in the air, reminding him why he fell in love with her.

The plane landed, and the crew was moving expeditiously. Something about a long plane ride becomes depressing after a while, so exiting the plane was music to their ears. Milly Mill was driving the sprinter. She paid the driver to go take his family out for dinner. Milly Mill wanted to take that time to update the ladies on Nicolette and Stone, plus she missed her girls. This was the first assignment she could not attend, and she was slightly sad. "What's up? I miss y'all nagging assess," Milly Mill said excitedly.

"Girl, that plane ride is not for the weak," Zen laughed.

"Fill me in on what I missed. I feel complete again," Milly Mill said, placing the last bag in the sprinter." "Sis, I got you. We have a round table meeting tomorrow to split up payments. We will give you the hype and all the facts later because right now, I'm going home to relax and overdose my husband on some pussy," Zen said while licking Mario's ear. Pound Puppy looked at Raz with his puppy dog eyes. "Nigga I got you too," Raz said, rubbing Pound Puppies shoulder and relaxing him.

Nicolette was one week clean. She became more cooperative with the whole recovery procedure. Nicolette was weak from throwing up, and the migraine headaches became unbearable. That was the side effect of her detoxing. Nurse Kelly explained nausea would go away soon.

Al loaded his girls up with the information they would need in the States. Their phones and tablets were going to be their lifeline. Maps, addresses, pictures, and profiles were some information stored away. Rainbow, Selena, and Gucci were all set for their journey to the States. Heavy would be joining them days later. "I want that bitch Zen so bad I can taste her. Them niggas act like she's unstoppable," Selena said to Gucci and Rainbow.

"Hell, yeah, she has an impressive profile, but she has not come across any females on our level," Gucci spoke. The girls headed to the airport to catch their flight and will soon find out what life on the other side is like.

Zen and the crew were meeting to discuss their next move and divide the currency they made from the London assignment. Lady J and Nena were the first to arrive. The other ladies arrived late as usual, even Zen was late, and she was always early. "Damn y'all bitches on COLOR PEOPLE time, I see Lady J fussed at them for their tardiness."

"I'm sorry, Lady J, don't kill me," Zen replied. Lady J frowned up, ready to get things popping because it was her anniversary, and she had epic plans. "Ok, I deposited the money in everyone's account. As you know, we scored three million dollars, divided six ways. We all cleared five hundred thousand each. I have the U-Haul truck parked in the back of Sweeney Street duplexes. It's full of gas, which we confiscated from our Jamaican lovers, Al and Face. We will be splitting that equally as well. Mario and I already have our share, so the rest of you grab yours. Raz, be sure to pick up Pound Puppies stash too. I will be working on my properties and managing my sweet business. I will be around as usual, throwing parties and hosting whatever events you ladies have planned for me, and of course, our usual foolery and fuckary. Margarita nights are mandatory. That is our holiday. We are forever them bitches ain't shit changed. If a mutha fuckar wanna get grimy, we step and roll as one," Zen spoke to her sister crew.

"AIN'T IT?" Said Milly Mill co-signed by the others. The ladies continued to exchange pleasantries while they smoked a few blunts of Al and Face exotic weed.

In London, Teola did not want to hear Martin's name or even watch the Martin sitcom reruns. Teola learned her lesson and was ashamed of how dozens of men mutilated her pussy fucking her wild and rough. Teola thought her and Martin's fling would last forever. Now she was bitter and scarred for her life. Teola cried and shook badly from the thought of a man touching her sexually, she has been used and abused, but that is the consequence you face when you fuck another woman's husband so freely.

Martin was receiving the ultimate payback; BB and Nathan were fucking like rabbits all over each other. They were loud with the sex sounds and kept the door open so Martin could hear them clearly, while he was locked in his cage in the guest room. Martin was feeling degraded and less of a man. Martin finally gained sympathy for how he treated BB, but it was too fucking late. Martin drowned himself in his misery and guilt as he cried like a bitch every day. Weeks later, Martin committed suicide, shooting himself under the chin with the neighbor's double-barrel shotgun. He broke into their garage and stole it when he was let out of the cage to hose himself off in the yard and cut the grass, but he ended his life instead. Nathan removed sharp objects, firearms, chemicals and lighters from around the house. He was afraid of what Martin might try to do to him. Nathan was one lucky man because the average man would have come for him strongly until they succeeded. Martin felt so guilty he wanted to repay BB and let her be happy because he knew his actions caused her terrible pain.

Gucci, Rainbow, and Selena were now on American soil. Their plane landed, and they were headed to the Bright Light motel off highway 85. Stella, Face's old chubby buddy, was meeting them at the motel to provide them with fake identification. Stella's hand-picked her white Jewish friend to rent a three-bedroom apartment from the Pickle Tower. Ashley screened all applicants before they even made it to Zen and Mario. If Ashley shut it down, it was a no-go with no exceptions.

Ashley was doing callbacks to the applicants that qualified for rental at the Pickle Tower. One particular applicant raised a red flag, so Ashley called Zen. "What up, sis?" Zen answered.

"We have an applicant name Amanda Crosby that applied for a three-bedroom at the Pickle Tower. Something just doesn't seem right about her. When I called, she talked to a few females in the background who were coaching her on what to say. I tracked her number to see if any familiar numbers were close by her phone, and Stella Rammings, the fat bitch who Face was having fuck sessions with popped up. And check this out, sis. The other three numbers were from Jamaica, but the names were unknown," Ashley interacted with Zen.

"That means they have untraceable phones, and yep, they were sent by Al and Face," Zen said in a low tone. "If they came all this way for us, eventually, we're going to cross paths with the OPPS, so go ahead and rent them the apartment. Let them feel like they have the upper hand for now. We need to act dumbfounded and stay on top of their every move. Have the maintenance crew install micro vision cameras with sound throughout the apartment before they move in," Zen added.

"I'm on it, sis," Ashley said before the call ended.

CHAPTER 12

MAKING ENEMIES

Zen texted the entire crew, along with Mario and Pound Puppy. *"Round table ASAP."* Zen was pacing back and forth, waiting on everyone to arrive. Mario drove up at full speed, thinking Zen was harmed. Seconds later, Pound Puppy came whipping in. "Zen, what's good? You alright?" Mario said, reaching for a hug. "Yeah, bae, we just have some visitors here from Jamaica that will be coming for us soon." Zen briefly gave Pound Puppy and Mario a small review before the others came. Everyone came in strapped and ready as usual. Joining the round table was Kash, White Boy and Big Mike. "We have a situation with a female by the name of Amanda Crosby. This female has applied for an apartment at the Pickle Tower. She is affiliated with Al and Face somehow. Stella Rammings is also in the mix," Zen explained.

"Wait, ain't that's the fat bitch that is down with Nicolette?" Pound Puppy asked.

"Yeah, that's the Michelin Tire mascot-looking bitch," Zen responded. Sundae and Nena laughed so hard; you would have thought they were at a comedy show. Zen even laughed herself. After everyone's giggles were out, Zen resumed with the information Ashley had dug up. "Ashley went deep, finding out what she could about Amanda. Amanda is a Jewish chick with two degrees from the University of Louisville. Amanda has no record, not even a speeding ticket. Her parents are from Kentucky and work at their family-owned farmers' market. Someone is using

Amanda for bait to get the apartment. I have agreed to rent the apartment to her. Cameras will be installed before they move in. Does anyone have any suggestions?" Zen asked.

"I feel like we let White Boy and Kash move in next door to keep an eye on what's coming and going," Mario added.

"White Boy and Kash will be the perfect neighbors if we're dealing with females like Ashley think we are. Make sure y'all dress to impress, smell nice and wear plenty of gray sweatpants," Bleu spat. White Boy and Kash gave Bleu a crazy look.

"You had me until the gray sweatpants," Kash said, looking confused.

"It's a female thang, men that wear gray joggers or sweatpants that enhances the illusion of their man muscle. A hot rental ride parked outside will seal the deal too. Females have a weakness for a good-smelling man with a big boy ride," Bleu sounded off, looking at White Boy and Kash as if she was teaching a class.

"That's small things to a giant that could be handled," Kash sounded off.

"So, are we pimping these Jamaican bitches or getting pimped out because I don't mind putting some dick in their life," White Boy said.

"Nigga, just ride the wave. Fake it to you. Make it. If you fuck you fuck but remember, these bitches are the enemy," Mario said still laughing at the look White Boy displayed across his face.

"Let's beef up our team by placing Big Mike in the apartment on the opposite side," Zen added. "Sounds good. We must keep our eyes and ears open and watch our surroundings. I'm sure they will be gunning for us," Mario stated to the crew.

"Our best move is to wait on their play and go hard when the enemy decides to strike," Pound Puppy said firmly.

"No doubt, I will instruct the maintenance guys to move and set up furniture in both apartments, so be sure to pack most of your belongings. No need to wait for y'all can move it in by tonight," Zen said, confirming with White Boy, Kash, and Big Mike.

Amanda received a call back from Ashley stating her application was approved. "Hello, Ms. Crosby. I just wanted to double-check the number of bedrooms you applied for. We have you down for a three-bedroom. Is that correct?"

"Yes, ma'am, that is correct," Amanda replied.

"Will you be adding anyone to the lease? If so, do we need also to check their name?" asked Ashley.

"No, ma'am, my parents will visit me a lot, and I have a teenage sister, so the extra bedrooms will be great," Amanda responded.

"Ok, sounds good. You can stop by the office anytime this week to pick up your keys and pay the deposit and first month's rent. The total amount will be two thousand dollars. One thousand for the security deposit and one thousand for rent," Ashley explained, "we would then go over the lease agreement, and you could move in whenever you like."

"Thank you so much. I will be by tomorrow morning," Amanda said happily.

Amanda shared the news with Gucci, Rainbow, and Selena. The three were inside their motel, plotting against Zen and Mario. Al solidified a plan for them, but the ladies were getting beside their selves because they were tired of hearing about Zen and her crew. Feeling like true crime fighters, the girls were about to ignore Al's plan.

The next afternoon Amanda was at the office completing her lease agreement and paying her fees. Amanda was giving her keys, and off she went. Kash and White Boy were set up at the apartment, and so was Big Mike. Gucci and the girls rented a U-Haul truck to pick up some furniture from the Good Will. One of Stella's cousins was selling a living room set, and they also purchased it. They were limited on money, so they patched up the apartment the best they could. After purchasing air mattresses from Wal-Mart, the girls made their way to the Pickle Tower to move in.

Gucci, Rainbow, Selena, Stella and Amanda drove to the apartment and began moving items out of the truck. "Damn, this U-Haul smells like weed," said Rainbow.

"Sure, does damn it smells good too," Selena spoke. It was a coincidence Gucci rented the same truck that stashed Al's and Face weed. After the girls completed three trips, Kash set up the bait by walking outside with his gray sweatpants and no shirt on. Selena and Rainbow were walking by carrying a sofa. "Hold on. Ladies let me get that for you," Kash said, signaling for them to place the sofa down.

"I see you buff around the shoulders, but how are you going to carry this sofa alone?" Rainbow asked. Right after, she said that White Boy came out of the apartment with a towel wrapped around his waist. He was wet from the shower. "You need some help, bro?"

"Yeah, let's help these beautiful ladies with this sofa," Kash responded.
"Ok, let me get dressed. I'll be right out," said White Boy.

"You don't have to get dressed," Selena spoke loudly.

"I don't want to scare you, ladies, away. You're just now moving in," White Boy teased.

"Scare me, you sexy mutha fucka," Gucci said while eyeing fucking White Boy. Kash and White Boy continued helping the ladies move in. Gucci, Rainbow and Selena continuously flirted with their two new neighbors. "These American men are too much," Selena stated.

"Girl, we've only been in America a hot minute, and your pussy is dripping cum already," Rainbow responded to Selena.

"Bitch, your ass been lusting too, putting on lip gloss every five minutes and asking for help with the smallest boxes," Gucci sounded off. Rainbow suggested to the girls that they should convince Kash and White Boy to take them out and show them a good time. The girls forgot about their mission. They were anxious about seeing what the American streets had to offer. Rainbow took a bottle of Hennessey down to Kash and White Boy's apartment. "This is from my girls and me; we really appreciate all the help you and your partner did for us today," Rainbow said, looking directly into Kash's face.

"No problem, lil Mama. We're glad we were able to help. Kash replied while White Boy nodded his head.

"If you guys are not busy tonight, how about showing us around and taking us to the hang-out spots," Rainbow asked, pointing at them both.

"No doubt I have the perfect place for you ladies. By the way, I'm Kash, and this is my brother from another mother, White Boy." Kash reached out for a handshake.

"Nice to properly meet you two. I'm Rainbow, and my two girls are Gucci and Selena. We can get further acquainted tonight," Rainbow said with a wink.

"Alright, it's settled. Meet us in the parking lot at nine o'clock," Kash sounded off.

White Boy saw the aggression Selena displayed for some dick. White Boy had planned on stroking her walls sooner than later. After he visioned sexing Selena, he made a call to Mario. "Hello, what's good, fam," Mario said when he picked up the phone.

"Shit, we're getting ready to take these Jamaican chicks out on the town."

"Damn already, don't tell me the gray sweatpants, " Mario said with a laugh."

"Nigga these bitches ready to fuck, one of them whispered in my ear for me to show her my dick," White Boy explained to Mario.

"Nigga don't forget these whores are after us." Mario said, "This could very well be a plot for them as well, concerned."

"Bro, I promise you these freaks are not thinking about handling no business. From what we gathered in the few hours we've known them. All three of them are hot and ready for some American pipe. But I'm on it. I'm doing exactly what Bleu and Zen want me to do. I'm Keeping them close, hopefully, real close," White Boy spoke.

"Text me when y'all get settled at the last party location, Zen and I will pop up," Mario sounded off.

Kash and White Boy brought Big Mike along to join in on the Jamaican fun. Everyone was in the parking lot as planned. "This is my homie Big Mike; he will be tagging along with us tonight. As you can see, we all have small sports cars, so each one of you can ride shotgun with us. Rainbow, I was hoping you ride with me. Selena and Gucci, my brothers, are harmless," Kash said while opening the door for Rainbow.

"Big Mike, let's ride. You look like you know where the wing spots are at," Gucci said loudly.

"No doubt," Big Mike responded while reaching for her hand. Selena and White Boy followed everyone's lead. Kash led the way. Their first stop was Sizzles, a Karaoke and Hookah bar. Sizzles was laid back and lots of fun. They started with a game of pool, then headed to the go-cart track to race. After competing for hours on the track, their hunger pains kicked in. The waitress seated them at a booth for six, but Big Mike and Gucci settled for a table next to them. "So y'all want to be antisocial table, huh?" asked Rainbow.

"Nah bitch, the way our bellies set up that booth ain't going to cut it. Besides, I might what to rub Big Mike's belly under the table," Gucci said jokingly.

"That sounds good, love, but if you're going to rub on something, don't let it be my belly," Big Mike said with a Casanova smile.

"Ok, nigga don't make me retire from eating pussy, and start choking on your American dick," Gucci spoke, lusting after Big Mike. The guys dug deep, pumping the girls for information, trying to get their back story. The girls revealed they were only in the States for an assignment. "This assignment seems very important Kash said, speaking aloud."

"Hell yeah," Gucci answered.

"Do y'all happen to know Zen Fuller?" Selena asked.

"Duh, we're living in her and her husband's Condos," White Boy said, looking at her dumbfounded. Selena tried to recover quickly. "No, I meant I would like to meet her."

"Hell, we all would," said Rainbow. They finished their food, ordered a few more rounds of Quavo shots, then enjoyed the Hookah. The strawberry and vanilla flavor was the best. Kash led them to a few more spots. The final stop was club Neuvo. The hottest, most exclusive nightclub in Greenville. The ballers, hustlers, movers, and shakers would all be in attendance on a Friday and Saturday night. White Boy Sent Mario the text. Just so happened that he and Zen were already in VIP living it up. Mario texted back, telling White Boy to come to join them. White Boy was reluctant because he had just bumped into Raz and Pound Puppy making their way to VIP. He at least wanted to rub the pussy. White Boy knew Zen and Raz were in the same place as the enemy. It was not about to be cute. White Boy pulled Kash and Big Mike to the side, telling them the news. "Damn, it is what it is, fam. Let's go," Big Mike said, shaking his head."

Since her mom died, Mario had not seen Zen drunk and crunk like this. Kash, White Boy, and Big Mike walked in VIP with their Jamaican girls. "What's up, Kash? Who is this dragon you have with you?" Zen said aggressively.

"Who the fuck you're referring to, you drunk bitch? I bet this dragon will beat your ass," Rainbow shouted. Gucci pushed her way up beside Rainbow, screaming at the top of her lungs.

"What the fuck you wanna do? Cause clearly you got us fucked up." Gucci had a serious mug on her face and was in a fighting stance.

"It's whatever ever, sir," Raz said to Gucci. Gucci swung at Raz, hitting her in the lip. Zen grabbed Rainbow by the neck with one hand, then grabbed Selena by the face, causing them to collide. The men tried to break it up, but it was a rumble. Not wanting to touch one of the other women, Pound Puppy finally got a hold of Raz and backed her up in a corner. Mario did the same with Zen. "You just signed your death certificate bitch," Selena said to Zen.

"I doubt that. Y'all bitches ain't shit. Y'all came over here to America for my husband and me, taking orders from two dummies that could not succeed at handling us themselves. What y'all need to do is boss the fuck up. Get your own fuckan money. I know y'all low-budget Jamaicans are working for Al and Face making pennies. Al and Face will keep you ladies below level if you allow them. Y'all are staying on my property and have the nerve to come for me. I and my boss bitch crew already knew you bum bitches were coming. We are top-tier status. We're way above grade level, so you will never be able to pull one over on me. Go back to the lab and re-strategize your plan because clearly, y'all have failed at your mission. If you ladies work for me, I will double your pay and give y'all a tutorial on how to become legendary boss bitches. Fucking with me is a mistake because I will wipe my ass with y'all frail cum rag whores. This bitch looks like she has received more plastic surgery than Lil Kim. Zen laughed, pointing at Rainbow. Baby Huey over there is tired already and ain't even gone around. This time, Zen was pointing at Gucci. And this bitch is just a follower. She looks like her pussy stank." Zen laughed, pointing at Selena. Raz joined in on the laughter, and she was ready to step if either one of them Jamaicans had moved wrong. "We can put this behind us and start fresh it's up to you. You can either be a begging bitch or a boss bitch, but you can't be both," Zen stated firmly.

"What if we don't accept your bogus offer, and you can stop with the jokes and insults? This is not Def Comedy Jam," Selena spat.

"Jokes, girl, I'm so serious, and nothing is more bogus than that tie-dye overall you're wearing and that bootleg body that your girl received from the Jamaican kindergarten class. If you decline, you can leave my Condo, return to Jamaica, and tell your bosses that Zen wins again." Zen walks off, picking up her Crown Royal bottle and taking a big boy swig.

Outside of the club, the girls huddled up before loading into the cars. "What y'all think?" Rainbow asked.

"Fuck her. That fat bitch. She just belittled us, and you want to side with her. That makes no damn sense. Please tell me y'all or not considering her offer. Fuck that. There is no way I'm about to work for the enemy," Gucci sounded off.

"How do we know Zen is the enemy? We only know what Al and Face have told us, and besides, they are only paying us five hundred dollars," Rainbow added.

"Rainbow is right, Gucci. We don't know shit about Zen. She could be nice and help lace our pockets with some American cash that we so need. I strongly feel like fucking with her will put us on top. The struggle is real out here if you haven't noticed. We're only going off Al's experience. This is not our fight," Selena said, "Five hundred dollars is not enough to rob somebody and risk our lives."

"Look, I'm not trying to get in you ladies' business, but if you know what I know, you will take the deal. Going up against Zen is not easy. A matter of fact, it is impossible," said Big Mike.

They all drove back to the Pickle Tower in silence. Gucci was not feeling the guys or the situation. Everyone exited the cars, and Gucci went straight inside their Apartment and slammed the door. Rainbow and Selena decided to hang out with Kash and White Boy. Kash gave Big Mike a signal for him to go check on Gucci. Big Mike knocked on the door lightly. Gucci snatched open the door with a pre-roll lit. "What the fuck do you want?" Gucci spat?

"Hey, hey, young lady, slow your role. I did not want our night to end. I also wanted to check on you," Big Mike said softly.

"You said I should do whatever Zen says, so you're down with her too, huh?" Gucci asked while passing the blunt.

"I'm not going to lie; I love Zen, and she is cool and impressive," Big Mike added.

"People act like she can't be stopped. What the fuck? She is not invincible," Gucci spat.

"You must believe that too because you seem a bit nervous. As you should, because Al and Face don't give two fucks about you ladies. Sending you ladies on a dummy mission like this was a major fuck boy move. They niggas knew the danger they were putting you, ladies, in. Y'all came to a gunfight with only built-up emotions. Emotions built up from what Al and Face amped y'all up to believe. " Big Mike spoke seriously. "Whatever play you ladies have for Zen will backfire and get you killed."

"My crew and I are no mutha fucking rookies at this game, Gucci screamed out. We have a track record in Jamacia. Bitches and niggas fear us."

"That may be true, but you haven't come across no team as thorough as Zen and her band of bitches. Al and Face were no match for them, so I would chill unless you ladies are made of Teflon. Apparently, you have your mind on how you will move, so if you want me to leave, I will. Big Mike said while blowing out a cloud of smoke, getting up to go.

" I want you to stay Gucci said in a low tone." Big Mike hugged her, then pulled out a fat bag of weed. He was about to roll a few blunts hoping the weed would bring Gucci to her senses. "Damn, that's a fat-ass bag. I'll make us some drinks," Gucci said, looking at Big Mike like he was a three-piece dinner from 'Churches Chicken'.

Rainbow and Selena convinced Kash and White Boy to play a game of Charades. The vibe was nice the laughter was nonstop. "How the fuck you did not know I was doing?" Bugs Bunny, Selena asked Rainbow.

"Bitch, shut up. You missed my greatest impression of Mike Epps, so we even bitch," Rainbow clapped back.

"Mike Epps, you were completely off, sis. That was more like Redd Fox," Selena and the guys laughed. After things winded down, Kash broke the silence. "So, what do you ladies think about Zen's proposal?"

"I personally thought she was full of shit at first. Only because her real character blinded me," said Rainbow.

"Man, I'm not sucking her pussy or anything, but she is a bad bitch on the real. Zen was so right about them fuck niggas Al and Face. I am game, with or without Gucci," Selena bragged.

"Me too, sis." Rainbow co-signed. The girls started spilling the tea on the plan Al and Face conjured up for them. After Kash touched Rainbow between her thighs and blew his minty breath in her ear, Rainbow started singing like a Canary bird. Kash knew the specifics about Heavy coming to the States in a few days and their plan to take Zen and Mario down.

Rainbow continued being talkative while lusting over Kash's body. Rainbow was being recorded. Before Kash gave her what she was yearning for, he whispered. "Good girl, now you must join our team because you leaked their entire play. If they were to find out, you snitched. You know the consequences of snitching. None of y'all would be safe. I'm about to fuck you because I see that's what

96

you want, but just so we're clear, I'm on team Zen and Mario all day." Kash sent the recording to Zen and Mario. Mario quickly texts back. *"Good looking nigga. Your ass better wear a damn condom. Everything that glitter ain't gold, fam."*

CHAPTER 13

SWITCHING SIDES

The next morning Zen and Mario were up bright and early. They decided to drive to the Pickle Tower to meet up with the Jamaican trio. They arrived, and Zen rushed out of the car as if she was going to war. Zen beat on Kash and White Boy's door. White Boy came rushing to the door, half asleep, feeling good from the Jamaican head he received up until a few hours before Zen's knock. "I need everybody woke around this bitch ASAP," Zen spat.

"No problem, let me piss and get Rainbow up," Kash responded.

"OK, NOW!" Zen said out loud. Mario bumped Zen with his elbow, meaning for her to shut up and mind her business. Mario stepped over to Big Mike's apartment and told him to come over. Minutes later, Pound Puppy, Raz and Bleu walked in. Sundae, Nena, and Lady J joined on a face time call. "I need to know right now what you Jamaican whores plan to do?" Zen blurted out.

"I'm all in because what you said made perfect sense to me. I have put much thought into the whole ordeal and had time to sleep on it. The conclusion is plain and simple. We're getting played," Rainbow answered.

"Seems to me like you didn't get much sleep," Zen said with a laugh.

"Regardless of what I did, it's none of your GAWD DAMN business. Now you were not going to talk to us and handle us any kind of mutha fuckan way. You may outpower us while we're on your soil, but I will be damn if I sit back and let you bully my girls or me, you fat bitch," Rainbow yelled out at Zen.

"Ok bitch, calm the fuck down and go put some fucking clothes on because you built like a deep freezer. Save that energy so we can get this nigga Heavy and send Al and Face a final message," Zen spat.

"What about Selena and Gucci? You two are quiet," Zen added.

"If Rainbow is in, then I'm in," said Selena.

"I guess I'm down, but I still don't like your flabby ass," said Gucci.

"Yep, flabby fat and whatever else y'all dusty backpack shape, nappy head whores wanna call me. I can give two fucks if a mutha fucka doesn't like me. My money like me bitch, I have more than five hundred you jumped for," Zen said as she gave Gucci the finger.

"OK, let's kill this catfight. We need to come up with a plan to get Heavy when he arrives tomorrow, and…" Pound Puppy sounded off.

"Right, we can handle Al and Face once that is done. Then you ladies can go back to Jamaica and do what you do because over here in the States, this is Zen's turf, rather you like it or not," Mario spat. "That's if they make it back, bae," Zen said with much attitude. Gucci reached over Mario and snatched a few of Zen's locs out of her head. Zen draws her pistol so fast; you would have thought she was in a showdown in the Wild Wild West. Zen shot Gucci in her kneecap and then aimed for her head. Mario quickly recovered Zen's gun. Gucci screamed in pain, blood and flesh splattered everywhere. "Oh snap. Big Mike, take Gucci to your apartment, and I'll get nurse Kelly over ASAP," Pound Puppy instructed. Pound Puppy looked at Mario shaking his head, "That's your wife."

"I can put up with y'all bitches talking shit, but don't put your mutha fuckan hands on me PERIOD," Zen yelled. Raz and Bleu immediately started pushing and roughing up Rainbow and Selena. Rainbow and Selena weren't scared, but they assured the ladies that Gucci was on her own with her actions. They had no ill intentions toward none of them.

 Kelly cleaned and patched up Gucci's gunshot boo-boo. Kelly gave Gucci some bandage wraps along with some anti-infection cream. Gucci was beyond mad at Zen for shooting her, but she was more pissed at her girl alliance for switching up on her.

Heavy was scheduled to ride the Amtrack until he hit the States. Heavy then would ride a fish boat to Charleston, South Carolina. From there, he will uber to Greenville. Heavy has cut off his long dread locs, and he will be disguised as an old sugar daddy with a walking cane. Heavy made it to Greenville and immediately contacted Gucci. Gucci started going into detail about how Rainbow and Selena had flipped. Before Gucci can go any further, Big Mike points his pistol directly at her and quickly mutes her phone. "Give him the address and end the mutha fuckan call," Big Mike said firmly with the nose of his pistol touching Gucci's head.

Gucci did exactly what she was told. "Now, why the fuck would you try some fuck shit like that? Big Mike asked.

"Fuck it, go tell your boss bitch I ain't fuckan scared," Gucci said nervously.

"That was the wrong move you just made. You are the enemy now. No turning back from this, Big Mike spoke as he tied Gucci up with duct tape, her mouth included." Gucci has a wide body, so; he duct taped her body as if UPS was shipping her.

Big Mike Joined the others inside the girl's apartment, waiting on Heavy to make his grand entrance. Big Mike sent Heavy a text from Gucci's phone, telling him the coast was clear. The Crew indulged in drinking and blunt smoking until Heavy knocked on the door. Rainbow and Selena opened the door, and Heavy rushed in, taking off his old man disguise. "What's up? Tell me the process. What have y'all learned?" Heavy asked, talking fast while looking around for Gucci. Mario came from behind the kitchen pantry door with his gun pointing at Heavy's chest. "What you wanna know, fam, Mario asked with a frowned face?" Heavy reached for his gun, but Kash was close by his side and hit him across the head with a Crown Royal gallon-size bottle. Pound Puppy patted him down, taking his phone and money. Heavy was tied up and dragged to Big Mike's apartment to join Gucci.

"I would like for you ladies to try and convince Gucci to play ball with us, but if her answer is still the same, she will hit the Lion's Den ASAP," Zen said directly to Rainbow and Selena.

"What is the Lion's Den?" Selena asked.

"Duh, a pit full of Lions," Rainbow said as if she was correct in her answer.

"Nope, but your very close. The Lion's Den is a six by twelve cement box with only one air hole, filled with thousands of non-venomous snakes. Pound Puppy just recently added four deadly reptiles to the party," Zen explained two King cobras and two Cottonmouth's snakes to the ladies. The snakes were donated to Pound Puppy by his brother Tilly. Tilly's wife Lucinda was about to leave Tilly if he did not get rid of his snakes. Two of the snakes escaped from the aquarium and bit Lucinda's Shih Tzu dog, he was bitten multiple times filling his small body with venom, then one of the snakes swallowed him whole. "What's the play on Heavy? I would like some get back on him for the shit he did to Kool Breeze," Big Mike asked. "Say less." Zen added, "You and Sundae will take him to the funny farm and let Bossy have his way with him." Bossy was Sundae's dog. He was the roughest, most challenging, meanest four-legged canine that barked in Greenville. Bossy was kept on the funny farm because that's the only place that relaxed him and kept him in a chill mode. Clowns and balloons were decorated throughout the farm to keep Bossy happy. Any intruders will be devoured and eaten down to the bone by Bossy. The only people allowed on the funny farm besides Sundae are her two sons and Pound Puppy. "Good luck, nigga. Bossy is going to rip a hole in your ass," Mario spat. Mario knew firsthand what Bossy was capable of. Zen and Sundae instructed Bossy to attack Mario for cheating on Zen in the past.

Zen planned to leave them in Big Mike's apartment tied up for a few days while she played phone games with both of their phones, texting Al and Face. Zen text Face from Heavy's phone. *'Bro, I'm here. Everything went smoothly as planned. The girls already have Zen. Gucci and I have Mario cornered right now. I'll call with the details."*

"Don't underestimate them. Bro, keep your guard up. Check with me as soon as you get Mario," Face responded.

"I'm about to call Rainbow to see the business," Zen texted.

"Ok, bro, Gucci and I our rolling on Mario as we speak while Rainbow and Selena handle Zen. Zen is fucked up too, bro."

"Good, I hate that bitch," Face texted aggressively. Zen and Rainbow quickly plotted up a skit for when Face placed his call. They would be on point. "Hello. I just spoke with Heavy, and he gave me a brief plan. So, what do you and Selena have in motion for Zen?"

"Right now, she's tied up. We had to beat that ass because she kept trying to fight and throw shit. We're waiting to see what Heavy suggests our next move should be," Rainbow added.

"Put the phone on speaker," Face instructed Rainbow.

"Ok, bro."

"You thought your fat ass won, didn't you? I'm about to have that fat pussy delivered here to Jamaica just for me. Imma sucks that pussy while you suck this dick, then imma fuck you in your ass while you're doing a handstand," Face said with a smirk in his voice.

"Fuck you nigga, and your bald head, mammy. Come suck the shit outta my ass. That's what you can suck. I hope you catch the Coronavirus in the throat, then die slowly. Your hot mouth, dirty, smelly, muddy skin, crabby bitch," Zen spat with much rage. Selena pretends to hit on Zen.

"OOCH, OOCH, STOP DON'T HIT ME NO MORE, PLEASE STOP," Zen yelled into the phone.

"Y'all beat that bitch till she passes out, then call me with an update," Face said before he hung up. Zen high-fived the girls and handed them two stacks each. Rainbow and Selena's eyes widen big as donuts after counting the money. They both displayed Kool-Aid smiles and repeatedly thanked Zen for her generosity.

An hour later, Mario decides to do the same skit with Face, but this time with Heavy. Mario briefed Heavy on what to say. Mario aimed his gun directly at Heavy's head, just in case he said something off-script. Heavy assured Mario he would participate. Heavy begins to beg for his life with the saddest look. "Shut the fuck up, cry, baby. We're just at the beginning, so hold up on the begging because shit is going to get really bad for you," Mario said in his boss-man voice. Face answered the phone.

"Wud up, bro? You got that pussy nigga?"

"Fuck yeah, I got him. The girls and I must move fast to another location just to be safe. Pound Puppy will soon send out a search party for them. I have the video of you and Al killing them niggas. Check this out, bro, them mutha fuckas were impersonating cops. They niggas were a part of Mario's squad."

"What the fuck? Are you serious?" Face asked loudly.

"Yes, we got a confession out of Mario after we threatened to kill Zen," said Mario.

"Good job, bro. Now we can relax. We were off balance and discombobulated, thinking we were cop killers," Face said, blowing his breath as a sign of relief.

"Now I need you and Al to come back to the States so we can take over and get our money back, plus come up on some extras, ya feel me."

"Fosho bro, we're on the next thing smoking," Face added. "Bet we're going to lay low and stay out of the way until you guys arrive," Heavy said as he ended the call.

"You see how I finessed that shit, come on man, you need to be a stand-up guy and let me go. I went against the grain for you nigga, play fair Mario," Heavy pleaded.

"Nigga we don't trust y'all Jamaicans. We will not keep playing this tic-for-tac game with you faggots, either. Besides, Big Mike has dibs on you for orchestrating the brutal death of his partner Kool Breeze," Mario sounded off.

Stone was receiving complaints; he had not been generating as much money without Nicolette. Most of his heavy spenders wanted Nicolette to fulfill their sexual desires, and most men needed a partner to get high with. Nicolette would smoke crack, sniff cocaine, and pop pills. Whatever her buyer was into, she was with it. Nicolette became popular in the streets for sex. Sad as it was, Nicolette was the goat of selling pussy. Plenty of girls were on Stone's roster, but none were knocking the shit out of the park like Nicolette. Stone put his men back on a search for Nicolette. He did not give a fuck about Pound Puppy and his threats. Stone was hurting financially without Nicolette; he was about to repo his whore.

Nicolette started to gain weight; her daughter Allison braided her hair in a feed-in style. Nicolette was beginning to look human again. Nicolette attended anonymous narcotic meetings and sat with her mom during chemo treatments. Nicolette became interested in writing when nurse Kelly gave her a journal to start her therapy process, working her twelve steps. Nicolette was active with her kids; she was feeling good about herself. "Nurse Kelly, I would like to thank you so much for putting up with me and my disrespectful behavior," Nicoletta said softly.

"Girl, you're good. I can handle you. You see, I was all gas and no breaks on your ass. I want you to kick that disgusting drug habit. You have so much potential, and your writing skills are amazing. Use your time wisely, and write a story about your life. I am sure Allison would love to assist you in branding your book. You have a testimony, young lady," Kelly said as she continued giving Nicolette a motivational speech.

CHAPTER 14

CREATING BEEF

Pound Puppy received word that Stone's men were looking for Nicolette. He did not like to be lied to. If a man gives you his word, that should be his bond were his thoughts. Pound Puppy and Big Mike went to hang out at the pool hall where they knew Stone would be. As usual, Stone was engaging in his wild pimp activities, rehearsing to find the sluttiest thot that could hold his cum down the longest. Pound Puppy stepped up beside Stone interrupting him, fingering a ratchet young girl beside the jukebox. "Nigga I thought we had a deal; you were supposed to leave Nicolette alone," Pound Puppy said with attitude.

"Deals are made to be broken, and in this case, that's what happened," Stone said while taking his hands out of the young girl's panties.

"Deal breakers don't sit well with me, especially coming from a street nigga. Now, this thang is bigger than Nicolette," Pound Puppy added, "You've just made unnecessary beef with me, and that beef will not disappear until you submit."

"You're right. The beef is unnecessary. Submission doesn't set well with me, so I'm game. However, you serve it up. Nicolette can't hide out forever. Tell her to get all the rest she can. Because that pussy belongs to me," Stone said firmly, standing his ground. Stone was a street pimp, but he was no match for Pound Puppy. Pound Puppy grabbed Stone by his neck and choked him till he passed out. He then beat his bodyguard to a pulp, breaking his jaw and nose. The bodyguard needed immediate medical attention. After Stone came, he was destroyed as well. Pound Puppy snatched Stone's chains from around his neck, then tossed them to the young girl Stone was fondling. Pound Puppy was sending a message. This was considered a warning. "If we revisit this topic again, his whores are going to be carrying his body wearing black dresses instead of bras," Pound Puppy said to Big Mike.

Pound Puppy went straight to Zen to put her on a mission to add some extra stank to his plan. "Wud up, Pupp? You're looking good nigga, besides that blood stain that's on your pinky ring," Zen said, laughing. "Damn, shit gets around," Pound Puppy said, looking shocked.

"Nigga, you know I got eyes on your ass too. You have your connects, and I have mines," Zen sounded off.

"That is why I'm here because I know whatever I need involving any female, you're my go-to bitch," Pound Puppy said while dapping up his sis.

"Talk to me, bro. All you got to say is the word," Zen confirmed.

"I need you to get with the McFarlin sisters. All the sisters fuck with the men Stone has on his so-called pimp squad. I need the sisters to make them niggas flip on Stone. Toss a lil money if you must, but I need no member of his squad to follow any of his requests," Pound Puppy elaborated to Zen. Zen has done plenty of business with the McFarlin sisters over the years. Cheryl, Paula, Beverly, and San were a force to be wrecking with. The sisters were Zen's silent weapons when she needed something handled quickly, or when she and the crew were busy on assignment, the sisters would show up and show out.

A week passed, and Rainbow and Selena tried to persuade Gucci to stop the bullshit against Zen. Gucci was still tied up alongside Heavy. They both were pissy and shitty and looked pitiful. Heavy tried maneuvering out of his chair when she saw Selena and Rainbow. Heavy mumbled through the duct tape loudly, wishing he could curse them out. "Ok, Gucci, this is your last chance. If you don't cooperate, then it's lights out for you, sis," Rainbow said with the duck lips. Selena took the tape off Gucci's mouth to hear her response. "Fuck y'all trading ass bitches, keep on with the ass kissing because I'm not," Gucci said right before she spit in Selena's face.

"Bitch imma let you have that one on credit because what they're going to do with your dumb ass is punishment enough," Selena spat.

Al and Face made it back to the States. Exiting the plane, looking more like Americans with fresh haircuts. Ashley handed over the video footage of Al and Face to her dad Seth, who was in his last year with the FBI before he retired. Murry and Bruce's families knew how their loved ones were killed. The burnt bodies were recovered, and both families could give them a proper burial. Charges were already filed against the two Jamaicans for two counts of first-degree murder. Airport security cleared the way for the FBI to make a clean arrest. Al and Face walked through the airport sharing a bag of skittles when suddenly the FBI surrounded them, giving them no room to run. "Fabian Badrick, and Alden Thompson, you're under arrest for the murders of Murry Scott and Bruce Holden," one of the FBI men yelled. Face immediately tried to run and was ambushed by a team of agents. Al went to his knees and locked his hands behind his head as instructed. The families received much support, so the trial was scheduled for that week. The media was all over the case. People were intrigued by how two Jamaicans killed two Americans and buried them. Al and Face were sentenced to life in prison without the possibility of parole. They would be doing their time in the States, in separate prisons. Zen made sure Heavy and Gucci were tuned in to the trial coverage.

Zen and Mario were about to handle Heavy and Gucci. Big Mike placed a gas mask over his head because the smell in his apartment was so horrendous, from Heavy and Gucci defecating on themselves for weeks. Big Mike snatched up heavy while he was still tied to the chair. He was thrown inside a utility van that Big Mike borrowed from his cousin. Heavy felt his life was close to expiring. He just didn't know how. When Big Mike reached the Lion's Den, Pound Puppy and Mario were already waiting. Mario placed a hundred field rats and baby mice into the Den to get the snakes riled up to attack. Big Mike picked Heavy up out of the van and slammed him on the ground. Breaking the chair and, from the looks of it, his back. "Nigga you know what time it is." Big Mike said as he snatched the tape from Heavy's mouth. Heavy begged and pleaded for his life. "I'll do anything. Please let me live. I have a family." Heavy continued with his plea. Big Mike cut Heavy's sweatpants off and removed the tape from his hands and feet. Big Mike felt it would be fun to watch him run around. Heavy was tossed into the Den, and the screams began. Heavy did not know where to run. Snakes and rats were all over. Pound Puppy and Mario joined in on the laughs watching Heavy run around before they closed the doors to the Den.

Rainbow and Selena begged Zen to spare Gucci. They were not questioning Zen but didn't want to see Gucci die. Zen was utterly indecisive about what to do with Gucci, but she would learn to respect her, was all Zen knew. Milly Mill completed the setup and design for Zen's hair factory she recently invested in. She makes her bundles and several types of black hair weave. Milly Mill has two of her Asian friends, Whunda and Sawija, running the factory. They are certified in the sewing manufactory business. Milly Mill also has a few bitches that owe her money working on the line for free, pushing out products. Gucci will fit right in; she will be chained by her feet, so she will not be able to run. Milly Mill's security team was tight in the factory. "Damn, anybody else owe you some money, Milly? Because we damn near, have a sweat shop going on," Zen sounded off.

"I need twenty bundles of thirty-inch Brazilian hair for my sister in Atlanta, plus her colleagues have ordered fifty bundles," Bleu added.

"Gucci just found her new home, that bitch with live, eat, sleep, shit in this mutha fuckan factory sewing bundles," Zen said, laughing.

Zen called a round table meeting to discuss what they were going to do with Rainbow and Selena. They did come through with helping them with Heavy, but at the end of the day, they started as the enemy. Selena begged Zen to let them stay in the States, but Zen ignored her pleas. "I think we may be able to use them whores for more than riding White Boy and Kash's dick," Raz sounded off.

"They bitches are not our friends, and they are lot legal. A passport is not a green card," Zen responded.

"If they go back to Jamaica without Heavy and Gucci, that's going to raise a red flag to the niggas Al and Face have down with them in Downtown Kingston," Pound Puppy added.

"I agree with pup bae. They can continue staying in the condo and pay rent. They damn sure won't be getting freebies. At the same time, they can work in the hair factory, perfecting their craft and getting trained by the Asians along with their girl Gucci. We can put their ass on the line, which means more hair products can be moved. In a few months, the chicks will be making great products," Mario explained that Silky -N- Wet hairline would be top ten in the hairline industry within a year.

"I have a few gigs I can use them for as well, but soon as they trick decided they want to get out of pocket, I'm shooting them all in the head," Bleu sounded off.

Zen explained to Rainbow and Selena what the plan was. Zen took their cell phones and replaced them with new ones. "First off, you will no longer contact anyone from Jamaica. You will not share your location, nor will you discuss Me or any member of my crew. I trust you, ladies, to stay here in the States and work in my hair factory. My crew and I will use you both to handle street business. We will not sit around and babysit yall, but we expect nothing but loyalty. You must always do as you are told and not speak about the assignment to no one. This is a trial run, so don't fuck up. We are not friends. This is only business, and please do not mistake the two. You, ladies, can come and go as you please, but the first sign of betrayal, you will be killed on the spot, with no second chances. This is not blackmail or a threat. This is just what it is. I cannot forget that you two came here to the States to target my husband

and me, so basically, I'm breaking my G code to help you, ladies, out," Zen continued to explain the dos and don'ts to Rainbow and Selena.

Stone was continuously patching up the injuries he received from Pound Puppy. Stone remained furious and mastered a revenge plan during his recovery process. Stone called a few of his day-one partners to execute a plan further. Stone desperately needed to collaborate with Benzo and Payday. Benzo and Payday were the muscle behind Stone with his street pimping. Benzo and Payday gave Stone the cold shoulder, explaining to him their family issues were more important than his situation. "Come on, Payday, man. I need you, fam." Stone begged through the phone.

"Happy wife, happy life nigga," Payday responded. The McFarlin sisters understood Zen's assignment and handled what was asked of them. Stone was confused and ready to kill Pound Puppy, but he was scared to face him alone. Stone immediately called his following best two-foot soldiers, Buster and Fizz. Stone received the same cold treatment. This time, he was hung up on. His bodyguard was fucked up just as bad as he was, so he was a loner with his revenge plan. Stone popped a perk thirty and sparked up a blunt to re-strategize his thoughts.

Al and Face were back at the county jail waiting to be shipped. Face started a fight every other day for not being able to use the phone. Pound Puppy was in a partnership with several of the correctional officers at the county jail. Face and Al's phone privileges were revoked per Pound Puppy. Aza Dennis was a young new correctional officer. Aza had the hots for Face. Face would hear her beginning her rounds, so when Aza reached his cell, he would have his dick out to a full stretch stroking it slowly, looking her in her eyes as she stopped in her tracks, smiling, licking her lips.

Face knew then he had her attention. Aza went back to the break room to tell her friend Theo, a new hire, about how big Face dick was. "Bitch don't get caught up with these jail niggas. What the fuck can y'all do together besides live in a fantasy world?" Theo spoke?

"Girl, I know, but that Jamaican is fine as fuck, and his accent drives me insane," Aza sounded off.

"All I'm saying is don't do no dumb shit. Just because the nigga has a big dick and made your pussy a lil moist don't mean shit. You see what happened to them women they told us about in training," Theo spat. Theo tried to get her new best friend to face reality, but she could tell she was a loose cannon and was about to blow. During the next round count, Aza made sure her lips were poppin with her grape lip gloss. When she reached Face cell, he was standing at the cell bars with a note for her. Face slid the note to her and rubbed her hand slowly. Aza smiled and finished her rounds. She took a break to go read the note from Face. "*I need a phone ASAP. Please call this number and ask for Glo and read her this message.* **Glo, Al and I are locked up in the county jail here in the States in Greenville. Heavy is probably dead by now. Zen and Mario are behind this shit. We will be shipped soon to start a prison sentence. You know what to do, but you need to hurry.**"

Back at the hair factory, the Asians were handling shit. Everything was going smoothly with teaching the girls how to thread the machines, sew the hair and adequately pack the hair. Milly Mill somehow convinced Kelly to go out on a date with her. Kelly was intrigued by the hair factory and loved hanging out with Milly Mill. Kelly even stepped over to the boss's table with Whunda, and Sawija. She took over their blueprints, laying down some of her ideas. Whunda and Sawija did not like her cockiness, but her ideas were awesome. "Let me find out you're not just a nurse," Milly Mill said to Kelly.

"I just know what women like, and I know quality," Kelly responded.
"So, am I quality? Milly Mill asked.

"More like mid-grade," Kelly joked. Milly Mill frowned and began to massage Kelly's shoulders when she took a seat. Kelly was feeling Milly Mill and vice versa.

CHAPTER 15

BEING GULLIBLE

The following week Face put on some extra charm with Aza because she was slacking on getting him a phone. Aza was doing her hourly rounds and quickly tossed a note into Face cell. "I will not be able to get what you asked for, but I did make that call. Glo will be arriving with Bobby in the States three days from now."

Bobby was Glo's boyfriend from Downtown Kingston. Bobby experienced several mental issues; he enjoyed raping women and shooting people with authority. Glo knew Bobby was unstable, but he fucked her good, so she was cool with his fuckery. Glo was a bit twisted herself because she lured women to Bobby so he could rape them. When Bobby could not get his fix, Glo would play victim to his sick fantasy.

Delyse Cabera was a beautiful college girl studying at a community college on the outskirts of a Jamaican village near Downtown Kingston. Delyse would normally walk home with her friends, but she stayed late to sign up for financial aid for the next semester. As she was walking, Glo and Bobby were at the laundromat washing clothes so they could pack their bags and head to the States. Delyse was busy talking on her phone, and her earbuds were in her ears. Bobby looked at Glo with the look that she was so familiar with. "No, Bobby, we need to get packed, our plane leaves in a few hours," Glo said, looking pitiful.

"Bitch I want her, and hurry the fuck up before she gets away," Bobby spat as he undressed, getting naked. Bobby closed the laundry mat door, then pulled down the homemade blinds. This was a spot he and Glo lured several girls into getting violated. Glo was hesitant about making this move because she had seen Delyse walking home before with her friends. Glo knew she was a college student. She could not do it; instead, she brought Bobby, one of the prostitutes, from the corner store. "What the fuck is this?" Bobby screamed out.

"It doesn't matter who it is. She can serve the same purpose, Bobby. We can't take that girl's innocence from her," Glo pleaded with tears falling down her face. Bobby smacked Glo hard to the floor. He put on his clothes and left the laundry mat to go after Delyse. Glo cried hard. Out of all the women she brought back for Bobby, she could not do this. She left the clothes and headed home. She was not about to witness this shit. Bobby crept up behind Delyse and grabbed her. Delyse maneuvered out of her shirt and quickly grabbed her mase from her bra. She sprayed Bobby directly in his eyes and kicked him hard in his nut sack. Bobby bucked down to his knees, moaning in pain. Delyse dialed her father, Anton, who was a Jamaican police officer.

Delyse ran to the station, but her dad and partner were already en route to catch up with Bobby. Delyse gave her description of Bobby, and it matched twenty others that were in the police system. "Is this the man here? A nice lady officer asked, holding up a picture of Bobby. "Yes, ma'am, that is him," Delyse responded. Bobby Dyers, age 32, spent seventeen years in jail for sexual assault. The Police were scared to go to Downtown

Kingston, so he was never apprehended for all the other rapes. Anton did not give a fuck where he was from. He was out for his ass for attempting to rape his daughter.

Bobby was officially a wanted man in Jamaica. His picture was plastered everywhere within hours, and the police were on a manhunt looking for him. Other women begin to come forward with rape charges on Bobby, inspired by Delyse's story from the news. Anton beats down the door where Glo and Bobby live. BOOM, BOOM, BOOM. Seconds later, Glo came to the door with a confused look because she knew Bobby never got caught for his rapes, and she was surprised to see the police in Kingston. "May I help you, officers?"

"We're looking for Bobby Dyers. Do you know him? Anton asked loud and clear.

"Yes, I let him crash here some nights, but I haven't seen him today, Glo explained to Anton.

"Well, if the mutha fuckar comes back here, let him know he is wanted for over thirty rapes and one attempted rape on my daughter," Anton screamed. He and his partner Chang cased the neighborhood for hours looking for Bobby. Several neighborhood people were looking and chattering, trying to figure out why the police were in Kingston. "Whoever runs into Bobby Dyers, please let that raping mutha fuckar know there is a warrant for his arrest. I am paying three thousand JMD for whoever leads us to the arrest of Bobby Dyers. My name is Anton Cabera. Contact me ASAP," Anton yelled loudly throughout the neighborhood. He removed a sharpie from his shirt and wrote his cell number on several houses while his partner gave out cards to the onlookers.

No one knew about the secret room inside the laundry mat. That is where Bobby conducted eighty-five percent of his rapes. Glo waited until three AM. Then she sneaked inside the laundry mat, knowing Bobby would be awaiting. Glo finished off the clothes she had left earlier. Glo was filled with paranoia, looking over her shoulders non-stop. Glo felt she was being followed, and her stomach was turning flips from the bubble guts. Glo finally sneaked into the secret room. Bobby was waiting at the guard door, but he felt it was Glo because nobody else knew the room existed. "Nigga I have our bags packed and hidden in the bushes a few blocks over. We must leave fast. The police are looking for you, and you have over thirty active warrants for rape and assault. We missed our first flight, so I booked us another one. I booked the flight under my son Dreus's name, and I have his passport for you to use," Glo said, full of shame and guilt.

"Damn, that lil bitch got me wanting to put dick in her ass now," Bobby said, sounding like the rapist he is.

"Nigga, are you fucking listening to what the fuck I am telling your disease to carry ass?" Glo spat, feeling disgusted. Bobby was diagnosed with HIV ten years ago. Yet he never used condoms with any of his rape victims, including Glo. "Bitch, fuck you," Bobby said, sounding pitiful.

"Nigga your mutha fuckan priorities are all twisted. We must leave now. Let's go but first, put this hat on," Glo instructed. Bobby moved nervously around the laundry mat. They grabbed the clothes from the table and left the laundry mat without being seen. Once they grabbed their bags from the bushes, Dreus was waiting to ride them to the international airport. Security was beefed up at the airport. Police were watching people checking in and boarding the planes. Luckily Glo and Bobby boarded the plane without being noticed.

Aza was being watched closely by Theo. Theo noticed Aza taking extra trips down the block where Face was housed. Aza slipped her phone to Face, and he sent a message to Glo with the information about his and Al's transport date, which he found out about Aza. Face turned his charm up on ten, and Aza ate out his palm. Aza was waiting to receive the text from Glo so she could pick her and Bobby up. Aza will allow them to crash at her house until further notice from Face.

Days later, Bobby and Glo made their entrance to the States. Glo immediately contacted Aza. Aza and Theo were both off that day. They were out getting a manicure and pedicure. "Come on, friend. I need to run a few errands really quick," Aza said to Theo.

"What kind of errands? I thought we were going window shopping and did us a layaway at TJ Max," Theo responded.

"Girl, I promised that nigga Face I would do him favor, so imma keep my word," Aza said, sounding like she was in love.

"Aza, are you stupid or slow? This nigga is about to be shipped tomorrow to start a life sentence in a maximum prison. Please explain to me what the fuck he can do for you besides lead you down a path of drama," Theo said, trying to be convincing.

"He has a plan; I think he is going to escape," Aza said with certainty.

"I am going to act like I didn't hear that and walk away from your ignorant ass. I'll catch a Lyft home bitch," Theo sounded off. She was furious with Aza.

Aza met Glo and Bobby at the Crab Shack near the airport. Aza introduced herself, and Bobby instantly started drooling. Glo made sure to sit in the front seat, but she knew that would not keep Bobby away if he were interested. He began strategizing a plan in his head of how he would get Aza. His dick was problematic from the smell of her lotion. "Face told me that he sent you the information y'all needed. Y'all will be staying with me for the night," Aza explained.

"Do you live alone?" Bobby asked lustfully.

"Yes, sir, I do. I will make you two feel at home. Don't worry," Aza answered.

"I'm sure you will," said Bobby. Glo dropped her head and hoped Bobby was not on the same shit that got him kicked out of Jamaica.

Aza stayed on the other side of the Pickle Tower, in Valley Breeze apartments with two bedrooms. The complex was quiet, and elderly neighbors surrounded her. Aza parked her car, and as they exited Glo, Bobby grabbed their belongings. Once inside, Aza showed them around, and they began to get settled. Bobby could not keep his eyes off Aza. Aza went into her bedroom to relax and called Theo. After three tries, Theo picks up. "What is it, stupid?" Theo said sarcastically.

"I'm sorry, the friend, can you come over so we can talk?" Aza begged.

"Hold up. This is my room; you're not allowed in here," Aza screamed out at Bobby when he opened her bedroom door.

"Who was that?" Theo asked.

"Just hurry up this nigga looks creepy." Aza was now nervous.

"We're not here for your shit Bobby," Glo sounded off. "I must have this American girl. She is so beautiful, and she smells like peaches." Bobby went on for minutes raving about Aza. Glo spoke her peace, but Bobby's mind was made up. He sent Glo outside, giving her the right now look. Glo went out on the patio and smoked a cigarette. Bobby went back inside Aza's room. This time he was naked. Aza was about to shower, so she was down to her panties and bra. "So, you're feeling me too?" Bobby said with a smile.

"Get the fuck outta here, you sick freak." Aza reached for her phone and began to scream, "HELP, HELP." Bobby made his way over to Aza and manhandled her on the bed. Bobby had a death grip on her small frame body. He grabbed the back of her head, slamming her face down on the bed. He was damn near smothering her. Aza's screams were muffled by the force of Bobby's hand holding her down. He ripped her panties off and began inserting his nasty dick inside Aza, penetrating her roughly. Aza's vagina began to tear and rip. Bobby was stroking with all his power, devouring this young girl's insides. Theo made it to Aza's apartment; Glo greeted her.

"Can I help you?" Glo asked.

"No, you can't. I'm here to see my friend if that's ok with you," Theo responded with much attitude.

"Well, she's not here. She stepped out for a second," Glo said nervously.

"Bitch bye. She called me less than forty-five minutes ago. Plus, her car is right there, so move out the damn way," Theo spat. Glo pushed Theo, causing her to fall on two patio steps. She quickly pulls her firearm and shot Glo three times in her hip. She busted through the front door calling out Aza's name. When she got closer to the bedroom door, Theo heard the light-muffled screams. She opened the door, and Bobby was going bananas, fucking Aza. Theo shot two times, but she missed. Bobby jumped up and quickly ran out of the bedroom. Bobby sprinted out the front door and stumbled over Glo, who was laid out squirmy in pain. Bobby stepped back inside, grabbed the keys from the counter, and dragged Glo to the car, and they sped off. Theo called 911 while she attended to her friend. Aza cried so hard; her body was shaking badly. Aza was in disbelief that she was just been brutally raped.

Aza was transported to the hospital by ambulance. She was given oxygen to steady her breathing; she was hyperventilating and traumatized. The hospital performed a rape kit, checked her for sexual diseases, and immediately assigned her a rape crisis therapist. Afterward the police placed Aza inside a family room, where she gave her statements. As she was wheeled to the room, Theo kneeled to hug her. "Make sure you tell them fucking thing too, friend. This animal needs to be caught. I wish I had shot him, but I was so scared of shooting you," Theo whispered to Aza. She was being questioned for over two hours, giving the police helpful information but leaving out the part about Face. Her story was, she met them online and decided to rent them a room. Theo also gave a statement about her attacker and how she fired shots wounding the woman suspect. Theo was licensed to carry, and most officers knew her and Aza from the county jail working as correctional officers. Bobby's DNA was stamped in the worldwide database, so a match quickly appeared. Bobby Dyers was now the most wanted man in the world. The detectives notified the Jamaican police giving them information about their fugitive making it to the States, raping another woman.

CHAPTER 16

THE JAMAICAN MONSTER

It was Five o'clock in the morning, and the guards loaded the inmates for shipping. Al and Face and six others were shackled from the waist down to the ankles. Aza delivered a note to Al days ago, so he was up on the plan, Face made with Glo. The guard was so sleepy putting the cuffs on Al he did not secure the cuffs completely, leaving Al room to move his hands. Thirty minutes into the ride. A black Tahoe pulls in front of the correctional van and smashes hard into the front end, causing the van to spin multiple times. When the van came to a halt, Al quickly grabbed the gun from the guard closest to him and fired three headshots at all three guards. The driver slowly came and pulled his pistol. That's when Bobby came from the side of the van and reached through the broken window, then bashed the guard in the head with a hammer.

Bobby helped Al and Face from their restraints, and Face freed the others. Al told the other men they were on their own as he and Face ran to the jeep. Glo was bent over half dead in the hatch, moaning in agony. "What the fuck is wrong with my cousin?" Al spat in anger. Bobby ignored his question and focused on driving. "OMG, she's been shot, bro," Face sounded off.

"Bobby, you have half of a second to respond to me, dammit," Al said as he leaned from the back seat so Bobby could see how serious he was.

"We ran into some trouble back at the young girl's house," Bobby said in a low tone.

"What kind of fuckan trouble?" Al asked loudly. "She and Glo got into a fight, and her friend shot Glo." Bobby was a terrible liar. Face felt through Glo's pockets, retrieving her phone. He then calls Aza but does not get an answer.

Face sent back-to-back text messages, begging for a response. Aza sent the mugshot picture of Bobby explaining what he did to her. He was silent for a few minutes, he knew his plan was over. There was no way Aza was going to trust him after that shit. "Pull over, Bobby," Face yelled.

"We need to get a lil further. The police will be flooding this area soon," Bobby responded.

"I'm sure they will, especially since you just raped Aza, you nasty sick bastard," Face spat angrily.

"What the fuck, dude, you still with that crazy shit, damn who rapes women when they have a whole bitch following them around. Pull this mutha fuckar over right now," Al screamed. "Glo, why the fuck do you bring this dumb ass nigga with you? You know he ain't right," Al continued cursing Glo out. Once Bobby stopped the car. Al shot him twice in his temple. Face snapped a picture, hoping he could show Aza he had eliminated the problem and she would open back up to him. Al and Face dumped Bobby's body in the middle of the road. "What about Glo? She's going to slow us down. Besides, she brought this fuck boy over here, creating unnecessary problems for us. She's dead weight, bro," Face sounded off.

"Say less," Al reached over the hatch and took Glo out of her misery, shooting her in the middle of her forehead. They dumped her body next to Bobby's. The duo of fugitives proceeded to Aza's apartment because they needed help.

Gucci was getting treated like a real stepchild. She scrubbed floors, made coffee and sandwiches, and prepped the packaging items for the hair to be shipped. Selena, Rainbow and the others were becoming close friends. They were producing excellent work and continued to do what was asked of them to prove their loyalty.

Chunchi reached out to Milly Mill about another assignment. One of Chunchi's close friends, Bethany Kaufman, was having some heavy issues and needed assistance. Bethany lived in Switzerland. Bethany and her tea party friends were old but filthy rich. Maylee Pfister, Lasonya Weber, and Kizzy Tanner were all fed up with getting played. The men in their lives were cheating with call girls and giving the girls large amounts of money from their bank accounts. The ladies became aggressive, and they were about to handle things on their own. Chunchi mentioned she knew a few American friends who were certified in handling business and, for the right price, would make a professional move and eighty-six their problems. Ten million dollars was the hefty ticket on this assignment. Chunchi sent the itinerary and a three million dollar deposit to Milly Mill's private account. Milly Mill responded, stating she needed to confirm and go over things with her crew before giving a complete thumbs up. *"That's fine. These ladies are anxious and ready to drop that money."*

I will relay the message that you will reply at your earliest convenience," Chunchi texted back.

Pound Puppy was out for blood and was totally devastated when he received the news about his niece Aza being raped. Raz rolled up several blunts and kept him a glass of Crown poured up. "That's why I did not want her to work at the county jail, because I know how niggas prey on young girls," Pound Puppy said in a rage.

"I can't say calm down because I totally understand how you're feeling. But I can say Pound Puppy reached for a hug from Raz. He tried to stay positive, but a nigga violating his only niece in that way made him wanna go bonkers. Pound Puppy called his sister Egypt, and she was also a wreck. Egypt and her boyfriend Marvelous were riding around asking questions, ready for war. Egypt and Marvelous agreed to meet Pound Puppy and Raz at Aza's apartment. They all were chasing the same thing; they wanted this creep dead.

Zen called Pound Puppy as he was en route to see Aza. "What's up, sis? I'm sorry I didn't call you back. I have been dealing with this shit about Aza," Pound Puppy spoke.

"Your niece Aza?" Zen asked.

"Yeah, sis some nigga she met online brutally raped her, she's home now Raz and I are en route to her apartment now," Pound Puppy explained.

"Oh, hell nah, send me the address. I'm on my way." Zen sent out the massive text, and everybody headed to the known location. Mario rounded up his crew as well. After everybody heard the news and the graphic details, that made the crew's blood boil. Immediate family was off limits. The crew stood tall for each other in any family situation. Revenge was a must for whoever was responsible for harming Aza.

White Boy heard about the escape from one of his lady friends. When Mario called White Boy, he dropped a bomb on Mario with the news. "Nigga you know Al and Face and six others were being transported to a prison from the county jail when they managed to escape," White Boy slowly explained.

WHAT THE FUCK, ARE YOU SERIOUS?" Mario screamed out.

"As a heart attack," White Boy replied.

"Ok, let me call my wife, but you and Kash will meet me at the address I just sent," Mario spoke with rage.

"Copy dat," White Boy responded. Mario called and told Zen the news. Zen immediately calls Ashley to dig for the coverage and forward her the details.

Everyone pulls up at Aza's apartment at the same time. Zen and Raz went in with Pound Puppy, but the others were there for support until they came up with a solid plan and a suspect. Egypt held her daughter close, and tears just flowed down her face. Aza was positioned a certain way on the bed because she was so bruised and sore after a few hours of small talk and comfort to Aza. Pound Puppy and Zen needed to interrogate her to find the smallest details. Before they went into her room, Theo told Egypt her side of the story. Zen overheard the name Face. "Hold up, sweetie, did you say Face?" Zen asked.

"Yes, ma'am, Aza was love-struck by that grimy nigga. He was housed in her assigned block. She made calls and sent text messages to his family. I tried to warn her about that nigga. He was clingy with her, stroking her ego and heavy with his charm. Face told her he was about to escape to be with her, and she fell for it. She will kill me for telling," Theo said, crying hysterically. "I tried to shoot the man raping her, but I was scared I would have shot Aza," Theo said in-between sniffles.

"You did damn good. You put three hot ones inside of his lookout bitch," Pound Puppy sounded off. Zen and Pound Puppy walked into Aza's bedroom. She was so happy to see her uncle. Pound Puppy always gave Aza two crispy hundred-dollar bills whenever he saw her. This time he gave her two thousand dollars of big face hundreds. "You know you're quitting that job," Pound Puppy said firmly.

"Once I heal unk, I can go back to work," Aza said like a little kid.

"That's not happening. No fucking way will I allow that. I did not want you working there in the first place, but I knew you were trying to be independent, so I backed off," Pound Puppy explained.

"I have a job for you and your friend, the county jail is no place for you two beauties to be working anyway," Zen spoke.

"Aza, I need you to tell me the complete truth about Fabian Badrick, AKA Face. The nigga used you to access a phone, and now he has escaped from jail. The two people that he hooked you up with, we have no idea who they are. But the man was brought here by Face, and the nigga raped you," Pound Puppy said in a soft tone.

"NOOOOOOOOOOOO," Aza screamed out, crying. "Face told me he was going to be with me. He said he was in jail for no reason. He was set up by a couple of jealous pussies," Aza cried out.

"My husband and I are the ones who put Face in jail because he is an evil man. That nigga has taken advantage of you and finessed his way outta jail with your help. You're a rookie correctional officer, blinded by this nigga coming through the jail with street swag. Face-fed you a mouth full of game. Those Jamaicans have the gift of gab. You made a stupid decision by helping this nigga," Zen explained slowly so Aza could feel her words.

"What the fuck? I know you did not just call my daughter stupid," Egypt yelled out.

"Girl, bye, your daughter made a STUPID ASS decision, just like the one you're busting up in here like your bout that life," Zen said as she gave Egypt the duck lip face.

"Y'all not about to do this, Sis. Zen and I got this," Pound Puppy said as he walked Egypt out the door. Zen flipped Egypt the finger as the door closed. "Pupp, you better get your sista," Zen said, looking serious.

"Zen, shut up. This is not the time." Pound Puppy said, walking back over to Aza and rubbing her back.

"Ok, Aza, I apologize for the hostility, but I am angry about what happened to you. You're my niece too, and I love you dearly," Zen said as she grabbed Aza's hand.

"I know, Aunt Zen. I fucked up badly. Y'all must hate me, huh?"
"Never that. No mistake is worth the pain and humiliation

you have endured." Zen held Aza's hand a lil tighter, displaying affection.

"We love you no matter what, Aza, don't ever second guess that. Do You understand, love? Pound Puppy asked. Aza shook her head yes, then wiped the last tears from her face. "Now take a deep breath, speak slowly, and tell us what you know, Aza. This is very important," Zen said in a low tone.

"Face texted a girl name Glo from Jamaica. Glo and her boyfriend Bobby are responsible for wrecking the correctional van. That was the plan so Al and Face could escape. I instructed Face when the transfer ship date was scheduled. I provided him with the routine route that the drivers usually take. I agreed to let Glo, and Bobby stay with me until Face got out. I'm sorry, I know now that was stupid as fuck, he gave me a note that mentioned Aunt Zen and Mario's name, and I said nothing. I had no idea he was after you, Aunt Zen. I feel like an idiot," Aza explained as she cried harder.

"Your uncle and I will handle the rest; you just get well and stay with your mom for a few weeks until this blows over. You are lucky nobody but your girl Theo knows about this ordeal because you could be facing a lot of jail time. You're considered a behind-the-scenes accomplice on the street, but by law, that's, aiding the escape of a felon; you must stay under the radar for a while. We don't need anything pointing back at you. This is a major learning experience for you. After you heal and you're comfortable telling your story, your testimony can help vulnerable young girls worldwide," Zen said in her auntie's voice.

Zen and Pound Puppy made their way outside with all the others. "First off, we're pulling an all-nighter this mutha fucka must die. Egypt, you can stop looking at me sideways and get Aza's phone. I am sure we need it because Face will be trying to contact her. You can send Theo to get her a new upgraded phone for a replacement. Give Theo this stack from me. She's an awesome friend. She can buy her something nice to calm her nerves down a bit. Whoever lives in that brick house facing these apartments, Bleu, let them know they must leave willingly or unwillingly. We need to see everything moving in front of this apartment, which is the perfect spot. A few of us will stay in Aza's apartment. She will be at Egypt's house. This nigga will call her phone or pop up, and we will be waiting, no more, saving these niggas first one that sees a kill shot, take it on sight," Zen continued with her tutorial while Pound Puppy sent Marvelous to the store for pizzas and snacks.

Not long after Zen retrieved Aza's phone, Face sent a text. *"I hope you're not blaming me for what happened. I did not know that nigga was coming. Look at the picture I sent you; I took care of him. I wanna see you. Do you think that's possible?"*

"I wanna see you too, but that man really hurt me. How do I know you want to do the same fuck shit?" Zen texts back, pretending to be Aza.

"I would never hurt you; we can go away together, I know you like me, and I like you too. I need your help badly," Face begged.

I'm having trouble trusting you at this point. I stuck my neck out for you and ended up being a fucking rape victim. That is no damn fun, so your promises are not believable. The results are one-sided. You get what the fuck you want, and I'm healing from an assault."

"I understand. I have sisters myself my family is predominantly women. I would never violate a woman in that way. In no way, to be exact. Just let me see you. I don't have to come inside your apartment. Two minutes is all I ask." Face was hoping he convinced Aza.

"My mom is leaving in about ten minutes; she thinks I'm sleeping, so you can come over in an hour. You promise I can trust you; I have a gun now, and I'm not afraid to use it."

"I know you have an itchy trigger finger; you can aim that mutha fuckar right at my head, all I want is to hug you and prove that I am that nigga, and we can be good together." Face was feeling himself while texting. He did not have any ill intentions for Aza. He really wanted her help.

Raz, Bleu, Lady J, and Sundae were all looking out of the big bay window of the brick house. They were on guard for any strange and unwanted activity. Nena, Pound Puppy, Mario and Zen were in Aza's apartment, patiently waiting. White Boy and Kash were outside down the block, letting the crew know whatever moves their way. Anxious energy was floating amongst the crew, and excessive nail biting and constant pissing were a few of the many things they were experiencing. Finally, White Boy sent a message that an old lady was walking up the street wearing jail boots and a lime green dress. Indeed, it was Face trying to camouflage his look. He was doing an awful job. Kash did not take the kill shot because an elderly couple was walking on the opposite side of the street closures in the distance. When Face reached the front step, Nena snatched him inside, taking him straight to the kitchen, where Zen and Mario forced his head into a sink full of bleach and ammonia. Pound Puppy poured more bleach on Face's head as Zen and Mario continued with the death grip around his neck. Face consumed bleach and ammonia through his nose and mouth. He could not produce any air bubbles from swallowing large amounts of the concoction. After Raz, Bleu and the others noticed Al was nowhere around, they all went on a search for him, thinking he'd be close by. Zen and Mario did not ease up on Face, his neck was broken, and his shoulder was crushed from the aggressive force against the sink. Face was not able to resist. He was a limp vegetable. After five full minutes, Face was drowned and suffocated from the toxic chemicals. Face was dead as a doorknob. "No bloodshed, just how I like it, easy clean up. Now let's dead Al's bitch ass. That mutha fuckar has more lives than a stray cat," Zen sounded off.

"You're the boss. Let's make it happen," Mario co-signed."

CHAPTER 17

ARE YOU SERIOUS?

The Search for Al had dragged into two weeks of exhaustion.

He was still nowhere in sight, and anger and frustration built up with the crew because they wanted Al dead like Face. Somehow, he managed to hitchhike to a farm shelter and did hard farm labor in exchange for a bed and food. It sucked for him to shove cow manure six hours a day, but it beat jail and being dead. The shelter did not allow any electronics, so no one knew he was a fugitive. Al changed his name to Steve Jones and shaved his head bald. He also purposely burned the left side of his face in a bonfire, so he would be hard to recognize.

Two acres down from the farm shelter lived two retired police officers, Croy and Vinnie Middleton. Croy and Vinnie trained police officers straight out of the academy that had passed with the highest-grade point average. The brothers were hands down the best detectives to grace the South Carolina police force. The brother's property was a training field with a gun range containing multiple firepower choices. Handguns, rifles, and sawed-offs were just a few located on the property. Smoke bombs, bulletproof vests, uniforms and tons of other police attire and gadgets were also available. Vinnie built a thirty-by-thirty fence to secure the canines; he also trained police dogs.

After days of hearing the gunshots nearby, Al finally asked one of the men from the shelter, Jim, what was going on.

Jim explained to Al about the brothers and their police duties. Al was having trouble concentrating on his work because he kept a visual of the activities going on at the Middleton farm. He was very intrigued to know much as possible about that farm.

Meanwhile, Nicolette's demons begin to test her. She left her apartment to go hang out with Misty, her old snorting buddy. Misty was three shades in the wind. She was high off coke, weed, and was popping a Roxi thirty while talking to Nicolette.

"Girl, I know you want a bump of this shit. I shopped with Fendi, and she blessed me with an eight-ball," Misty said, slurring her words.

"I heard Fendi started lacing her shit with fentanyl, two niggas just died from a bad batch of that shit," Nicolette spoke. "Fendi straight, it's them young niggas you gotta watch, Misty defended her coke bag."

"Just take a lil bump for old times. I know you want to too; this shit gives you an instant drain, Misty said as she pushed Nicolette's shoulder and fell."

"It was a mistake coming here. You finish wilding out, I'm good. Nicolette never thought she would see the day when sniffing coke would discuss her." Nicolette was still in her honeymoon stage, but she did well dodging playing in the devil's playground. That experience just gave her another chapter in her book. (GROWTH) was all she could say to herself. As Nicolette was walking back to her apartment, she felt she was being followed. When she looked back, it was a Crown Vic, so she brushed it off, thinking it was a police officer patrolling. Stone was riding with his nephew

Zahge, checking out the car he recently bought from the police auction. Stone quickly mustered up a plan.

"Neph, I need you to pull up next to that girl to your right with the jean shorts on and throw her ass in this car ASAP," Stone instructed.

"Hell nah, unk, just because I'm in a police car does not mean I can do police shit," Zahge said, looking at his uncle with a confused look.

"Nigga that's one of my whores, that bitch thinks she has got away from me, but I got her ass back now," Stone said with a devilish smile.

"That's bullshit. You already have enough whores on your squad. My homeboy Tim and I fuck with them tricks all the time, and we get the full treatment when they find out you're my uncle," Zahge said, smiling and thinking of his last dicksucking encounter with one of his uncles' tricks. Stone was not fully equipped to handle the task of snatching up Nicolette, but he was about to try. Stone was not about to waste time mouth battling with his nephew.

"Pull up close and let me talk to her," Stone demanded.

"Nigga you do the most," Zahge replied, pulling up to the curb.

Nicolette slowed down. "This muthafuckin' cop thinks I'm out selling ass, I bet," Nicolette said to herself.

Stone jumped out of the car quickly with his head down, grabbing Nicolette tightly, and tossing her in the back seat as he got in behind her.

"GO, NIGGA GO," Stone yelled out to his nephew.

"OMG, I am an accessory to a fuckin' crime now, I'll never get into college with a record," Zahge said, pissed at his uncle.

"Nigga you were an accessory when you were fucking my whores too, big pimp. Drive this muthafuckin' car and stop acting like your punk-ass daddy. Imma compensate you very well nigga, just chill," Stone said to Zahge with his pistol pointing at Nicolette. Nicolette screamed and tried to get out of the car until Stone placed his pistol on her forehead.

"Why the fuck are you fucking with me? I'm doing good for myself. You should be glad I'm not out tricking anymore," Nicolette cried.

"Why the fuck should I be happy? You were bringing in mad clientele, you can't just walk away from that shit," Stone spat.

"What if I pay you double what you were making? Then you wouldn't be losing shit," Nicolette tried to plead her case.

"Fuck no, I'd actually lose more. These street niggas want good wet pussy and monster head, and you have the best pussy and mouth action money can buy. None of these other whores are taking dick up the ass and bouncing it back like you. You're the muthafuckin' pussy crook, so get ready—your break is over," Stone said as he looked Nicolette straight in her eyes.

Nicolette started struggling, giving Stone everything she had. She tried her hardest to get out of that car, and Zahge even slowed down; he was feeling sympathy for Nicolette.

"DRIVE NIGGA," Stone yelled, just before Nicolette laid a few punches in his chest. His pain came surfacing back, and Stone was about to buckle. Stone tried to fight her off, but Nicolette overpowered him. That's when Stone made a cowardly decision and shot Nicolette in her shoulder to gain control of the situation.

"You sick fuck," Nicolette screamed out in pain. "You're not going to get away with this nigga," Nicolette continued to curse Stone; blood was pouring profusely from her shoulder.

"WHAT THE FUCK UNK, I know her pussy ain't that scrumptious, nigga. No wonder you stay in jail; you're always fucking up. Ain't no fucking way imma let you drag me down with you," Zahge spoke as he burned rubber all the way to Stone's crib. "Get the fuck out nigga, and cash app me my fucking coins. Send extra for all this damn blood too. I can't believe this shit," Zahge kept repeating to himself as he sped off."

Stone's house was full of tricks and pimps in training. Stone forced Nicolette to the kitchen table and ripped her shirt off. Everyone quickly gathered around the table, trying to assist.

"OMG, it's Nicolette," Sammie said as she began to cry. Sammie and Nicolette were good friends; they used to get high together and tag team men, making double the pay.

"Don't come in here with that sentimental shit. Help me get this bullet outta this bitch; she has work to do," Stone sounded off. Everyone started scrambling around; Sammie went looking for alcohol and scissors. Another old friend of Nicolette's, Carrie, found some clean rags. Greg, one of

Stone's wannabe pimps, handed Stone a cup of water with two Roxi thirties.

"NO," Nicolette screamed out. She didn't want to take those pills; she wiggled around, trying to avoid Stone placing the pills in her mouth.

"Bitch, either you take these pills, or I will pop you in your other shoulder," Stone said angrily.

Nicolette took the pills crying and shaking, wondering why this was happening to her. Greg Googled a video of a gang member taking out a bullet out of another gang member's shoulder. After Nicolette was good and drowsy, Stone and Greg followed the video step by step, taking the bullet out of Nicolette's shoulder. Sammie filled in as the nurse, she cleaned the wound with alcohol and wrapped her shoulder with torn t-shirts. Nicolette's body was limp; her two months of sobriety had been taken away from her by force.

Gucci was causing too much trouble at the hair factory.

Gucci constantly started fights with the other girls; she even managed to cut one of the Asian women, Whunda, with the paper-cutting scissors, and Zen couldn't lose Whunda. Whunda was her lead worker with the brains and skills behind her hair factory. Zen was done with babysitting Gucci, and instructed Raz and Milly Mill to assist Rainbow and Selena in taking Gucci to the Lion's Den. Zen wanted Rainbow and Selena to see firsthand what crossing her would get them. Rainbow sent Selena a text.

"Do you have any idea what the Lion's Den is?"

"The zoo is all I can think of. I begged Gucci to chill out," Selena texted back.

"Well, I know I am not fucking up. I think I'm in love with Kash, and I like it here in the States," Rainbow explained.

"Me too," Selena responded.

"Fuck all of you American bitches; I won't sell out like these two pussy poppers. Y'all can kill me, I don't give a fuck," Gucci yelled out from the back seat of Raz Suburban."

"Imma hurry the fuck up so we can shut this yup mouth bitch up—she's killing my nerves," Raz spat.

"Yeah, bitch we're the wrong muthafuckas to play games with. You came all this way to become a test dummy, go ahead and say your final goodbyes because it's lights out for your ugly ass," Milly Mill said, laughing."

"Suck my clit, you manly dike," Gucci yelled at Milly Mill.

"Imma suck a clit and lick some ass too, but it damn sure won't be yours," Milly Mill said while licking her tongue out. Rainbow and Selena were quiet; they knew Gucci was going to die—they just didn't know how. Pulling up at the Lion's Den, Milly Mill hurried out of the car, dragging Gucci out behind her.

"Okay, here is the key to that shed. Y'all go ahead and throw her in," Milly Mill said to Rainbow and Selena."

They wanted to prove they were gangsta, so they did as they were told. Selena opened the shed and immediately started screaming when she laid eyes on the numerous snakes and rats crawling around. The bones from Heavy were visible and were eaten clean. Gucci pushed Rainbow and Selena out of the way and tried to run; Raz immediately put two hot ones in Gucci's back. She went to the ground instantly, screaming so loud she made their flush cross. Rainbow dragged Gucci to the Den and kicked her inside. Gucci pissed, shit, and vomited all over herself and continued to scream out in pain.

"With the mixture of bodily fluids oozing from her body, she won't last long. The rats and snakes are going to fuck her funky ass up," Milly Mill spoke.

"You brought this on yourself, big baby," Rainbow said as she walked away. Raz called Zen via facetime to let her see Gucci panic and crawl around in the Den, trying to avoid the snakes and rats.

"Damn, all she had to do was act right. Oh well, lock it down, sis," Zen said to Raz.

"Gladly," Raz responded.

Zen and Mario were trying to come up with a plan to catch Al. Pound Puppy placed a half-a-million-dollar reward on his head. Niggas were looking in their mom's panty drawer for Al's grimy ass.

CHAPTER 18

FUGITIVE ACTION

After two weeks of searching for Al, Zen and her crew continued to come up short. Al was scheming to stay a free man. He knew the tight schedule of Vinnie and Croy, so he was going to snoop around and hope to find an advantage.

Al was making his way to their shed when he saw the brothers leave in the police training car. He knew they would be gone for exactly three hours, and picked the lock, stealing a full police uniform and placing it in his duffle bag. Al planned to return to the shed and cuff a few firearms. He knew he had to wait because he had no one he could trust at the shelter. Al was moving solo; he did not want a co-defendant. Al returned to the shelter, telling his roomies he went for a long walk picking pecans.

Pound Puppy, the crew, and the Greenville County police were all looking for Al. Gang members, prostitutes, homeless men and women were all involved in the man hunt. Crime stoppers hotline kept receiving false leads, which further pissed the police off. Ashley put a crew together to check all the local shelters, churches and hospitals. The airports and train stations were completely locked down by police. All passengers were being screened for identification, and the staff was on a thorough look out as well.

Stone was not playing any games; he was a monster for making Nicolette turn tricks with an injured shoulder. He forced Nicolette to do lines of coke and fed her Roxi's by the hour. Nicolette was a walking zombie. Soon as Stone put the word out that Nicolette was back, niggas were lined up for a turn with her. Stone made sure the men came to his home because he was afraid of Nicolette running away or calling someone for help. Stone did not want any run-ins with Pound Puppy or Zen; he knew the outcome would be deadly.

A few days later, Al managed to sneak into the brothers' shed and cuff two loaded hand pistols: a thirty-eight caliber and a Beretta. Al cased the shed for more findings. He discovered a police car covered up; inside, were keys, walkie-talkies, and a cell phone. Al hid the guns under the seat and thought of away he could steal the car without being noticed. It would be damn near impossible, being on a farm with nothing but field and more field. Al remembered that the director of the shelter, Conrad asked him to fix the riding lawn mower. Al was going to do a switch. Al was going to cover up the lawn mower in replacement of the police car. Al decided to wait patiently for the brothers to go back out for driving training tomorrow, then he made his move.

Maggie and Allison begin to worry about Nicolette. They knew something was wrong because Nicolette was not answering her phone. Her voicemail was continuously picking up for days. Allison called Milly Mill, giving her the specifics about the length of time her mom has been missing in action. Milly Mill was headed over to calm them down since they were so worried. Milly Mill arrived with Zen in tow.

"Ms. Zen, something is wrong with my baby, I just know it. Nicolette has been doing so well and focused on her writing. She is determined to write a book and make up for lost time with the kids and me, Maggie said with a face full of tears."

"Ms. Maggie, now you know your daughters background, I guarantee you that she has relapsed and is with one of her fuck-ass friends. Nicolette will return when she's tired," Zen sounded off."

"I disagree with you this time Ms. Zen. No disrespect to you in any way. You must believe me, please I'm begging you, it's a mother's intuition. I know something is wrong," Maggie spoke with certainty.

"Well, we'll investigate and see what we can find out, only because we like you, and we know you love your daughter. But we can't keep forcing her to change. We aren't her keeper; she must learn on her own," Milly Mill said, feeling sorry for Maggie. As Milly Mill and Zen walked away, Milly Mill called Kelly to get her input. She explained the situation and Nicolette's mom's concern.

"What d'you think, bae? I have you on speaker," Milly Mill asked.

"I agree with her mom. Nicolette has made tremendous progress. She would not have abandoned her family at this point. She is a changed woman; I have witnessed her growth and struggles firsthand as she became clean. I bet my right arm something is wrong," Kelly explained to Milly Mill and Zen.

Today was the day the brothers instructed driving training classes. The brothers needed to cover a lot of new techniques on safety and when should an officer stop a speed chase. So, today they were going to be out much longer than usual. Al grabbed the tool bag, along with his duffle bag. He placed the bags on the riding mower, and he began to push it towards the brothers' shed.

"Where are you going, Steve?" one of the shelter men, Justin, yelled out.

"I'm about to fix the mower if that's alright with you," Al answered sarcastically.

"Mr. Conrad said I could help, because I fixed the farm tractor two weeks ago," Justin explained."

"Well, I don't need any help; I work better alone," Al said, pissed off.

"I don't mind Steve. I am really handy with the equipment; you can ask any of the guys, they'll tell you," Justin was not letting up.

"It's best if you let me handle this one, please," Al continued trying to convince Justin to stay but Justin was not taking no for an answer.

"Why are we going to the Middleton farm? Do you know them?" Justin asked, nagging the hell out of Al.

"Will you shut the fuck up," Al yelled, picking the lock and pushing the mower inside.

"I don't think we need to be in here, man, these guys are cops, and they told Conrad if the ever caught any of us guys meddling around their property, they'd *kill us*," Justin said as he started backing out of the shed. "I'm going to leave; Conrad won't like this."

Al knew Justin was about to rat him out. Quickly retrieving the Beretta pistol from under the seat of the cop car, he snatched Justin by his shirt and placed his head between two stacks of hay. Al shot Justin directly in his head, before placing his body on top of the mower. Al changed into the police uniform, then drove the police car out of the shed. Al placed the mower where the car was parked, covering it up, and it look the same. Al placed the lock back on the door, and he rode off in the police car. Al proceeded to speed up the country road. When Al passed by the shelter, he saw a group of people walking up to the shelter looking around.

Sundae, Lady J, and Nena, along with Ashley's college friends made their way to the shelter. They spent countless hours visiting shelters in search of Al. Conrad greeted the group with a paranoid look and asked what the urgency was.

"Have you seen this man around?" Sundae asked while holding up a collage of mug shots of Al.

"Yes, that's Steven Jones, he's been here with us for a few weeks," Conrad explained.

"His real name is Alton Thompson, and he is a wanted fugitive. He escaped from a correctional transport van on his way to the big house to do a life sentence," Lady J slowly explained.

"Where's he now?" Sundae asked.

"He and Justin—one of the residents here—went to fix the riding lawn mower. They've been gone for hours," Conrad said, looking concerned. Nena called Zen with the news before she and Mario left immediately to join them at the shelter.

"Should I call the police? This seems serious," Conrad asked.

"Yes sir, and tell them they need to hurry because if we see him first, you're going to be calling for a coroner next," Lady J sounded off.

The police were at the shelter for hours, looking for any sign of Al. As the officers were riding down the farm, officer Chad spotted Vinnie. "Hey, old fellow. We miss you on the force."

"Hey there Chad, what brings you fellows out to the country?" Vinnie asked.

"We have an escaped inmate that has been staying at that shelter on the next farm," Officer Chad explained.

"It's some strange men around that farm. I made it clear I don't want none of them sumbitches around my property. Croy and I will help with the search if you like—we just came from training some of the men at the academy," Vinnie said.

"Nah, were about to wrap it up, but you know to call us if you see anything suspicious," Chad said as he drove off.

Zen and the others left; they were not hanging around with the police scattered everywhere. "I'm going to kill that muthafucka when I catch him," Mario said in a rage. "Al is on his A game; he knows Face and Heavy are dead, so he's dotting his I's and crossing all T's."

"Just give him time; he'll slip up," Zen said with a serious look."

Al's mind was made up: he was going to find Zen.

His plan was to use her as bait; he needed leverage to leave the country. Al knew Zen had multiple connections; he was going to do whatever it took to get her.

Pound Puppy leased a ten-room Airbnb so all the ladies could stay together until Al was apprehended. Egypt and Aza were the first to move in. Zen and Raz met at Chillers, a frozen drink bar in downtown Greenville. Zen was beating herself up for not being on top of things with Al. Revenge against Al played heavily on her mind. The two ladies enjoyed different flavored frozen drinks and hit the dance floor doing the wobble line dance. After Pound Puppies' twentieth call, they decided to leave. Raz was tipsier than Zen, so Zen drove. She was about to get her clothes from her house, and they were headed to the Airbnb.

Al, meanwhile, was en route to Zen's house to scope out the scenery. Al was a few minutes away from Zen's house when he spotted her jeep cruising down the street, headed towards her home. Al quickly did a U-turn and hit the blue police lights behind Zen.

"What the fuck," Zen yelled out.

"Calm down, sis. Don't give them pigs a reason to fuck with us," Raz said calmly.

"You right, sis. I hate these faggot-ass cops," Zen said nervously." Al walked up to the car. Zen's window was half down.

"What seems to be the problem officer?" Zen asked.

"I'll be asking the questions here, young lady. I need you to step out of the car, please," Al spat.

"What the fuck for? All I can do is give you my license and registration," Zen responded.

"I won't ask again. Step out of the muthafuckin' car, please," Al spoke loudly.

"Raz call my husband, *now*," Zen instructed. Raz proceeded to call Mario; she texted Pound Puppy their location and situation. When Al noticed Raz raise her phone, he shot her twice in the side of her stomach. Zen scrambled for her gun, but Al snatched her door open, and manhandled her from the jeep.

"I promise on everything I love that I'll shoot you if you try anything," Al said to Zen as he placed the gun to her head. He threw Zen in the back seat, and he resumed in the car and sped off fast with the lights still flashing. Raz was losing blood quickly; she called Pound Puppy and screamed in the phone.

"Raz, what's wrong? I'm almost at your location," Pound Puppy asked.

"I've been shot, hurry bae," Raz said faintly.

"OMG, where is Zen?"

"The cop took her, call Mario," Raz said, feeling weak.

Pound Puppy did just that. Mario was on two wheels after receiving that news. Pound Puppy arrived minutes later; he heard the ambulance coming. Pound Puppy called as soon as Raz said she was shot. The medical crew jumped right in, working on Raz as she passed out and began to hemorrhage. After hooking her to an IV and placing her on oxygen, she was transported to the county hospital. Pound Puppy called Bleu and Milly Mill, who instructed them to meet Raz at the hospital.

"Please keep me posted, and make sure y'all take care of my baby Bleu," Pound Puppy said frantically.

Pound Puppy and Mario took a few minutes to collect their thoughts, and they both came up to the same conclusion—they were about to get down and dirty.

CHAPTER 19

KIDNAPPED

"This shit has Al's name all over it," Mario screamed out.

He was carrying around assault rifles and handguns with extended clips, pacing back and forth, chanting.

"Bro, you must put that heavy artillery up for now. No need to cause any distractions; the police see you carry that shit around, they're going to focus on us instead of Zen. Let's report this to the police and see if we can make out if this fuckin' cop was real," Pound Puppy said, trying to sound convincing.

The police arrive on the scene asking their normal questions.

"Look, officer, my damn wife was taken. Do you have her in custody or what, because y'all fuck ass officers are moving too damn slow for me," Mario said as he paced back and forth.

"Mr. Vanhorn, I'm officer Barry Provon. First, let me get your wife's full name.

"Zeneta Fuller-Vanhorn. She goes by Zen," Mario said dryly.

"I assure you we will apply pressure on this situation. We do know that none of our officers were in this area tonight, so whoever took your wife was not an officer of the law. Our forensic team will be out to scan for fingerprints. We are also checking with the traffic light specialist to retrieve the camera footage at all surrounding traffic lights. Whoever has your wife must have passed a few," the Officer continued to explain to Mario.

"We have a female officer at the hospital to speak with the victim as soon as she's out of surgery and able to talk. Hopefully she can shine some light on this, may I have her name please?" Provon asked politely.

"Her name is Razia Parks, and she's very special to me. We happen to believe that Aldon Thompson is involved with this; he and his friend Fabian Badrick escaped from the correctional van a few weeks ago. We just recently found out he was staying at a farm shelter on Millions Road," Pound Puppy added.

"That's impressive to know, we have two ex-cops that live close to that shelter. I'm sending some of our men that way now," Provon extended his hand for a shake, and he informed the other officers of the details.

Mario called Ashley to tell her the news, who instructed him and Pound Puppy to meet her at the Garage ASAP. Ashley began to cry; Zen was her everything. They have been inseparable since high school; when the other kids would bully Ashley, Zen protected her. She taught her how to fight and hustle—and street crimes were on the list as well. Ashley started changing grades for cash and taking lunch money. Ashley and Zen used her quick wits to keep them ahead of their peers.

Zen could not get out of the back seat of the cop car. However, she was calm. "What the fuck, Al? You're losing your damn mind. You'll never win fucking with me, so stop while you're ahead pussy-boy," Zen said, laughing loudly.

"Shut the fuck up, bitch," Al spat aggressively.

"Or what, nigga?" Zen replied, still laughing.

"I got your pussy-boy; imma show you just how pussy I am when I put my dick inside your pussy," Al spat with attitude.

"*Oooh*, I'm scared of your dick. Threaten me with something I aint never experienced nigga," Zen blurted out.

"What makes you laugh makes you cry, you fat bitch," Al sounded off.

"Yep, I am fat and tasty; you're drooling over this kitty right now. I know you wanna get up close and personal with this fat pussy. You're a fuckin' scrub; you need to go play in traffic. I hate your Freddy Krueger looking ass." Zen showed no fear as she continued to insult Al to the highest degree, she'd been trained by Victor Lee and Pound Puppy to handle situations like this. Zen knew how to inflict pain; she would never submit, regardless of the circumstances.

Al drove to a camper park he'd seen as he left the farm. As Al rode through the entrance of the park, the park ranger working the gate was shocked to see a police car coming through.

"Can I help you officer?" the ranger, Kaleb, asked.

"Yes, I'm here to rent out a camper. I'm on a secret assignment. I have a hostile female prisoner that is in the witness protection program, and we need to stay here until my chief tells me otherwise, Al explained.

"This muthafucka is lying! Call the real police, this nigga has kidnapped me," Zen yelled from the back seat. Zen beat on the window, trying her best to raise a red flag. "He's a fugitive; he's wanted by the police!" She continued to yell and make movement. The park ranger was trying to speed up the process as he looked at Zen with disgust as if she was a hostile prisoner.

"Here are the keys to camper number twenty; I put you far in the back away from the other guest. No one can hear her screaming back there, and you will have more privacy to conduct your business, officer," the park ranger Kaleb said, trying to be helpful, still frowning at Zen.

"Thank you so much," Al responded.

"Just sign here, and you can pay for the number of days you have stayed when you leave," Kaleb explained.

"I will make sure I come back and fuck you up, white boy. You fuckin' queer, I hope your asshole blows up," Zen yelled out at the park ranger. Kaleb gave Zen the finger.

Zen was down to fight and get away from Al. As he parked the car and opened the door to let Zen out, before he could grab her, Zen pulled her twenty-two pistol from her boot and let off two shots in Al's arm. Al dove in the back seat on top of Zen and choked her till she passed out.

Al drugged Zen's limp body into the camper with his good arm. He cuffed Zen to the island table in the camper and quickly found the medical kit, and retrieved the alcohol and peroxide. Al then used a fork to try and remove the bullets from his arm, but it was an utter failure. Al was in pain; he found more gauze and ointment from the police car, and tried to do a surgical procedure on his own. Al made a bigger hole with the tweezers trying to get the bullets out of his arm. Zen woke up panicking when she realized she was cuffed.

"Bitch you're going to take these fucking bullets out of my arm," Al spat.

"Fuck you nigga, I ain't doing shit. Besides I'm cuffed to this table like a puppy dog," Zen sounded off.

Al knew if he removed the cuffs from Zen, she would get away. On the other hand, he was bleeding profusely; he needed medical attention badly. The more he tried to get the bullets out, the bullets begin to travel throughout his arm.

"You dumb muthafucka. I hope you bleed to death," Zen said continuously.

Al wrapped his arm tight as he could and left the camper to go seek help from Kaleb, the Park ranger.

Luckily for her, Victor Lee had trained Zen to remove herself from hand cuffs. Zen had already loosened the cuffs before Al left the camper. Zen removed the cuffs completely in minutes, and grabbed a few knives from the drawers. When Zen was about to open the door to leave, Al reappeared with Kaleb in tow. As Al opened the door, he bent down feeling drained from losing so much blood. Kaleb entered first, and Zen stabbed Kaleb in the side of his temple with a steak knife. Zen gave the knife a twist, making sure it was stuck. Kaleb dropped to the floor as Zen sprinted out of the door. Al looked up and immediately shot Zen in her shoulder.

"*Fuck*," Zen screamed, but she didn't stop running as she fought through the pain. Al got into the police car and began to chase Zen, leaving Kaleb's lifeless body on the floor. After a few minutes of running, Zen crawled inside a shielded dog cage. Al rode around for hours trying to find Zen; he knew she could not have gone far, but exhausted, he was forced to return to the camper to rethink some things. Al dragged Kaleb's body to the back of the camper and shut the door.

Zen saw Al drive down to the bottom of the park, so she exited the dog cage. At that moment, a redneck family noticed Zen coming from there camper area. Caught, she immediately started to run.

"Hold it right there, you *nigger*," a fat white mess of a man named Jim Bob yelled out.

Zen continued to run. Jim Bob's brother Roy hopped into his pickup truck, and alongside his son Roy Jr., chased Zen down. Zen didn't make it far before they blocked her off. Roy Jr pulled out a rifle and pointed it at Zen.

"What the fuck were you doing around our camper?" Roy asked.

"I was being chased by an escaped prisoner, so I hid in the dog cage until I saw him leave. His name is Aldon Thompson; he just shot me in the shoulder. I just need to get to a phone and call my husband," Zen explained.

"I don't believe her Paw; she looks up to no good," Roy Jr said.

"Looks like you're coming with us," Roy said to Zen. She tried to run again, but Roy Jr cocked the rifle and she was forced to surrendered for the moment.

"Please let me use your phone. I'll pay whatever you ask; I'm desperately in need of contacting my husband. His name's is Mario Vanhorn; 675-1223 is his number. Please, just call him," Zen put on her best sales pitch, but the rednecks had other plans and calling Mario was not among them.

Zen had been missing for a week now, and Mario hadn't been sleeping. He was looking for Zen night and day, and his anger was through the roof; Mario felt like the police weren't doing shit.

And so he formed a squad of his own: vicious niggas that didn't give a fuck about jail or losing their life. They were terrorizing and fucking shit up around town. Mario bust into Stone's crib, and manhandled him to the floor. Placing the barrel of his snub nose revolver deep down Stones throat, Mario said, "My wife is missing; do you know anything about that?"

Stone shook his head no.

"Well, who do you know around this muthafucka that would?" Mario asked angrily.

Stone shrugged, indicating he didn't know shit.

"Your pimp ass knows everything that goes on in these streets, so we're not leaving until you find something out for me," Mario said firmly. Mario walked around the house looking around. He signaled for his men to do the same.

Then Mario saw Nicolette and shook his head in disgust. Nicolette threw herself at Mario grabbing his leg tightly. "Please help me! This nigga kidnapped me and took me away from my kids. I was doing good, I swear to you," Nicolette cried, begging on her knees.

"Bitch you don't owe me no muthafuckin' explanation, my wife is missing. I don't care about your ass, Mario said as he kicked her away from his leg."

Buthere was no way Nicolette was going to stay another day, being forced to fuck and do drugs. "Al contacted Stone. He knows where Zen is," Nicolette shouted out.

Mario instantly cocked his riffle.

"Everybody get the fuck out, and I mean *right fuckin' now*," Mario screamed viciously. Nicolette sprinted out, leaving everything behind, crying all the way home to her mom and kids.

"I hate liars," Mario said to Stone, as he shot both his knee caps off. "This is my last time asking you, nigga. Where the fuck is my wife?" Mario spoke loudly.

"Al called me, telling me he needed supplies because Zen shot him in his arm. I sent one of my men over to the camper park to help with getting the bullets out of his arm, he's staying in camper twenty at the bottom of the park!"

Mario grabbed Stone's phone and nodded at Kash, who immediately blew Stone's brains out with a double-barrel shotgun. Meanwhile, White boy packed up the dope and the money.

Nicolette made it home, exhausted from running. She was breathing hard with barely enough energy to knock on the door. After a few light knocks, Allison swung open the door.

"GRANDMA, GRANDMA," Allison screamed loudly.

Maggie dropped what she was doing and rushed to the door. Nicolette took one look at her mom and collapsed in her arms. Maggie called Milly Mill and Nurse Kelly for help.

CHAPTER 20

MIND GAMES

Zen was being held in a small room inside the redneck's camper.

Roy and Jim Bob figured they'd make a man out of Roy Jr. They'd always heard a black woman's pussy was superb, and their curiosity and anticipation were on a high volume.

Despite of the myth that had floated around for generations about black women having cooties, Roy and Jim Bob insisted Roy Jr go inside the room and have his way with Zen. Roy Jr was a thirty-year-old virgin about to break his virginity with Zen, and he made his way to the room, ready for some excitement.

"You let her have it, son, and make sure she sucks it real good," Roy said, laughing alongside Jim Bob.

Roy Jr opened the door as Zen was trying to untie herself.

"I don't think you should be doing that," Roy Jr said nervously.

Zen noticed how uneasy Roy Jr was, so she was about to use that to her advantage. "Paw said you need to get naked, and I can have my way with you," Roy Jr said with a hard dick. "Muthafucka, I am tied the fuck up—how can I get naked, dummy?" Zen said, aggravated." "I'll untie you but don't do anything fancy, because paw and Uncle Jim Bob are outside of the door ready to kill you," Roy Jr explained.

"And if I don't get naked, what the fuck are you gonna do, white boy? You look borderline retarded," Zen sounded off.

"I'm not playing with you," Roy Jr said trying to be firm, while pointing his gun.

"Don't worry, sexy, Imma, give you want you want… but you better be ready for what comes with fucking me. My pussy is so good it will knock you out and have you sleeping for days. Then I'll take your gun and kill your paw and uncle. So, what you can do is, untie me, and I can play in my pussy for you, and you can play with that big dick of yours. Your paw and uncle will think you're becoming a man," Zen explained.

"Is it true that blacks have the cooties," Roy Jr asked with a concerned look.

"Yes, we do have the cooties. If you put your dick in me, it will have pus bump, and eventually, fall off."

"Oh, hell no. But paw will bust my ass if I don't do it."

"Just do as I told you; it will still feel good, trust me," Zen said seductively.

Roy beat on the door. "I don't hear nothing in there, Roy Jr," Roy yelled through the door.

"Hold on, paw. I got this," Roy Jr untied Zen. She took off her clothes and began to play with her pussy, moaning loudly. "Take your dick out and jack it off—I know you know how to do that, Zen instructed with a giggle, before turning it up a notch. "Yes, yes, give me that dick," Zen faked.

Roy Jr was beating his meat so hard he started to moan out too. "Oh, fuck yes, keep going," Roy Jr was extra loud. Roy and Jim Bob were high-fiving each other on the other side of the door.

Macy was a young redhead that had a deep crush on Roy Jr. She stayed in one of the back campers with her mom and sister. Macy decided to pay Roy Jr a visit to discuss their relationship goals. Macy already claimed him as her boyfriend, but she needed further confirmation. Jim Bob and Roy tried to turn her away from the house, but she shoved her way inside. Macy heard the sex sounds, and her face instantly turned the color of her hair. Macy pushed the door open with her shoulder, and she was not ready for what she saw. Zen was playing in her pussy while Roy Jr was in front of her, beating away at his pea-sized dick.

"OMG, Roy Jr, you're nasty—you're going to get cooties," Macy screamed as she ran out the door. Roy Jr grabbed his clothes and ran behind her. Zen jumped up as well and attempted to run but was roundhoused by Jim Bob. The brothers tied her back up, only this time, she was naked.

Roy Jr begins to plead his case with Macy. "Baby, my paw made me do it, he and my uncle have her kidnapped, and they won't let her go. I was forced, I promise. I love you, baby," Roy Jr explained. Macy pushed Roy Jr away, and she left him standing in front of the camper with his confederate flag boxers on.

Macy wanted revenge in the worst way. She knew Zen came to the camper park in a police car and was in custody by the police officer. Macy scrambled her brain trying to figure out how Zen got away and ended up with Roy Jr and his paw and uncle. Macy grabbed her mom and told her the story as they walked to the bottom of the camper park to tell the officer.

"Hello," Macy yelled out as her mom knocked on the camper. Al looked out the small window of the camper, paranoid. Macy and her mom were not going away.

"Hello, Mr. Officer, Jean," Macy's mom yelled this time. Al held his pistol in his good hand, then cracked open the door.

"Can I help you ladies with something?" Al asked with an attitude.

"That black girl you came in with is up in camper eleven fucking my boyfriend. His name is Roy Jr, and his dad and uncle are in on it, too," Macy explained.

"I know she's a fugitive, but she doesn't deserve to be raped, but that is what Jim Bob and Roy are going to do. I know them fools very well," Jean added.

"Thank you, ladies, so kindly for the information. I'm about to call back up, but you ladies make sure you go inside your camper and stay there. This park is about to be surrounded by canine dogs and police. It will not be safe for any bystanders," Al explained.

"Yes sir, Jean," Macy said with a head nod.

Al wore his riot gear, a bulletproof vest, and combat boots. He secured both handguns in the pockets of his army fatigue pants. As Al was hurrying out of the camper to enter the car, Mario and his crew of men were riding down the hill in an eighteen-wheeler truck. Mario was riding shotgun, while White boy, Kash, Big Mike, and Pound

Puppy were loaded in the back with twenty other niggas strapped with heavy artillery; they were ready for war.

"Crash right into that police car," Mario screamed to the driver Tokeyo, and he did just that. Mario leapt out of the truck and started firing away at Al, hitting him twice in the same arm had Zen shot. The army of men quickly joined Mario, weapons were drawn at Al.

"Where is my wife? I know you have her," Mario spat angrily.

"Hold on, Mario, please. I was just about to go get her from these rednecks up in camper eleven," Al screamed out in pain.

"Why the fuck would Zen be with some muthafuckin' rednecks," Pound Puppy sounded off. White Boy and Kash came from the camper choking and coughing from the smell of Kaleb's body.

"Man, there's a dead body in that camper, in the back room," White Boy explained. Al was shot twice more in his other arm by Pound Puppy.

"Take me to my wife right now," Mario spat as he beat Al across the face repeatedly with his rifle.

Al couldn't raise either arm to protect his face, and was receiving hard strikes from the butt of the rifle. Mario snatched Al up and dragged him up the hill to camper eleven. Mario instructed Tokeyo to turn around and meet them at the camper. Mario threw Al next to a tree beside the redneck's camper, then instructed one of his men to keep Al at gunpoint.

"I want you to blow the horn while we stand at the door," Mario spoke directly to Tokeyo. As the loud truck horn sounded, Roy came to the door with a concerned look. Soon as the door opens, Mario shoots him multiple times in his chest. Jim Bob and Roy Jr reached for their weapons, but White Boy and Pound Puppy shot them both in the palm of their hands. Their weapons clattered to the floor.

"Where is my fuckin' wife?" Mario demanded.

"Mario, I'm in here," Zen screamed out. Pound Puppy ran to the room; Zen was still on the floor naked, tied up and shivering from the cold air coming from the floor vent. Pound Puppy took off his shirt and passed it to Zen to put on. Zen walked up to the front and hugged Mario tight.

"What took you *so long* nigga? Kill all these muthafuckas, bae," Zen yelled.

Mario immediately sprayed Jim Bob and Roy Jr with over fifty rounds.

"Let's get the fuck outta here," Kash screamed out.

"What about your boy Al?" Big Mike asked.

"Somebody gotta take the blame for this shit. Al can't move and the police are on the way. He is already a wanted fugitive, so he's responsible for these bodies whether he did it or not. They can't tie shit to us. Tokeyo will stay behind and collaborate on the story," Mario explained.

"Good play, fam, Pound Puppy spat. They all rushed to the top of the hill, where Mario had left a utility van.

The ride home was filled with excitement, and Zen was happy as hell to be free. Mario and Pound Puppy felt like they could breathe again. Zen changed their smiles to frowns once she explained her horrible experience. She was very anxious to get cleaned up so she could see her girl Raz. Zen felt bad about Raz being shot behind her issue—but Raz was beyond tough, and Zen was sure she'd be giving Pound Puppy hell about leaving the hospital. Raz was going to be released today, and Zen would pick her up.

Zen reunited with her girl team, and they were rolling Raz out of the hospital. Sundae was waiting for the right time to tell Zen about T-Baby's drama. T-Baby was out in Houston Texas caked up with a rapper, Sincere. Sincere was good to T-Baby, but his fame has gone to his head; the groupies had become a serious problem. Sincere had begun to explore other women, creating an unstable, hostile environment for T-Baby.

T-Baby had been mugged and attacked by several groupies. She shot one of the attackers in the face, and the bitch turned around and placed a lawsuit against T-Baby, earning the attacker jail time for her stupid decision. The other attackers now felt some type of way about T-Baby not going to jail, and her still being in the spotlight as Sincere's number one girl. The jealousy was real in Houston. The other female attackers caught T-Baby coming out of her penthouse garage. They maced her in her face and broke her arm; the garage security man only just got there just in time. The ladies were about to pour gasoline on T-Baby and set her on fire. T-Baby's skin had been badly burned from the high quality of mase the attackers used, and she'd gone into a deep depression while Sincere continued to carry on with his life as though everything was okay.

Serena, T-Baby's daughter, reached out to her Aunt Zen for help, but Zen had been kidnapped by Al. And so, when

Sundae called to inform T-Baby about Zen, Serena loaded Sundae with the information about what her mom was dealing with.

Days later, Milly Mill called everyone for a round table meeting to discuss another major assignment. Sub Way catered the meeting; a variety of subs and other goodies were spread along the table. Sundae brought bottles of liquor. She knew after she shared her secret, they were going to need it.

CHAPTER 21

HOUSTON BOUND

The ladies begin the meeting by eating and taking shots.

Milly Mill had designed an area just for Raz to relax and chill with her feet propped up. Milly Mill then discussed the urgency of the situation that the ladies from Switzerland are proposing. She went over the ticket and the pre-itinerary that Chunchi had emailed her.

"Wow, that's some great fuckin' money to eliminate them Switzerland men," Lady J spat.

"Before we get too hyped about this Switzerland gig, we have some bigger fish to fry. Zen, I need you to take two shots and sit back before I go any further," Sundae explained.

Zen poured up two double shots of crown and fired up her Hooka.

"Ashley has already been notified to book our flights and hotel rooms. T-Baby has been jumped out in Houston by some jealous ass groupies. Her rapper boyfriend seems to be enjoying the fame and isn't paying T-Baby no attention. Long story short, our girl is having some serious mental health issues right now. T-Baby is out in Houston, Texas, without her squad. I know she feels all alone and terrified, like the world is against her. Serena can only do so much, but you know this is where we step in," Sundae explained.

"What time does our flight leave?" Zen asked with a face full of tears, pouring two more double shots. Sundae continued giving the ladies the details she received from Serena.

"This nigga has lost his muthafuckin' mind," Raz said as she rose from her cot. Zen was quiet; the ladies hated when Zen would shut down because they knew shit was about to get ugly.

"Call Ashley and give her Zatima's information. Have Zatima and the models meet us in Houston," Zen spoke directly to Lady J.

When Raz heard Zen was calling in Zatima and the Models, she knew Zen was not letting her go on this assignment.

"Zen…" was all Raz could say before Zen let her have it.

"Raz, you are not well enough to join us. I cannot risk you reinjuring yourself. You stay here with Pupp and rehab, so when we swing to Switzerland, you will be ready," Zen spat.

"You're not the only one who cares about T-Baby," Raz sounded off. "That's not fair for you to say, Raz. Don't get me off my game; I don't have time to fight with you, sis. Chill the fuck out," Zen spoke firmly as she walked away.

The next morning, the ladies were picked up by the airport shuttle and taken to Greenville's international airport. The ladies arrived early, it was nine o'clock am, and the flight was scheduled for takeoff at nine forty-five am. During that time, Zen was going over a few plans.

"Once we check on T-Baby, we're going in, all gas and no breaks. Nobody involved will be spared. We will be aggressive; we must give these muthafuckas our best shit," Zen said.

"Heard," Sundae replied, followed by Lady J, Nena, Bleu and Milly Mill. The ladies boarded the plane and spread out to have more room to relax. Zen set with Bleu to comfort her because she knew flying wasn't her strong suit. After the flight attendant finished the safety tutorial, the plane took off a moment later. Raz was disguised during the boarding of the flight and no one knew she was there. Raz took a seat next to Zen and Bleu.

"Excuse me, ma'am, is this seat taken?" Raz asked.

Zen looked around, ready to respond, then noticed it was Raz. Bleu shook her head at Raz pointing her finger while saying, "You gonna get it."

Raz sat down, and Zen leaned her head back against the headrest and giggled. Zen knew she would have done the same thing, so she wasn't going to be so hard on Raz.

"I don't have the energy to kick your ass right now because my mind is in overdrive thinking about these bitches fucking with T-Baby. Your disobedient ass will be staying with T-Baby so you can bounce her back. You gotta get her out of this funk, Raz. I can't have my sister going nuts behind this fuck boy. I've seen plenty bitches confined to a padded room because of a nasty ass nigga," Zen stated sadly and began to cry. Raz hugged her tight, and the rest of the ladies moved in closer to console Zen too.

When the ladies landed in Houston, the shuttle bus took them to their hotel. After settling in, a rental van was waiting for them at the valet station in front of the hotel. The van was loaded with all the firepower they needed. Ashley was on her job. The ladies moved quickly and anxiously to T-Baby's crib. T-Baby was not expecting them, but she desperately needed them. When they arrived, Serena was there washing T-Baby's hair. When Serena opened the door and discovered it was her Aunt Zen and all the other familiar faces she loved. Serena was so happy; she leapt into Zen's arms and began to cry. Zen consoled Serena but was more worried about making her way to T-Baby. T-Baby was sitting at the dining room table with a towel wrapped around her head. Zen noticed the burn marks on her face from the mace the attackers sprayed her with.

Zen and the others hugged T-Baby, letting her know they were there for her. It was a bittersweet moment. The ladies played catch up by talking and reminiscing, and T-Baby told the ladies much more information that they needed to know about what she had been dealing with.

"You already know we didn't come all this way to play patty cake. That bitch ass nigga of yours will pay dearly for his betrayal. Those behind-the-scenes groupies will pay, too," Zen spat. The crew knew how Zen was coming about T-baby, so they matched her energy. Nobody on the opposite side was safe.

"Don't worry because that nigga is about to pay for a skin graph to reconstruct your skin back to its natural tone," Sundae spat.

"Sis, I know this nigga has hurt you tremendously, and you feel like the world is over, but you survived when Alonzo fucked over you, and this is no different. You gotta flip this shit, sis; take all your built-up hurt and frustration and transform that into your grimiest, evilest, most corrupted side. If you need to cry, let that shit out, we are here to help you through this with no judgment. This fuckboy is just a young thug nigga with some Houston fame, because nobody knows about him in any other states. I need you to put your big girl panties on, and let's suit up and bust a move on this wannabe rapper. I will handle shit from here on out, so get Sincere out of your system, *damnit*," Zen spat aggressively. T-Baby wrote down the address of the studio where Sincere and his dancers practice.

Zen and the ladies went to pick up Zatima and the models from the airport. Zen and Lady J began explaining what was going down when they entered the van. Zen pulled up at the studio building and parked right in front. The ladies exit the van and enter the building. They followed the arrow sign to Ballistic studios on the second floor. Zen was the first to enter the studio. Sincere was in the booth with his headphones on, rapping to the beat. Two other guys were smoking a blunt and controlling the amplifier. Lady J and Sundae immediately fired multiple shots into the amplifier. Bleu followed up by pouring bottled water on top, causing dust clouds of smoke to fill the air.

 The two young guys reached for their pistols, but they were too slow. Zatima and Claudia shot them both in the hip, causing them to drop to the floor, and they quickly retrieved their pistols. Zen and Milly Mill entered the booth, and Sincere was backing up against the wall, scared senseless.

"What the fuck is this about I have twenty stacks in my backpack. Please don't hurt me." Sincere begged Zen.

Zen pulls out a large can of mace from her inside jacket pocket and unloaded the spray directly into Sincere's face. His skin begins to burn and dissolve.

"Now you see how my sister felt when those fuck bitches' maced her, and you did nothing to defend her." Zen spat.

"Who is your sister? What the fuck are you talking about?" Sincere cried out in pain; he couldn't see anything, and everything was a complete blur. Lady J and Bleu entered the room and sprayed more mace on Sincere's face while Sundae removed his pants and maced his dick and balls. Sincere was in excruciating pain. He screamed loudly, and his body jerked back and forth. Sincere begged for water but was ignored. Milly Mill placed a dog chain around his neck and dragged him to the elevator to exit the building; she threw him in the van hard against the side, causing him to hit his head and pass out. Bleu was constantly torching him by placing gunpowder down his ears.

The two guys were left on the floor. Nena grabbed their backpacks, jewelry and firearms, taking the stairs to meet up with the ladies in the van. Sincere woke up, screaming in agony all the way to T-Baby's crib.

Raz was at the door, ready for their arrival. Milly Mill continued to drag Sincere by the neck with the dog chain; once they were inside, Raz covered the kitchen area with trash bags and bed sheets. Zen pushed Sincere to the floor, then threw hot water in his face. He was already burning from the mace, so he barely flinched when the hot water hit him. Sincere was finally able to see out of a small corner of his left eye.

"Please tell me what the fuck this is about. My ears are stopped up, my face is on fire, I am wounded… Damnit get me some fuckin' help!" Sincere said, begging loudly to be let go.

"Nigga you will not be going any muthafuckin' where. T-Baby has been dickmatized and lovestruck by your punk ass. It seems that you have lately lost your way and forgot that you have a woman who moved to Houston to be with you," Zen said.

"T-Baby is my everything! I wouldn't harm her at all, you ladies are under some misunderstanding… T-Baby hasn't spoken to me in weeks. She won't answer my calls or nothing," Sincere explained.

"Look, pussy boy, we need to know who these freak bitches are that attacked my sister, and we need to know now," Sundae spoke.

"I have no clue, who these girls are," Sincere explained.

"So, you didn't try to find out? You're just as guilty nigga," Lady J yelled as she shot Sincere in his kneecap. Sincere screamed at the top of his lungs and buried his face into the floor. After hours of torture, he refused to give up the attackers.

"One of the attackers must be related to him, because I can't see him protecting a random," Zatima added. When T-Baby woke up and entered the kitchen, she noticed Sincere on the floor fucked up. T-Baby walked over to Sincere and stepped over his body, she pulled up her gown and pissed on his head. She farted loudly directly over his face. T-Baby then pulled out her bloody tampon and stuffed it inside his mouth, before walking away and returning to her room to shower.

"Please tell me our girl didn't just DNA this nigga." Raz spoke.

"Yep, she nasty—just like her Zen." Sundae spoke.

The girls were tripping about T-Baby's sudden move; they laughed till it hurt.

"And you better not spit it out, or I'll shoot you again," Lady J screamed at Sincere.

Zen instructed Ashley to tap into Sincere's social media and his phone to see what may come up. Sincere had a secure password on his phone; he would not break and give the password to the ladies. Ashley discovered that Sincere had a sister name Bridget Davidson, and they were extremely close. Bridget had pictures on her Facebook page that fit the profile of the ladies T-Baby described. Ashley sent the pictures to Zen's phone to confirm their identity with T-Baby. Ashley manually unlocked Sincere's phone, so now the ladies had full access to scroll through and find more valuable information.

Zen approached T-Baby with the pictures from his phone.

"Yep, that's them low-budget bitches. The one with the red wig is the ringleader," T-Baby explained. Lady J recognized Bridget's post advertising a few sew-ins and colored wigs she completed on her client's head. Sincere's sister Bridget worked at a hair salon in downtown Houston called Bundles.

Zen insisted that T-Baby take this ride and claim her victory against these bitches. T-Baby was down as usual, but she shocked them all when she pulled a sawed-off shotgun from under her bed.

"What the fuck has Zen created? First, she's pissing on niggas, now she has a fuckin' sawed-off, oh hell nah. T-Baby is corrupted fo-sho," Sundae spat.

"She's *b-a-a-ack*," Zen yelled with joy as T-Baby lubed her face down with coco butter, ready for revenge.

"Let's ride," T-Baby said as she threw the rifle in an upward position and walked out like a gangsta. Raz was given T-baby motivation about picking up the pieces with her life. She encouraged T-Baby to stand on what happened to her; once she healed, she could have the skin graph to repair her damaged skin.

Zen, T-Baby, Lady J and Sundae went into the salon. Zatima, Milly Mill, Raz, Bleu, Claudia, Oliva, and Isabella stayed outside in front of the salon, armed and ready. All the chairs were occupied with customers receiving hair service from their stylist. T-Baby shot up into the ceiling and instructed everybody to get down on the floor. The women were screaming and moving to the floor quickly. T-Baby walked over to Bridget and snatched her up by her face. T-Baby hit Bridget in her face with the rifle; her head was moving side to side from the vicious hits. Lady J then pushed her down in the shampoo bowl and sprayed hot water on her face causing her to gasp for air. Bridget was sliding down in the chair, kicking and trying to gain control. The sink was filling up with hot water, but Lady J or none of the ladies gave a fuck.

"The next muthafucker that screams will be dealt with; I want total fuckin' silence," T-Baby yelled, snatching Bridget up from the bowl. Her face was red as an apple; it was burnt badly and was still steaming. T-Baby looked back at Zen, wondering what to do next. Zen sat down at a booth and gave her a nod indicating that the next move was all up to her. T-Baby grabbed the color volume peroxide and doused the entire bottle in Bridget's face. Bridget screamed bloody murder; she was so loud she strained her voice and shat her pants before passing out.

"The first person who can tell me who these girls are in this picture will be able to walk outta here untouched," T-Baby said loudly.

A woman raised her hand. "I am a club promoter, and I see lots of faces. I may help," T-Baby showed the woman the pictures, and she immediately responded.

"That is Layla in the short shots; the girl dressed in green with green lip gloss is Texas. She always wears the color green; she'll stick out like a sore thumb. The girl with the black scarf around her head, that is Co-Co. Strip City, or Magnolia Park is where you will find those three." The neatly dressed, sophisticated lady Stephanie stated.

"Sorry for disturbing your beauty day; you ladies may proceed where you left off. This burnt-face beauty will be coming with us, so her clients need to find another stylist because it will be a while before she recovers," T-Baby spat as she grabbed Bridget by her neck and forced her to the van.

The ladies drove to Magnolia Park since it wasn't time for the strip club to open. "Stop at the car wash to hose this bitch down; she stinks like hell." Nena spat. "I need something to eat. Can we fit that in before we bust up these she-devils?" Zatima added.

"Not right now; dinner's on me once we're done," T-Baby said while holding her nose.

Lacy J forced the information out of Bridget, where her co-defendants would be hanging at. She stabbed her down her side repeatedly with a syringe needle, which made her talk easily. The basketball court was packed with niggas betting on a three-on-three basketball game. The females were rolling blunts and being thots as usual. Several people were on Facebook live, just broadcasting their fun activities at the basketball court. Claudia stops the van directly in front of the court; people begin to turn and look when they noticed how deep the ladies were in the van. T-Baby dragged Bridget from the van and tossed her to the ground. Zen immediately spotted Texas with a green body suit on and her green lip gloss. Zen and Sundae walk towards Texas, and she was instantly loud and ignorant.

"Who the fuck is these whores walking up in the Nolia like they are running shit?"

"Apparently, you don't see your girl Bridget over there fucked up on the ground," Zen said to Texas.

"OMG, what the fuck?" Texas said as she hurried over towards Bridget. Texas was clotheslined by Milly Mill, then dragged to the side to join Bridget.

"Where are Layla and Co-Co?" Lady J asked.

"With your daddy—while he beats your mama," Texas spat.

Lady J stabbed Texas in her face with the same syringe needle she had just used on Bridget. Bleu delivered some monster kicks to their face. T-Baby poured lighter fluid onto Texas green body suit; T-Baby scooped it up from the young thugs that were grilling next to the van. Zen lit a thousand-pack of TNT firecrackers and threw them down the front of Texas fitted suit. Texas begins to jump around like a fool, just as they expected. Texas was on fire, and her body was popping and jerking. It was entertaining for the ladies and the crowd, too; so many people were recording the scene with their phones. The pain became so intense for Texas that she blacked out and lay face down motionless as the firecrackers finished popping.

Layla and Co-Co were getting a pass for now. The ladies left Texas and Bridget at the basketball court totally and utterly fucked up. No one tried to help the girls or stop the torture they received; they were disliked by many. The look that the crowd displayed on their face said only: *about damn time.*

Claudia drove off, and the ladies went to Harold's Steak and Shake, apparently the best steak house in Houston. T-Baby had been bragging to them for months about how delicious the food was. The ladies ordered their food and several pitchers of Margaritas.

"T-Baby, don't you scare me like that no fuckin' more. I was about to go crazy, bitch," Zen said.

"I'm good; I just needed that boost. Zen brings the animal outta me," T-Baby said, laughing.

"Zen brings the animal outta *everybody*," Nena spoke.

"I know one thing; we're going to the TURKEY LEG HUT before we leave Houston." Zatima spat as she gulped down her Corona.

CHAPTER 22

NO REMORSE

The ladies spent two days at T-Baby's crib packing up her and Serena's belongings. T-Baby was moving back to South Carolina, and she was taking her daughter with her.

Serena wasn't thrilled about the move back, but T-Baby and Zen didn't give her much choice. The concoction of coco-butter and shea butter that Raz had blended for T-Baby's face had brought her skin back to normal, and she wouldn't need a skin graph—though Sincere would still compensate her. Sincere had been held in the kitchen at gunpoint; he was allowed to clean up his piss and shit from the floor and was sent right back into the position of a dog.

Zen allowed him to take a shower, because he was going on Instagram with a public apology to T-Baby. Sincere was performing at Strip City, and T-baby was about to be his special guest.

"Nigga you better floss to the world how much you love my sister; it needs to be known that no other female can ever come close to holding your heart. T-Baby will be on stage the entire time, and you are going to act like a pussy-whipped fuckboy. You will then close the show by bending down on one knee to propose to T-Baby." Zen explained.

"If you try any fucked shit, we will finish Bridget off and kill your daddy," Sundae explained.

The ladies gathered that Sincere loved his daddy more than life; he had pictures and posts of him and his daddy on all of his social media accounts. Sincere even had a tattoo on his back that says DADDY'S BOY. His phone call log was consistent with his dad's phone number.

"How the fuck you beautiful ladies expect me to perform when I can barely walk or see? I haven't eaten, and the only fluids I've consumed is a tall glass of T-Baby's piss. My face is scorched and burning like fire. You ladies are sick; I promise I'll be sending all y'all to jail."

"First, we're beautiful, and now we're sick? Which one is it? The sooner you figure out that this sick bunch of ladies you see before you are in control, the better off you'll be," Zen spat.

Isabella and Olivia went shopping for the power couple so they could look the part. The rest of the ladies got drunk and smoked some sour diesel from Sincere's backpack.

"Can I please get a sandwich and a drink? I need the energy to perform tonight." Sincere asked out loud, clearly agitated.

"Hell no, nigga. If you wanna eat something, come in this room and eat me for the last time." T-Baby sounded off.

"Damn, T-Baby, you're going to feed that nigga more blood, huh?" Lady J said.

"No damn wonder T-Baby's in a rage; she's on her cycle," Zatima added.

"Bitch, you seen that crazy heffa stuff her damn tampon in buddy's mouth, so you know she's on her cycle," Raz spoke.

The ladies kept repeating the play to Sincere because if he fucked up in any way, his daddy was going to be bleeding from his ass. Sincere and T-Baby left her house in a limo, and the ladies followed close by in the rental van.

"T-Baby, this shit is unnecessary. You need to call your people off," Sincere spoke.

"You don't know Zen too well, but what she explained to you is going to happen," T-Baby said as she blew Sincere a kiss.

"I'm glad y'all bitches are leaving Houston; you have been a damn problem since day one. How the fuck y'all sluts are going to beat a muthafucka to force them to like your slow ass," Sincere spat with venom.

"Zach, I need you to turn around and make your way to the county hospital," T-Baby instructed the driver.

"Yes, ma'am," Zach responded.

T-Baby straddled Sincere's lap and kissed him on his neck.

"I'm sorry you feel that way bae, I would have never stayed with you under false pretences. But you led me to believe what we were sharing was real. I thought you were feeling me; I thought you were my man, boo. I continued to ride your coat tale, so for the life of me, I can't see what gave you the power to mistreat me by cheating with them low-life sluts. My Team and I are known for doing damage to men who disrespect and cheat on a woman. So, *fuck you, nigga*. I'm about to ride your daddy's dick from now on and let him lick my ass crack—like father like son, huh. He looks like he can give me that work." T-Baby sounded off.

Just as Sincere gained the courage to slap T-Baby, she grabbed her twenty-two purple pistol and shot him thrice in the side of his neck—the same spot she left her lip-print. T-Baby then dug her nail down in the bullet wounds and poured the Absolute vodka from the limo bar inside of the wounds. When the driver drove up to the emergency room, T-Baby instructed the driver to throw him in the wheelchair that was sitting out front. "Do you what me to just leave him here ma'am?" Zach asked.

"Yes, sir, somebody will find him." T-Baby spat. Sincere was moaning in pain; he had no voice to scream. He vomited twice before the limo pulls off. Zen and the others put the puzzle together about the change of plans. T-Baby instructed Zach on what she needed him to do once they arrived at Strip City. T-Baby then texted Zen the play she had in mind. Zen text back with a smiley face emoji.

The ladies walk into the Strip club with Layla and Co-Co on their agenda. Zach made his way to the locker room to do as he was instructed. When the ladies entered the locker room, all eyes were on them. Zen cocked her gun.

"Everybody but Layla and Co-Co leave the locker room, please," Zen said, imitating Diamond from players club. The girls begin to scatter like roaches, except one rusty, dusty, thot stripper Riah who was placing body glitter on her legs. Riah was brave; she popped her gum while looking the ladies up and down and slowly moving to her vanity. Milly Mill pulled her by her thong and slammed her down in the restroom stall, pushing her head inside the toilet bowl. Bleu places her foot on top of her head, forcing her face further down in the toilet. Layla and Co-Co tried to exit the locker room, but were stopped by Lady J and Raz.

"This party is in honor of you two, so it will be rude if you leave," Zen added.

T-Baby walked up close to them both and slapped them repeatedly. Zach moved in with two chairs and rope. Zach tied the rope to the support beam in the middle of the locker room, adding noose-shaped knots.

"What is going on?" Co-Co asked.

"Oh, you two don't remember jumping my sister T and fucking up her skin? And to add insult to injury, y'all snakes fucked her man and swallowed a few of his kids," Raz added.

"I'm so sorry for my wrongdoings... please, don't hurt us. It was Texas' idea I promise. She's always bullying us, y'all need to kill that green-wearing bitch, please... *please*, I have kids," Layla pleaded for forgiveness, but the crew did not fall for her fake tears and apology.

"We either hurt you or your kids. Which one do you prefer? We don't do sorry or regrets. We're a different breed of bitches; y'all stank puss rug rats pick the wrong sister to fuck with, so enough of the small talk. We have a flight to catch," Sundae sounded off.

Isabella and Raz grabbed Co-Co and placed her ankles in the noose knots. They hung her upside down from the support beams. Zatima and Lady J, repeated that process with Layla. Once their bodies were dangling, and their legs were spread out like the red sea. T-Baby used the step ladder, and sprayed bug spray in between their legs, directly on their pussy. The spray begins to ooze from their pussy lips. Layla and Co-Co began to squirm, screaming from the burning pain; just then, Zen began to shoot their body with nails from a nail gun.

"Please stop, stop, please," The ladies screamed out in pain. Zen was shooting the nail gun like she was playing for a prize at the fair. Milly Mill took over while Zen and Bleu went to the bar for lemon juice. Bleu noticed a utility closet on their way to the bar. Bleu picked the lock and filled a paint sprayer with Clorox and ammonia; the concoction immediately began to fuzz and foam. Zen gave the bartender one hundred dollars for her sliced lemons and lemon juice that was in stock. When Zen and Bleu made it back to the locker room, the hanging friends continued to beg and plead to be let go.

"I was begging the same way when y'all bitches fucked my face and damaged my back. Chin up, chest out, suck that whining up," T-Baby said aggressively.

"They haven't felt shit yet, sis," Zen said. Raz began to spray the chemical mixture over their body while Bleu was popping them slave-style with a belt. The holes from the nails were soaking up the mix and began to display bubbles. Raz added more chemicals on top of the bug spray in between their pussy; no more kids were coming outta their holes. Both of their pussies were like a Nickelodeon slime show. Raz later sprayed their face, and Lady J and Zen began to pour pitchers of lemon juice over their now chemically burnt bodies.

Milly Mill used the rest of the nails from the nail gun to shoot them both repeatedly in the face, leaving them looking like Jason's hockey mask. Nena poured the rest of the lemon juice into Co-Co and Layla's eyes, the dripping from the lemon juice marinating inside the holes in their face. The pain the girls were feeling was unbearable. Layla and Co-Co were half dead; they were unconscious, and their bodies looked like they had been pulled from the swamp. The ladies were sure Co-Co, Layla, Texas, and Bridget would have rooms side by side in the burn unit at the hospital. T-Baby rewarded Zach for his help, and the ladies left the club, headed to the airport.

Sincere was admitted to the ICU unit; he refused to tell the police anything, fearing what could happen to his dad and sister. Sincere lay helpless in the hospital bed in pain, feeling regret and shame of the treated T-Baby. Bridget, Texas, Layla, and Co-Co were also being treated for chemical burns and other severe injuries. The foursome girl squad refused to talk to the hospital staff and police; Co-Co made up a bogus story, but no one was buying it. The police instructed the hospital staff to document their charts as gang retaliation.

Zatima, Claudia, Isabella, and Olivia decided to move to South Carolina. They needed to lay low from Los Angles for a while. Once Zatima explained her situation to Zen, she knew Zatima had created a hostile environment, and the heat was on her and the models.

"I have plenty of property; you ladies will be good. I can use some extra help in my hair factory." Zen responded to Zatima.

The flight back was fun for the ladies; they ordered several Peach margaritas and were drunk on energy. They were live and out loud thirty thousand feet in the air, enjoying the vibe.

"Look at Bleu; she's a big girl now, riding this plane like she's riding on a dick," Raz joked.

"Ha-ha!" Bleu said, rolling her eyes at Raz.

CHAPTER 23

THE BRAWL

Al was housed at Wire Fence Federal prison in Arizona. Wire Fence prison housed nothing but the highest-charged murder cases from the Federal court system. This prison was stacked with a mixture of killers. Every prisoner had a story to tell; they either persisted in claims of their innocence or were cold-blooded killers. Different scenarios led the men to lengthy sentences. Any prisoner that stepped foot onto Wire Fence Federal property knew they were there till death.

For his part, Al had received a double life sentence for his prior convictions, not to mention the four dead bodies found at the camper park. Kaleb, Roy, Roy Jr, and Jim Bob. Al knew he was fighting a losing battle trying to explain his innocence. However, he wanted revenge in the worst way.

He was roommates with Damion Dubose, AKA Olive. He was called Olive because of the dookie green round birthmark on his face cheek. Olive was briefing Al on how he could get revenge. As the longest living prisoner at Wire Fence, he was like the mayor of the prison. He'd helped men like Al on several occasions to attack their prey from behind the Wire Fence. Al was not intrigued by the idea because he'd come up short many times, trying to hurt Zen and Mario.

"Man, I am telling you these fuckwads have nine lives plus some. They have escaped death more than these muthafuckas in here jack their dicks," Al elaborated.

"If they're as caked up with money as you say they are, I know a few niggas that will handle the situations discreetly and professionally. This Zen chic that you wanted to fuck so bad? I'll have my niggas empty her bank account and fuck her in front of her husband on top of the bank receipts. I will even arrange for the entire fuckfest to be captured on video and forwarded to my phone, so you can enjoy the fruits of your labor while sitting comfortably behind these walls." Olive spat.

"I want that bitch badly, bro; I wanna see her punished and fucked hard and long," Al spoke firmly.

"I'll contact my man X and set up a play. He may need confirmation on the money situation, but other than that, he'll be ready to ride." Olive explained.

"This bitch and her crew are loaded with cash, but he must come with his best shit, or he'll be floating in a river with a plunger up his ass. I have two pounds of compressed exotic weed in an abandoned house in the floorboard of the attic. Both blocks are inside a gain-flings laundry container. I stashed it there when I was on the run," Al explained.

"That alone will make X move; you get busy on the information he's going to need while I make this call," Olive said, feeling good about the set-up.

Olive knew something good was going to be in it for him. Al began to feel a bit more at ease, glad to know that Zen was about to get what the fuck she deserved. Al knew if

Zen got fucked up, that was Mario's payback. Al begins laying out an itinerary of everything and anyone affiliated with Zen. Al was making sure not to leave anything out; he wanted her life just as fucked up as his.

Meanwhile, Zen was on a mission to expand the hair factory. She was doing great with business and generating legal money. Zen was now fully staffed with Zatima and the models living in the Pickle Tower; they would put in work four days a week to take care of their rental fee.

Mario reached out to Sundae about helping him with a special project for Zen. Mario wanted to handle this alone but needed someone from Zen's team to help him pull off the perfect fairytale day.

The round table meeting was taking place at Zen's pool house. The ladies had to decide on the Switzerland assignment.

"I honestly think we need to rethink the Switzerland deal. We just recently went to London and created lots of confusion. So, we need to lay low. If we use the same passports going to another country again and more people lose their life, that could be a fuck up for us. A total red flag," Zen said.

"What if I take the lead by getting a fake passport and taking the newbies along? Then we handle the task. Since I stayed back on the last assignment, let me get my hands dirty and bless the team with some coins," Milly Mill suggested.

"You're the only one with the proper training, so it would be suicide sending the others on a blindsided mission—unless you can get your girl Kelly to go. Kelly is certified to handle a task like this; she's always pushed that premium gas when I sent her to handle shit for me. Zatima will be the only other one to take if we decide that's the move." Zen spoke.

"That'll be perfect; people will only see Zatima wobble from restaurants to Dunkin Donuts," Milly Mill joked. Zatima gave her the finger.

"Zatima needs to loosen up her muscles and go through some intense training for a few weeks—shooting range exercise and a liquid diet is a must," Zen said.

"Zen, you're just as thick as me, Suga, so don't go there," Zatima spat.

"Yes, ma'am, I do have a lot of fluffy goodness, but I'm in shape. I work out, and I shoot guns more than I pump gas. So, it's a big difference, lil girl," Zen said jokingly to Zatima.

"I'm down; I need to get my body snatched anyway," Zatima added.

"I'll let Chunchi know that the assignment will take longer than usual, but it will be handled. I'm certain Kelly is down with the task. Milly Mill explained. "Okay, two weeks from now, y'all can head out; contact Kelly ASAP. Training starts right now. Take my membership and go hit up the gym." Zen said as she snatched Zatima's honey bun from her hand.

Al touched base with X over the phone, telling him the details verbally that Olive had sent to him. "This bitch is tricky, don't let her fool you. She carries multiple guns; she fights like a man. The best way and the only way will be to knock that bitch out and tie her up military style. Check her mouth for razor blades and her boots for any additional weapons. That's how she shot me; she pulls a pistol from her boot. I have the perfect female that can help you with luring her in. Zen absolutely hates this bitch. I will send over the name and address and Facebook profile of this whore I'm speaking on; you might wanna reward yourself and take that pussy for a test drive. She's dangerous with that kitty." Al explained to X, thinking about all the times Nicolette made him weak at the knees.

Zen often tried to do something fun and entertaining for her the ladies. She set up a family day color party at the park, with games and food. Zen delegated the grill duties to Zay, while Star handled the decorations. Pound Puppy created a playlist, and he was on point with the music. Kelly and Milly Mill were sucking face, and so was Lady J and Zatima. Zatima forgot about her liquid diet, because she was hiding behind Lady J fucking up a rib and a bowl of potato salad. Mario and Zen kicked it off with the dancing. They were smooching like they were in a liquor house, grooving across the pissy floor. Starr was there with her boyfriend Corrupt; they were passing love licks and posing for Instagram.

Corrupt had Star in a sticky situation; Allison Nicolette's daughter was pregnant by Corrupt. Star and Allison had even been in a brawl at the college football Jamboree, and Star, being the baby Zen, beat Allison's ass. She refused to stop until Allison was fucked up. The results of the fight caused Allison to lose her baby.

Allison blamed Star, and she wanted to get her back for stealing her man and causing her to lose her baby. Nicolette and Allison drove to the park to confront Star and rub in her face that she was going to jail. Allison started crying to her mom about the pictures they were posting on Instagram. Allison felt disrespected; her young heart was crushed. Nicolette wanted to protect Allison and make up for not being the mother Allison needed after many years of choosing drugs over her.

"That stripper-looking daughter of Zen's is going to be a bully just like her mama, but I'll be damned if she treats you how Zen treated me," Nicolette spoke. When Nicolette and Allison pulled up at the park, Star immediately squared off with Allison, punching her in her face. Nicolette then grabbed Star by her hair and dragged her to the ground kicking her, but that didn't stop Star. Star held onto Allison with a super grip and struck her with hard blows to the face. Zen and the ladies finally realized the commotion. As Zen made her way over and realized that her baby girl Star was on the ground being kicked by Nicolette, she totally blacked out. Her mind became twisted, and nothing but evil, corrupted thoughts danced in her head. Zen began to walk the dog on Nicolette.

Zen split Nicolette's face open from her hard and quick punches. Raz tried to jump in, but Sundae held her back. "Zen got this." Sundae spoke.

But, somehow, Bleu managed to maneuver her way around Zen and place Nicolette in a chokehold, while Zen continued giving her body blows. Mario didn't know what to do; his two favorite ladies were in a deep rage. Maggie showed up with the police following close behind. Star would not let go of Allison, and Zen and Bleu were still whaling on Nicolette. The police officers did not want to use force. Mario stepped in when he saw the aggravation from the officers; they could not get Zen to calm down or stop beating Nicolette.

"Zen, get your damn daughter and stop it before you go to jail," Mario spat.

"Oh, they're all going to jail," The white officer stated. Bleu went into defense mode and grabbed Zen as if she was breaking up the fight.

"Okay, sis, chill; you must listen to these nice officers. Let's not make matters worse," Bleu spoke softly.

Zen, Star, and Nicolette went to jail for disorderly conduct, and disrupting public property. Star was currently in the system with an active warrant for her arrest pertaining to Allison's assault that had caused the death of her unborn child. The officers place cuffs on them and proceeded to the police car to take them to jail.

"Mario, I want these freeloading dirt goblins off my property ASAP, fuck them ring worm oily skin bastards," Zen yelled.

"Bitch I should have let Al kill your bitch ass. If it wasn't for me, Mario would have never found your evil ass." Nicolette spat.

The officers hurried and placed them in the car.

"I'm sorry Ma."

"You don't have to be sorry for shit. Fuck that bitch and her grimy-ass mammie. I may get out before you, but you know your mommy got you, no matter what. Soon as you get a bond, you're outta there," Zen spoke.

Mario turned to Corrupt. "I know your young wanna-be player ass did not just get my daughter caught up in this bullshit," Mario said loudly with aggression.

"No sir, I was done with Allison. She never even told me she was pregnant. Allison was jealous of Star, so she started doing dumb shit to fuck with her until Star beat that ass," Corrupt explained.

"Look, son, my wife and my daughter do not handle confusion and drama well, so please, for future reference: if you plan to be with my daughter, do not cheat and keep them thirsty thot bitches away from you. You will not have to worry about me at all, but her mom and many aunts will fuck you up slowly." Mario said seriously.

Meanwhile, Raz and the ladies headed over to the Pickle Tower to evict Maggie from Zen's property.

"Y'all got to give me at least thirty days; I know the fuckin' law," Maggie spat.

"I can't believe you and your daughter would bite the hand that fed y'all. Zen went out on a limb to help y'all's raggedy asses. And for Nicolette and Allison to pursue charges on my niece—that shit was fucked up," Milly Mill spoke.

"Fuck the law, you have seventy-two hours to be out, or we're putting your dysfunctional asses outta here. That's final," Raz spoke.

Bleu became belligerent and began knocking over furniture and pulling down curtains. She threw her soda pop in Maggie's face. "Don't get shit twisted; you can get your old ass tossed up too," Bleu spat firmly.

Mario and Pound Puppy were down at the county jail, waiting for Zen's and Star's bond to post. The main judge was out due to Covid, and the jail was backed up with fifty people ahead of Star and Zen, waiting to see the judge. The desk officer explained the situation to Mario and told him he was better off leaving because there was no way they were being released tonight, and tomorrow wasn't looking too good either.

"What the fuck," Mario said, enrage.

X and his homie Mustard were on their way to South Carolina to wreak havoc with a mission to get Zen. Every criminal had that one partner that would ride or die, and for X it was his boy Mustard. Mustard was a high yellow skin criminal that stood seven foot tall, he entertained what every fuckary X was on. X's Suga Mama, Mildred, had given him just enough money so he and Mustard could catch the Amtrack.

The two delinquents were always trying to come up with a get-rich-quick scheme. Olive had never stirred them wrong, and so money was their motive to handle whatever needed to be handled.

CHAPTER 24

YOU'RE COMING WITH US

Nicolette and Zen were released after forty-eight hours.

Nicolette was called to the release room first. She gathered her belongings, and she was let out by a female guard, using the jail phone to call her mom. Maggie was upset because they only had one more day to move and nowhere to go.

"Calm down ma; I'll handle it when I get there. I need you to come to pick me up, please," Nicolette asked.

"The car has a flat. Allison's friend Teresa and her boyfriend are coming by to help us," Maggie spoke.

"Okay, but I'm not waiting. I need to take a long walk; it will do me some good," Nicolette said.

X and Mustard stole a red 2018 Audi station wagon from the Amtrack station. They went to recover the weed from the abandoned house. When the two arrived, several homeless men were hanging around the front of the house, keeping warm from the fire blazing in the old, rusted barrel. No one asked who they were; X and Mustard just went inside and headed for the attic. The Gain containers were in the exact spot as Al instructed. The next stop was Nicolette's house to see if they could get her to come with them willingly. When Mustard knocked on the door, Maggie answered.

"Hello, ma'am. Is Nicolette here?" Mustard asked.

"No baby, they just released her. She needs a ride from the county jail; are you the man to fix the flat tire?" Maggie asked. "Yes, ma'am. We're here to fix the tire; then we can pick up Nicolette," Mustard added.

"Praise God, you men are awesome," Maggie said throwing her hands in the air in testimonial praise. Mustard and X moved quickly to fix the flat tire; they couldn't refuse after seeing her excitement.

X googled the direction to the county jail, and they were on their way. When they were two blocks from the jail, X noticed a female walking, fitting the description of Nicolette. Mustard quickly turned the car around, and they slowed up beside her.

"We're here to pick you up; we just fixed your mom's tire." X sounded off.

"Yes, thank you so much. I was starting to get tired." Nicolette spoke. Nicolette entered the back seat, and Mustard proceeded into traffic.

"Where are Allison and Teresa? Which one of you is Teresa boyfriend?" Nicolette asked with a concerned look.

"Neither one of us are. We're here on a mission to capture Zen; we were sent by Al. We need your assistance to help make our mission successful." X spoke.

"That bitch is about to be released from the county; we both were locked up a few days back at the park. Please explain to me how the fuck I help you. That bitch hates me." Nicolette spat.

"That should be the reason you need to help us." Mustard added.

"Like I said, what the fuck can I do? All I know is Zen is about to be processed out and she should be walking out as we speak." Nicolette explained.

"Great. When we get her, you can go or stay with us and seek your revenge." X said. Mustard turned the car around again and went back in the direction of the county jail.

Meanwhile, Zen was briefing Star on how to handle herself until she got her out.

"I'm good, Ma. You get outta here; I'll see you at home soon. I got this; I am bossed up just like you. I will never show any weakness, just like you taught me." Star spat.

Zen hugged Star and walked with the female officer to exit the jail. Zen was about to use the free phone when X walked up beside her.

"Mario sent me to pick you up. I'm Kash's cousin X," X explained.

"Okay, cool. Get me the fuck away from this demon-ass place," Zen spoke, entering the station wagon in the back seat. Nicolette and Mustard were a street over, waiting for X to pick them up. X pulls up to the sidewalk and in jumped Nicolette and Mustard.

"Oh, hell nah. Let me outta this muthafuckin' car." Zen shouted.

"Looks like I'm not the only one who don't like your grimy ass," Nicolette said, looking back at Zen from the front seat, giving her the middle finger. Zen quickly leaped towards the front seat, grabbing Nicolette by her neck and starting to choke her. Mustard pushed Zen hard into the door, causing her face to smush against the window.

"What the fuck is going on? Who are y'all fuck niggas?" Zen yelled out angrily.

Mustard then begins to manhandle Zen. Mustard pushed her hard and held her head down in between her legs using much force.

"Is that all you got fuck boy? My baby niece got more stamina than your stanking ass. Nigga you need a muthafuckin' shower," Zen spat.

"Fuck you bitch," Mustard said, pissed off. He continued to punch Zen, pulling her hair and scratching her face like a deranged female. But Zen would not crack; she cussed and spat in Mustard's face, even sucker-punching him, causing him to bleed. Zen then reached for Nicolette again.

"Just chill, bro; soon as we stop, that bitch will act right, I guarantee it." X spat. He explained to Nicolette that he needed her to get a Motel room for him and Mustard.

"I don't have any cash on hand, but if you take me to my mom, I'll get the money," Nicolette said.

"Imma let you out at the end of your street, so we can avoid being seen. Just hurry, get the money, and meet us at the Spider Inn Motel by the Amtrack station." X sounded off.

X dropped Nicolette off and headed to the Spider Inn Motel. "Y'all some real live pussies. Who sent y'all? And why couldn't they handle me themselves?" Zen spat.

"Shut the fuck up. Al sent us to collect his money and then some from your entire crew." X spat.

"Nigga, Al sent you two leaches on a dummy mission, y'all mutha fuckas not getting shit from me. Get a muthafuckin' job, you fuckan bum." Zen said as she quickly grabbed the back of X's head, causing him to swerve into the road. Zen was able to get a few punches in before Mustard choked her out, putting her to sleep.

"This bitch cannot be a real female; she's cocky as fuck," Mustard said.

When Nicolette walked into the house, Maggie was at the table with Allison and Teresa. Allison jumped up and hugged her mom, landing a big kiss on her cheek. "Two men came and fixed the tire, but it was not Teresa's boyfriend," Maggie spoke.

"I know Ma; they were friends of mine," Nicolette said.

"Okay, sweetie. That was so nice of them," Maggie said softly.

"I need to borrow thirty dollars, Ma—and I need to take your car quickly. I'll be back shortly." Nicolette spoke.

"We need this money so we can get a place to stay. We must be outta here by tomorrow," Maggie explained.

"I have a plan, Ma. Just trust me," Nicolette said as Maggie handed her the keys and the money.

X and Mustard waited patiently on Nicolette to arrive at the motel. Zen woke up fighting, and this time X knocked her out, punching her in her face repeatedly. Zen's nose was broken, and she was bleeding heavily.

Nicolette paid for the room, noticing that X was parked in the back by the old motel furniture. Nicolette walked to the car and slid X the keycard. Nicolette took a quick selfie with Zen while she was out cold and bloody beyond recognition.

"Good luck, fellas," Nicolette said as she hurried back to her car to leave.

Mario was told by Star's lawyer that Zen had been released. He hurried down to the county jail, but Zen was nowhere in sight. Mario begins to ask the desk officer serious questions which the officer could not answer. All the officer knew was that she had been released over three hours ago. Mario called Pound Puppy and the rest of the crew to see if Zen was with any of them, but no one had seen or heard from Zen. They'd all assumed she was still locked down.

Several hours passed, and Mario and the crew began to panic.

"Meet me at Ashley's garage immediately," Mario sent a massive text to everyone. The crew came rushing in; everybody was in a rage. They knew something was off.

Mario instructed Ashley to pull the camera footage from the county jail and the surrounding areas. The crew notice Nicolette leaving first, then forty minutes later Zen walks out the jail's front door, approached by a freckle-faced albino man. He was identical to Tobias Whale from Black Lighting.

"Who the fuck is that scary-looking muthafucka?" Sundae spoke.

"I have no idea, but he's a dead man. I know that," Mario spat.

"Zen must know this nigga for her to move so freely and enter his car." Lady J said.

"I have a funny feeling, y'all," said Raz.

"Let me follow the car on camera to see what direction they headed in," Ashley spoke.

"Looks like the car's pulling over." Pound Puppy added. They saw Nicolette and another unknown man enter the car. The entire crew rushed from Ashley's garage, and Mario sped off with no intention of obeying any traffic laws. They were headed to the Pickle Tower to find Nicolette.

Mario opens the door with his property key. "Where the fuck is Nicolette?" Mario shouted.

"What the fuck are you doing? You can't just walk in here. We're leaving this raggedy muthafucka tomorrow," Allison spoke loudly.

"Y'all muthafuckas about to leave right now. Nicolette and two high yellow niggas have my wife, and I need to know where her pussy-popping ass is at," Mario spat.

"Ms. Maggie, where the fuck is your daughter? I'd hate to fuck you up, but I will if I don't get the answers I need," Milly Mill spat. Raz began to smack Allison and her friend Teresa around, asking questions about Nicolette's whereabouts.

"I'm not telling y'all bitches shit. I'm sick of y'all bulling my mom around like she's some damn kid." Allison said angrily. Lady J slammed Allison hard against the wall.

"Shut your dick-sucking ass up. You and your pissy, pamper-wearing grandma about to be floating in the nearest river," Lady J spat.

"Stop it, please. Two guys came by looking for Nicolette, and I told them she was just released from jail and needed a ride. They fixed my flat tire on my car and left to get her, I think. Nicolette came home and asked me for thirty dollars, saying she needed my car. She's been gone since then." Maggie explained to whoever was listening.

"No need to waste any more valuable time here. Let's just take her old-ass Mama with us. When Nicolette returns, her bumpy-lip-ass daughter will confirm that we have her grandma, and she doesn't have her medication." Nena spat.

"Y'all whores are going to hell," Ms. Maggie spoke.

"Nicolette will be there too, sucking flaming hot dicks," Raz sounded off.

Nicolette was across the street looking from behind a tree; she noticed the multiple cars when she was about to pull up, so she hesitated to go home and exited the car and took cover behind a tree. Nicolette saw Milly Mill manhandle her mom roughly into Sundae's car while Sundae smacked Maggie across the head.

"I need my medication," repeated Maggie as she was shoved into the car.

CHAPTER 25

DON'T GET TOO COMFORTABLE

X and Mustard were attacking Zen and raping her.

One would hold her down, covering her mouth, while the other would sexually assault her. X would face-call Olive, so Al could see the damage they were doing. Al's dick was dancing through his federal uniform, seeing Zen naked and getting fucked and tortured. Yet he wasn't satisfied; he wanted to see Zen fight and scream while she took dick up her ass and pussy.

Zen lay there, thinking about her family; that is what held her together. She did not give any kind of reaction, even with the excruciating pain ripping through her body. X and Mustard didn't like the fact that Zen wasn't begging for mercy or giving up information about her money. The two men repeatedly added force, trying to get Zen to acknowledge her pain. Zen was crying from the inside, but she'd been trained to show the enemy no weakness, and she mastered the class. Mustard and X were more frustrated than Zen; they were tired and sweating from force fucking Zen. X went to get ice to fill the ice bucket while Mustard lay naked across the worn bed.

Zen opened her eyes and focussed on the Barbie doll she noticed in the corner of the room when they first arrived. The prior occupants of the room must have left the doll behind. Zen also noticed an ink pen on the table between the two beds. Zen quickly grabbed both items; she leaped on the bed and forcefully gapped Mustard's mouth open, forcing the Barbie doll legs down his throat as she stabbed him in the eyes and face with the ink pen repeatedly. Mustard's eyes widened; he couldn't breathe, and he twitched, trying to reach Zen.

But Zen took the extra second to jam the doll's legs further down his throat. She then hid behind the door, waiting on X. AS X opened the door, Zen stabbed him in the side of the neck with the ink pen then she punched him with all her might like Craig did Deebo.

Zen bolted out of the door full speed and butt naked as X flopped down to his knees as he struggled to grab the pen from his neck.

"Gawd dammit, imma kill you bitch. Oh shit, my neck. Mustard, wake your ass up. Wake up, nigga!" X screamed. Then he suddenly heard Mustard gurgling lightly on the bed; he sounded a breath away from death. X made his way to the bed and held Mustard's hand. X didn't know what to do, Mustard began to foam from his mouth and nose, and his skin was turning blue. X began to remove the doll from Mustard's mouth, but his gurgling became worse. He was now certain that Mustard was not going to live, and he didn't want to be in the crossfire when the paramedics and police arrived. X wrapped his neck with a torn sleeve from a shirt, then grabbed the weed they retrieved had, and left the motel. X was assed out; he had no play on what to do, so he called Olive to deliver the news.

"I thought you said this nigga X was certified. I told that nigga he could not underestimate Zen. If he left an unopen move, she was going to take it. Now we're fucked."

"How the fuck are we fucked? It has nothing to do with us. We're in here serving double life sentences." Olive spoke.

"Trust me, that bitch and her nigga will be coming for us. They're going to kill us some way somehow." Al said, paranoid. "Nigga you're giving this bitch too much ammunition. I don't give a fuck about her street creditability. She can't get into a federal prison on her best day," Olive said.

But Al just paced back and forth through the prison; he was filled with nervous energy. He knew Zen was coming; he wanted to kill this X nigga for his fuck up.

Zen made it to the Amtrack station; she knew the police or security guards would be there. Two security guards happened to see people pointing in Zen's direction as she bent down to catch her breath.

When the guards noticed Zen was naked, they assumed she was high from smoking crack.

"Ma'am, you need to put clothes on, or you will be arrested for indecent exposure." One of the guards yelled out. But when Zen stood up, the guards noticed that she was beaten, they rushed to her side, and one guard wrapped his jacket around her. The guard radioed for an ambulance. Other bystanders were covering Zen with blankets while she lay there helpless. The ambulance arrived, and they dressed her in a gown and placed Zen on the gurney. An oxygen mask was being placed on Zen; she pulled it off and pointed at the motel. Zen was trying to talk, but she was choked so much her voice was strained.

"I was kidnapped and raped, and the men are in room 210, red station wagon." Zen said in a low tone while still pointing in the direction of the hotel. The EMTs performed a brief physical while they prepared to leave for the hospital. They noticed her vagina bleeding and damaged.

The police arrived on the scene and retrieved statements from the security men and the EMT. The EMT elaborated to the police that Zen was adamant that something happened at the motel down the street, because she kept saying room 210 and that two light skin men raped her.

Nicolette made her way back to the motel. She noticed the red station wagon was gone. Nicolette entered the room, and the door was cracked halfway open. When she was inside, Mustard was on the bed, dead as a doorknob with a barbie doll down his throat. Nicolette rushed to his side and began to shake him. Nicolette hurried to the restroom and vomited over the floor.

"OMG what the fuck happened," Nicolette screamed. Nicolette went to feel for a pulse and attempted to pull the doll from Mustards mouth. Nicolette heard some cars pulling up outside, she quickly went to the door, thinking it was X. To her surprise, it was the police. Nicolette ran out of the room, trying to get to her car.

"Ma'am, is this your room?" The officer asked. The other officers went inside and found Mustard's body.

The Spider inn motel was now a crime scene. The manager was notified, and he joined the officers at the scene to give his statement of what he knew.

The manager noticed Nicolette and became riled up. "That is the lady right there that rented this room," the old white manager explained to the officers while pointing at Nicolette. The officer immediately placed Nicolette under arrest; she was going down for murder and misprision of a felony if she could not explain who did it. "No, please, I didn't do this. I promise I'm innocent. You gotta believe me, sir." Nicolette was crying hysterically. The officer placed Nicolette in the car, and she was transported to the county jail.

Before the hospital contacted Mario, Ashley was alerted by her FBI tracker that a woman fitting Zen's description was being admitted to the county hospital. Ashley first called Mario.

"What's up, white girl? Tell me you found Zen."

"Yes, bro, I think so. Head over to the county hospital; I'm certain It's Zen. She's been hurt bad bro, so prepare yourself. I will contact the others; you hurry by her side." Ashley said, giving Mario the heads up on what to expect.

Mario was en route to the hospital when the triage nurse called him. He was listed as Zen's next of kin. He did not answer her as he was focused on getting to the hospital. Mario pulled up to the front and jumped out of his car, leaving it parked in front of the emergency center. Mario ran through the metal detectors, chased down by the security.

"Sir, we need to scan you, please," The security man stated.

"Sir, I need to find my wife she's been hurt." Tears were falling down Mario's face. He needed to see his wife now.

"No problem, sir. Calm down; I'll help you." The security guard was married, so he knew how Mario felt and understood his pain and frustration. A nurse came to escort Mario to the back where Zen was; she was getting cleaned up. The doctors just performed a rape kit exam on her, and gave her a tetanus shot, starting her on several antibiotic IV drips. She was given a high-dose sedative, so she was going to be relaxed and non-responsive for most of the night.

Mario walked into the room, and Zen's face was swollen; her neck was raw from being choked with a leather belt. She had received two black eyes, a broken nose, and she was covered in bite marks from head to toe. Zen's vaginal area was severely scared from X and Mustard playing and jamming their hands in her vagina. Zen's anal area was split open; she received sixteen stitches to repair the damage. She was also missing her two front teeth, and her lips were the size of burger buns. Mario cried loudly as though he was at Zen's funeral.

"Imma kill whoever did this to my wife," Mario screamed out.

The nurses and doctors enter the room to console Mario. Hours later, he finally calmed down. The crew were able to see Zen, one at a time. They all cried bloody murder seeing Zen fucked up in that way. "I don't give a fuck. I want Kelly to take care of Zen, I don't trust nobody. If they have a problem with that, let me know. I'll have her moved. I want someone here with her around the clock." Mario spat.

Ashley walked in through the door with balloons, flowers, and teddy bears. Ashley was always the behind-the-scenes one of the crew. Zen wanted her to always be low-key, so no one could ever place her in affiliation with her and the rest of the ladies. This was one time Ashley broke the rule; she was going insane sitting home in her garage while Zen was lying in a hospital bed. The ladies looked like they saw a ghost when Ashley appeared. Ashley motioned for everyone to gather close to listen in on what she had to say.

"It was a must that I come here, but imma get back so I can find out more details on what's going on. I do know Zen killed one of the men that attacked her. I also know that Nicolette is in jail for the murder of the man and most likely a conspiracy to Zen's attack. The other man is roaming free. So, if we want answers, we need to get to Nicolette ASAP." Ashley explained.

Milly Mill and Sundae went to Kelly's house to get Maggie. Milly Mill explained to Kelly that she needed to go and stay with Zen full-time at the hospital and assist her back to health. Kelly immediately packed a bag and left out with no hesitation.

"Your daughter is in jail for murder, and she knows who hurt Zen. So, I desperately need you to visit Nicolette at the county jail and find out what the fuck she knows." Sundae spat.

Maggie looked at Sundae and Milly Mill with a stank face.

"Maggie, don't make me beat your ass. This isn't optional; it's a muthafuckin' demand." Milly Mill spoke.

"Murder?! What the hell has Nicolette done? She just got out of jail for fighting and now this. Lord have mercy, between Nicolette and y'all damn thugs, imma be in an early grave, and it won't be from cancer. Well, can I at least have my medication before I go; I'm feeling dizzy. I haven't been to a jail since I beat Cora Mae's ass at bingo for stealing my money." Maggie sounded off.

Lady J went inside the jail with Maggie to schedule her visit to see Nicolette. The wait time for visitation was an hour. They both sit in the waiting area, looking at the other people sign in.

Nicolette was being questioned in the interrogation room. "I have told y'all all I know. Alden Thompson is the one who sent two men to pick me up from jail. The men forced me to get them a hotel room while they handled business with Zen." Nicolette said with a scared voice.

"So, you mean to tell me you knew what these men were about to do to Zeneta Fuller-Vanhorn, and you did nothing to stop it." Detective Rogers asked.

"Zen and I have a violent history together. You can check the files; of the number of times I have been to this jail, placing retraining orders and no trespassing papers on Zen stalking me and constantly beating me. Zen and I were just arrested for fighting in the park." Nicolette tried to gain some sympathy from the detectives.

"Ma'am, that makes you just as guilty. You're now being charged with aiding and abetting, as well as the obstruction of justice on top of first-degree murder. Your best bet is to find your co-defendant. Make yourself at home; this is as good as it gets for you." Detective Rogers explained.

Nicolette knew her life was over. She knew that even if she had any chance of getting out of jail, Zen and her crew were going to hunt her down and kill her. Nicolette has a zero chance of surviving in this world if she is released from jail. Jail suddenly looked appealing to Nicolette; she began to low-key make mind adjustments to gain momentum and be identified as inmate 7779311.

Maggie entered the visitation room. Nicolette was behind the glass with swollen eyes, and her face displayed a fearful look.

"What in God's creation have you gotten yourself into, Nicolette?" Maggie asked through clenched teeth.

"I know you don't want to hear it mommy, but I am so sorry for my continuous fuck-ups." Nicolette said as she dropped her head.

"This is the granddaddy of all your fuck0ups. Child, these police have you charged with murder. Please tell me what's going on?" Maggie asked firmly.

"The two men that fixed your tire, they were sent by a guy named Al. Al has a long-going vendetta with Zen. Al somehow got me in the middle of helping him get revenge on Zen. The men picked me up as I was walking from jail, they told me their plan and demanded I help them get a motel room, or they would kill you and the kids. That's why I needed the thirty dollars. So, I made my way back to the room to tell the men to let Zen go because I knew her friends were after you and Allison. When I entered the room, one of the men was lying on his back on the bed with a Barbie doll down his throat. I immediately went into a panic attack. I continued to vomit in the restroom for approximately three minutes. Seconds later, the police came; I was scared and confused, so I tried to run. Now I am here under arrest for something I did not do." Nicolette explained.

"So, who killed the man? And where's Zen? She can clear your name right?" Maggie asked, concerned.

"I honestly think Zen killed him; they underestimated Zen. They were talking about raping her and beating her to get her to transfer money to their CASHAPP." Nicolette spat.

"Damn, Nicolette, you could have saved Zen. That was so damn selfish of you. You're guilty by association, whether you like it or not." Maggie said angrily.

"Ma, she attacked me soon as the men placed her in the car. You already know how many times she has fucked me up with bruises and broken bones. But now she's the *gawd damn hero*." Nicolette sounded off as she walked out of the visitation room.

Maggie relayed the information to Milly Mill and Sundae. "I know Nicolette's involvement is about to catch her a jail sentence, but if I can convince Allison to stop the charges on Star, will you ladies help me out by asking Mario if I can stay with the small kids at the apartment? Allison can care for herself, but the smaller kids and I need shelter desperately." Maggie begged.

"We'll see, but nothing is promised. Right now, you can go back to the apartment and handle the kids, and we will get back to you." Milly Mill explained.

Milly Mill and Sundae immediately spread the tea to the rest of the crew. Pound Puppy, Mario and Ashley were strategizing a play of how to clap back at Al from the outside.

"That nigga Al definitely received some help with this attack on Zen," Mario said, fuming.

"Yes indeed, most likely his roommate placed a direct hit in exchange for something. That would make the most sense because he is at a level three prison, and the inmates are locked down for twenty-two hours a day. So, that's the one person who he could plan and receive help from." Pound Puppy added.

Ashley looked up the prison files and retrieved who Al's roommate was.

"Damion Dubose is the scumbag's name. He is from Phoenix, Arizona, and he goes by the name Olive," Ashley said as she typed away. She cross-referenced Damion Dubose and the name Olive with the state of Phoenix, Arizona, and came up with some hefty information. Olive was the man at Wire Fence federal prison. Two female correctional officers, Blanch Piles and Africa Smith became pregnant by him. The two ladies were fired and will never be able to work in a correctional facility or with male adults again. Most guards let Olive do as he pleases to keep from having confrontations each shift. Olive has tons of outside connections, and he has eleven kids, all daughters, the youngest two by the correctional officers were four and six.

"Let's gas up, bro. We're going to Arizona." Mario sounded off.

CHAPTER 26

HANDLED

Mario went to the county to visit and inform Star of what had happened with her mommy. Mario knew Star was so much like Zen. Star would make Nicolette pay dearly for her involvement with Zen's attackers.

"I need you to hang tight, princess. Your lawyer is working on your case around the clock. Worst case scenario, you'll serve thirty days here in the county jail and pay five thousand dollars in restitution for the loss of Allison's baby. Allison pertained alcohol and marijuana in her system when she was hospitalized for her miscarriage, so that helps your case tremendously." Mario explained to Star behind the dirty visitation glass.

"Pops, I really don't care about that right now, just kiss my mommy for me and get her well again," Star said with tears streaming down her face.

Mario held his hand to the glass. "You know your mommy as well as I do; she's a fighter. This is a minor setback before a major comeback." Mario said, encouraging his daughter.

Before Star left the visitation room, she wiped her face and turned to Mario. "I can make a whole lot of shit shake with some," Star paused, then rubbed her fingers together, indicating money. Mario winked and dropped a thousand dollars on his daughter's commissary before he left the jail.

Ashley emailed the crew the information with the names, addresses, and phone numbers of the grown daughters of

Olive, along with the two ex-correctional officers, Blanch and Africa. Mario and Pound Puppy tried to sneak away on their own to handle this, but Raz and Bleu spilled the beans to the crew, and they were going to follow behind the men. This was business and personal to the ladies; somebody had to feel their frustration. The crew hit the highway; they were off to see the wizard. They were expected to be on the road for over twenty-four hours.

White Boy, Kash, and big Mike were guarding Zen's room no one was allowed in but Ashley, T-Baby and Kelly. Kelly was the only person handling Zen's medications; she examined them closely before she administered them. Kelly exercised Zen's legs and constantly placed ice packs on her face. Zen's swelling was reduced a great deal by the repeated process. Kelly bathed Zen keeping her clean and fresh. Zen was still unable to say much, but Kelly was working on a healing herbal tea with lemon, honey, chamomile, hibiscus, and ginger. She used that concoction on her patients that suffered from throat cancer. For once, Zen was not in the lead, but she knew her team was ten toes down with her, and they were going to act a fucking fool. They would get revenge on her attackers.

Zen knew Mario was not around because he was out wreaking havoc. Zen noticed Ashley coming and going, she finally made eye contact with her, and she pointed her finger at Ashley, saying she was in trouble for coming out of her bubble.

"You can get on to me later; you just rest and get better for now, so you can show me how to do these trending Tik- Toks. I wanna do the Jagged Edge one, 'put a little uumpth in it." Zen smiled at Ashley and reached for her hand. Ashley rubbed her forehead and whispered in her ear. "Your white girl is in overdrive for you, justice believe that. Nobody that's involved is safe is." Ashley spoke softly to Zen as she kissed her cheek.

Star was pacing back and forth, ready to go out for recreational activities, where she would most likely see Nicolette. Nicolette knew Star was still in jail behind the charges Allison had placed on her. Nicolette's intentions were to throw in the towel with Star and try and create an easy path for her to survive in the county jail. Nicolette knew Star was coming after her once she got word about her mom. So, she wanted to approach Star first, but she was coming peacefully. The cell bars unlocked, and it was time for the ladies on the yellow pod to endure their recreational time.

Misty Colepepper was a white girl with a severe crack addiction. Misty smoked every drug that came through the jail. She'd been locked down in the county jail for two years awaiting trial for killing a cashier at Walmart. Misty had nothing to lose; she would do anything to score some drugs. Star made sure Misty was high, and she paid a guard to stash some drugs in the female lockup shoe where Misty was about to go.

Star was bouncing the ball when Nicolette approached her.

"Can you and I have a conversation, please?" Nicolette asked.

"Yep, if you can tell me where the second nigga is at that hurt my mommy." Star responded.

"I have no idea, please believe me. I am a victim in all of this as well. I was forced into this situation." Nicolette explained.

"Bitch you know your ass is grass soon as you hit them streets. Imma beat Allison's ass. Every time that bitch sneezes, imma be right there to bless her. You're lucky I'm on my way home, or I would spank your ass myself, so walk the fuck away from me with your sorry ass." Star sounded off.

Nicolette went to sit alone at the table, feeling sorry for herself when the guard motioned for everyone to return inside. Star was the first to walk through the door. Misty was lined up behind Nicolette. When the coast was clear, she slid her shank from her sleeve and jabbed Nicolette in her side and chest multiple times. Nicolette dropped to the ground bleeding profusely. Misty dropped the shank and raised her hands in the air to surrender. The guards handcuffed her and took her to lock up, where she had a week's supply of drugs waiting for her. Nicolette was rushed to the infirmary, but her injuries were far too severe for the nurse to handle. She was transported by Ambulance to the county hospital, along with a female guard.

Star called her Aunt T-Baby to relay a message, using one of the girls' cell phone a pod over.

"I sent my mommy some company; y'all got it from here," Star explained, saying just enough to give T-Baby a heads up.

"Lay low, niece. You're getting outta there soon." T-Baby spoke.

Mario Pound Puppy and the rest of the ladies arrived in Arizona in record time. They drove nonstop, except for gas and restroom breaks. They immediately get in touch with the ex-correctional officer and Olive's baby mama Africa Smith. Africa was doing security work at a local bus station. Mario and Pound Puppy felt useless, the ladies took the lead, and they went with the flow. Raz, Bleu and Milly Mill took a strong approach.

"Hey, are you Africa?" Raz asked.

"I am. Who wants to know?" Africa responded.

"I work at Wire Fence and I'm pregnant by Olive," Raz stated.

"Damn, he got you too. He's a smooth Casanova, I tell ya." Africa spoke.

"I would like to contact his daughters; I want them to know who I am. I plan on marring Damion Dubose soon." Raz spat.

"Damion? What the fuck, wait a minute. Olive never mentioned you, what's your name?" Africa asked.

"That's not important. Why would he mention me? I'm his sneaky link." Raz clapped back.

"Girl, this conversation is over, you best get the fuck outta my face before I spaz on your wannabe relevant ass." Africa sounded off. Milly Mill and Bleu opened their trench coats showing off the heavy artillery underneath.

"That's not friendly of you to say. I was trying to play nice with you. So, now I need for you to follow my ladies to the car or get your ass splattered all over these buses." Raz said with a smile. Africa dropped her head and followed close behind Bleu.

When Africa entered the car, Sundae was inside, mugging her to the fullest. "Look bitch we are tired and frustrated, so we do not want any lip outta you. We have many guns and are not afraid to use them." Sundae spat.

"And I haven't choked a bitch all week. I'm ready for a bitch to resist." Nena added.

"First you're going to get your daughter from daycare, and we're all going to your crib."

"Please don't bring my daughter into this, she's innocent and she's only six years old. Veronica can't help who her daddy is." Africa begged.

"It depends on you if Veronica walks away still beautiful with long pigtails." Sundae said with an evil grin. Africa cried hysterically, scared of what was about to happen when she picked up her daughter.

Sundae walked into the daycare with Africa. "If you try to send any kind of signal, I'm shooting your daughter in the head." Sundae spat.

"Don't worry, I will not jeopardize my daughter's life; you ladies are delusional and need to seek help," Africa spoke with attitude.

"Hello, Ms. Smith. Veronica is packed and ready for you. She has on her extra outfit you sent because she encountered an accident earlier after lunch." The teacher Ms. Carter explained.

"Yes, ma'am. Thank you, Ms. Carter. Come on, Veronica." Africa said.

"Mommy who is that? She's ugly." Veronica said, pointing at Sundae. Sundae licked her tongue at the little girl and gave her the finger.

When the crew pulled up at Africa's house, Mario reiterated the plan with the ladies. This was sure to get Olive to kill Al for getting him involved with his mess. Mario could not beat down the federal wall and kill Al himself, so plan B was in full effect.

Everyone entered the house close behind Africa. She was stripped of her cell phone and forced to sit down at the kitchen table. Lady J pointed a rifle directly in her face, giving her the I wish you would try me look.

"Mommy, who are these heathens." Veronica cried out.

"You better teach this brat some fuckin' manners." Sundae spoke.

"Veronica, shut your mouth and do what they say," Africa said to her daughter.

"Okay, this is step two. You need to call Blanch and the other daughters over here. Explain to them how this is an urgent matter that cannot wait, and no pussyfooting around." Milly Mill sounded off.

"No problem," Africa replied. Lady J passed her back her phone to place the calls. The first call was to Olive's older daughter Janae.

"I need you to come through quickly. I need to discuss something with you about your dad."

"I just spoke with him; he seemed nervous. He asked me to hide his friend X out in my apartment for a few weeks since I'm always at my baby daddy's house. I told him I'd do it, but I don't want to. X looks creepy as fuck; his skin looks like a deep-fried potato. Is everything ok, fam?" Janae asked.

"Yes, just hurry."

"Ok, I'm on my way," Janae added. Africa repeated that call to the others.

"I need to see a picture of this X dude. Can you provide that for me?" Mario asked firmly.

"Yes, he dates my co-worker Ms. Mildred. She posts pictures of him all the time on Facebook." Africa explained. She went to Mildred's Facebook page and showed Mario a series of pictures of X.

"Pup, we got action. This is that high yellow banana-looking muthafucka right here." Mario said, fuming.

"Oh, his ass is ours. Raz y'all hold this shit down; we're catching oh girl at the door. We're going to smash on this nigga." Pound Puppy instructed.

Janae exits her car and proceeds to walk in the direction of Africa's house. Pound Puppy stepped from the side of the house with a shotgun, and Mario crept up from behind her with his handgun.

"If you scream, you're a dead woman. Turn around and enter the black Range Rover parked on the curb and get in the back seat." Mario instructed Janae. Janae pissed herself and immediately began to tremble, but she did as she was told. Pound Puppy entered the driver seat, and Mario joined Janae in the back seat.

"This has nothing to do with you, but I desperately need to know where to find X?" Mario spoke.

"I was on my way to meet him at my apartment, but when Africa called, she said I needed to hurry, so I came straight over. I pushed the time back to seven o'clock." Janae said, still trembling.

"Call that faggot and tell him that you're able to come right now." Mario spat.

"Yes sir," Janae said nervously. She called X, and he picks up on the first ring. "Hey nigga, you can go ahead to the crib. Africa didn't need me after all," She explained to X.

"Okay, I really appreciate your help. Some fuck-nigga that's roommates with your dad has me caught up in some deep shit right now. I went to South Carolina to rob this bitch, and she fucked around and killed Mustard when I left the room for ice. So, I just need to chill for a week or two." X explained.

"You're good, fam. You shouldn't be discussing that over the phone, but thanks for the heads up." Janae said. She placed her address in her phone's GPS and passed it to Pound Puppy.

Blanch and four of the sisters were there at Africa's house. They were being held at gunpoint by the ladies.

"I need one of you to facetime your dad and explain to him the situation at hand. Explain to him that this is all Al's fault, and if he does not kill Al ASAP. He won't have any daughters left to bury him when he dies. Little miss Veronica and Solange will be sold to Hero, a Pakistani sex trafficker." Sundae spoke.

Solange was the daughter Olive shared with Blanch. The sisters were sitting in the middle of the floor with guns and rifles pointing at their head, the two little kids were in the front sitting Indian style crying loudly.

"Mommy, that lady is ugly and mean like Gargamel." Veronica continued to cry out.

Sundae picked Veronica up and hung her on the kitchen door by her overalls. "Who's ugly now, you little pissypants." Sundae said, annoyed by the little girl.

Blanch made the video call to Olive. When he clicked on, he was excited until he saw the scenery. Guns pointed at the heads of his precious family, including his two youngest seeds. Olive noticed Veronica hanging from the door, crying her eyes out.

"Dad, whoever this Al nigga is, you have to kill him immediately, or we're all going to get killed by these people. They aren't playing any games dad; they are so serious. We were told to tell you this is Al's fault, and you shouldn't have gotten involved." Lindy, Olive's daughter, explained. The other siblings added their input on the situation.

"Zen. I was warned about her, and you're right. I should have let this fuck nigga rot in his misery. I know how the game is played, but please: don't hurt my family. They're all I have. I'll eliminate this nigga as you wish." Olive spoke, impressed by how powerful Zen really was.

"Nigga you see the results of what medaling in another grown man's business will get you. So, you better make that shit happen within the hour." Bleu spat. Before the video ended, Sundae went to the smart-mouth little girl Veronica and cut her two front pigtails off.

"Please, no," Africa yelled out.

"I'll mail you a souvenir as a reminder not to ever cross us again." Sundae spat as she held the hair up to the camera and pushed the door, causing Veronica to swing back and forth.

Olive knew what he had to do. He began to jump up and down and box the air loosening up his body, so he could take Al out. When Al walked into the cell, Olive was on the floor doing pushups.

"Have you heard from X yet?" Al asked.

"No, but I should have listened to you about Zen." Olive sounded off while placing a pair of gloves on his hands.

"Yeah, that bitch is the mastermind of her whole damn team, I warned your boy to be careful, but you insisted that he was the best," Al added as he went to lay down on his bunk, shutting his eyes with thoughts of Zen getting away in his head. Olive set up his phone to record, then slowly grabbed Al by his neck.

Al was gasping for air but could not make a sound from the death grip around his throat. Olive added more pressure by placing the pillow on top of his head with his other hand before switching gears and gripping Al's neck with both hands applying massive force. After ten minutes of strangulation, Al was dead. Olive quickly ripped up Al's sheets and tied a long strip around his neck. Olive connected the sheet to the upper pipe in the corner of their room. Once Olive placed Al's body on the desk to lift him up by the sheet, he placed a chair underneath him, making it look exactly like a suicide.

Olive was well respected in the prison so no one would question what he said to them. Olive sent the video footage to Blanch and his daughter's cell phone. The sisters and two baby mamas walked away unharmed, thrilled that this madness was over. Veronica was still crying about her Pigtails being chopped off; in her six-year-old eyes, life was over for her.

"If you don't clean up your attitude, I'm going to come back and shave your head bald, and make you wear Huggies diapers to school since you can't go potty like the other kids," Sundae said with a mean voice, tormenting Veronica even more. Little Veronica screamed so loud that Africa and the sisters had to try and silence her. They wanted Sundae and the ladies to get the fuck away from them.

X was still driving around in the same red stolen Audi station wagon. He was at Janae's apartment when Pound Puppy drove up. Janae was instructed to let X inside her apartment, then excuse herself out the back door. Janae opened the door, and X began to thank her again.

"Hold on, fam, let me take my dog out for some fresh air," Janae spoke. Pound Puppy and Mario came rushing through the door. Mario grabbed X, benched-pressed him in the air, then threw him into the window. Glass shattered everywhere; his body was hanging from the window. Pound Puppy snatched his body, slamming him to the floor, viciously kicking his head repeatedly. His neck instantly cracked, but that didn't stop the Pound Puppy from kicking him. Mario removes his dagger from his pocket, then stabs X in his eyes, causing his eyeballs to pop out. X was then stabbed in his heart with the dagger, Mario twisted the dagger with much force while cursing at X.

"No man will ever live that touches my wife," Mario continued to scream harshly, going crazy on X. He could have easily shot X and gotten it over with, but he felt the need to put in work and exercise his anger.

Pound Puppy gently stopped Mario as he suddenly blanked out. The rage, sadness, and frustration came rushing back about how Zen was treated by X and his partner. Pound Puppy helped Maio to his feet; they quickly left the apartment to meet up with the ladies and make their way back to South Carolina to cater to Zen.

CHAPTER 27

YOU'VE CROSSED THE WRONG ONE

A week later, Kelly had Zen up and running. Her voice was completely back to normal and she was ten times stronger. Kelly continuously helped Zen rehab her body; when Zen's efforts would give out, Kelly would move her muscles for her. Kelly placed Zen on an all-fruit and vegetable diet, giving her Ensure for a snack to keep her muscle and weight up.

"I love y'all bitches to the end of time. I missed talking shit to Sundae and Raz. I missed Bleu nagging the hell outta me. I didn't get a chance to miss T-Baby, Milly Mill, Lady J and Nena. Those whores instructed Kelly to via face time me every second of the day." Zen said, laughing.

"Sure did, friend." Lady J yelled out.

"My white princess Ashley is the muthafuckin' goat. Everything she touches lights up; that's my white supergirl. I love me some of her. Special shoutout to my super nurse, Kelly, for bringing a bitch back together and wiping my pussy clean every day. I was at my lowest, and Kelly did not take no for an answer. Kelly bucked up to me and set me straight. She told me I was not in control, to shut the fuck up and stop drowning in my pain and get up and fight back. I owe you dearly; not only did you take care of my mommy, but now you have taken care of me as well." Zen stated to Kelly with tears in her eyes.

"No thanks needed, fam; I'll do whatever for you and the team," Kelly spoke.

"Let's get the fuck outta her and go to your pool house, so we can fill you in on our latest adventure. Sundae was about to fight a six-year-old kid." Bleu explained.

"I keep telling y'all Sundae is heartless when it comes to kids; she only cares about her fur baby, Bossy." Zen said, shaking her head at Sundae. She could not wait to hear that story. "Keep talking and see how I bring Bossy to swim in your pool in his speedos." Sundae joked.

"I desperately want to fuck Nicolette's Monkey-Pox-infected pussy-ass up, but she will be going to jail soon, so either way, I win." Zen added.

"Whatever you ladies decide to plan is cool but do know I will be tagging alone." Mario sounded off. Mario had his mind made up; he was sticking to Zen like glue.

"Y'all whores heard my husband. That's my big daddy right there." Zen said licking her tongue sexually at Mario.

"Uuuh, your nasty ass will have time for that mess later," Sundae said loudly to Zen.

"Girl, don't be a hater all your life, big sis." Zen joked with Sundae.

The ladies were talking about taking a trip when the hospital intercom started announcing a code blue. T-Baby joined the ladies in Zen's room with Dunkin Donuts and iced coffee for everybody. T-Baby was very cheerful and full of energy.

"Zen, are you ready to get the hell outta this place?"

"Hell yes, friend, I need a tall peach margarita with pineapples and strawberry toppings," Zen spoke.

"What the fuck is going on? The doctors are running around like crazy?" Pound Puppy asked.

"I think I heard them say a Jane Doe lady flatlined at the end of the hall," T-Baby spoke.

"She's in the right place for that." Raz added. The head nurse entered Zen's room. "Hello, Ms. Vanhorn. I'm your discharge nurse, Bella. I am so sorry for the constant noise and chaos, but soon as it is over, you'll be all set for discharge."

"What is the problem, Ms. Bella? Are we under attack, because I'm certain my colleagues here are able to assist?" Zen joked but was so serious. Zen knew her team was bypassing any metal detectors; some of them, if not all, were strapped.

"No, ma'am, not at all. A female prisoner was being treated on this floor for a severe injury that occurred in jail. She suffered some complications throughout the night, but she suddenly took a turn for the worse and suffered a massive heart attack and died. Once the coroner removes her body and the prison guards are all cleared out, we will be able to discharge our patients." Nurse Bella explained.

"Really," Zen said, looking at T-Baby. T-Baby gave the ladies a wink and blew her index finger. The ladies knew T-Baby took out Nicolette on her own; she was definitely Zen's best friend.

"Look likes Zen's mini-me has struck again." Sundae spoke.

"Christmas has come early for us. We're drinking to that process of elimination." Bleu spoke.

Star was released from jail, and she was under Zen being a true mommy's girl. Star rubbed Zen's feet, something she'd done since she was a small girl. Star was infatuated with her mommy's feet. Zen was waiting to give Star the big surprise she's been secretly working on for her. But today seemed to be the perfect time to expose her secret. Zen and Star drove up to a building with office spaces downtown. Zen pointed up to the big colorful sign that read: *DANCING WITH STAR*.

Zen had purchased Star her own dancing studio. The design was incomplete, but Zen felt Star would love to finish the rest of her studio with her added touches.

"OMG, mommy, I love you so much," Star exited the car and began to dance in front of her space; other people from other spaces were there getting things together for their property; they joined in dancing with Star enjoying her excitement. They were just as excited, they welcomed Star to the building, and Zen popped two bottles of Moscato, and she and Star shared with the others. They sipped the wine and talked about design ideas for hours.

Isabella, Claudia and Oliva contacted some woman they did modeling jobs for back in Los Angeles. They sent some samples of Zen's hair products, and the top seller was the twenty-inch Brazilian curly-or-straight silky bounce hair. The vendors were more than impressed; they passed the news and professed the superb quality of Zen's items. The production and professionalism coming from Zen's hair factory were top-notch; this placed Zen as the number one hair vendor in the south.

Zen automatically upgraded the models to a boss position right up under Whunda. Zen instructed Zatima to oversee things and micromanage behind the scenes. Milly Mill and Kelly were to design a perfect layout to expand the factory.

Rainbow and Selena became extremely jealous. They secretly contemplated a play to sabotage Zatima and the models. Aware of this, Zatima displayed her first complaint to Zen, showing off her boss-lady skills.

"Zen, these hot-head bitches Rainbow and Selena don't do shit. They're constantly mugging the models and me, and all they do is fuck White Boy and walk around like their shit don't stank. They're bragging to their Jamaican friends on the phone about how they're living their best life here in the States. These two are getting too damn comfortable. You handed them an inch of livelihood, but they're taking a mile," Zatima spat.

"I instructed them mouth-breathers not to contact no one from Jamaica. After this shit with Al, I don't trust them anyway. Gather them loose-pussy bitches up and take them to the Lion's Den." Zen spoke.

"Wait, the Lions Den?" Zatima said, confused.

"My bad, Zatima. Round up Raz and the others. You'll see once we arrive what the Lion's Den is about."

Zen sent a massive text to the crew telling them that Rainbow and Selena would be eliminated. Mario warned White Boy and Kash about the situation Rainbow and Selena had gotten themselves into. Neither one of them was pressed about the issue.

"Dang, there goes my late-night head action." Kash spat.

"Nigga, you're crazy. You can at least shed a tear or something." Mario responded.

"I will if Zen let me get some of that Jamaican neck one last time," Kash spoke.

White Boy was down for whatever. "That's a straight suicide mission for anyone to cross Zen. Guess they gone learn today." White Boy sounded off. Now White Boy didn't have to keep lying to his baby mama Peaches about his whereabouts because she was becoming suspicious of his constant phone calls and movement.

The ladies arrived at the Lion's Den, and Zen kept it cute and sweet. Rainbow and Selena thought they were at the Den for someone else. "I went against the grain for you two bitches." Zen said, pointing at Rainbow and Selena.

"OMG, what's the problem, Zen? We haven't done anything to violate your trust. We've been working our asses off at the hair factory, and campaigning for new clients." Selena spat. Zatima punched Selena in her mouth.

"Bitch y'all mutha fuckas haven't done shit but gossip on the phone all damn day." Zatima sounded off.

"I told both of you bitches the rules of the game from the gate. You two begged me to stay In the States and work for me. The crazy thing is, y'all know what I do to muthafuckas that cross me." Zen said firmly.

"Zen, everything was good until you brought this fat whale and her make-up-wearing bitches into the factory," Rainbow said, pointing at Zatima and the models. Zatima leaped over to Rainbow and pulled her hair until it was completely uprooted from the front of her head. Rainbow's scalp begins to bleed instantly. Zatima then choked Rainbow until she was out cold; she let her drop helplessly to the ground.

Selena continued to beg for her life. "Please, Zen, please. I'll do anything. Don't kill us, I'm begging you."

"Bitch shut the fuck up. You two mud rats have been calling and receiving calls from Jamaica since you have been working in my hair factory. I don't trust none of y'all Jamaicans, so now you both can join Face, Al, Gucci, Glo, Bobby, and Heavy. All y'all hopeless Jamaicans can burn in hell." Zen took out her nine-millimeter pistol as she stepped over Rainbow and shot her in the center of the forehead. Selena screamed out loudly, calling Zen fat bitch and other cruel names. Selena managed to get out a few words to clap back at Zen.

"You don't trust us, but you trust your cheating-ass husband? Word on the street is you're carrying around so much rage because you're not happy with the one man supposed to be your everything. So, all the killing and barking out orders is a front to stroke your own ego, because Mario is stroking bitches' pussy with his man stick. The sad thing is you keep allowing it. So, killing me is only the beginning; it's a long line of thots with their lady part cream dripping from Mario's dick. I was working on my chance to swim in the pond, too, because clearly, your pussy ain't it. Especially after the damage those two niggas caused digging in that thang. Mario don't want that worn-out pussy. Now shoot, bitch. Your trigger finger broken or something?" Selena sounded off, intending to dig deep into Zen's head.

"*Gladly bitch!* I should have been killed y'all muthafuckas from the start." Zen said angrily as she unloaded her clip in Selena in her face.

Selena had known she was about to die; she wanted only to plant a seed in Zen's head to fuck with her. Selena knew the way to fuck with any woman is to downplay their significant other or kids. For some reason, that message Selena just said left Zen feeling some type of way. Zen quickly shook it off, she did not want to show any weakness to her crew, but she was stressed behind the statement. Zatima and the models got the privilege to throw Rainbow and Selena in the Lion's Den, where the rest of their fuck-squad of Jamaicans had been eaten down to the bones.

Mario was planning something big for Zen; he was anxious and ready to prove himself. Mario put on his big boy boxers and carefully created a play that was going to surprise his Zen. He and Kash finally displayed a layout, and things were finally looking up to Mario's standard. Mario did not want the other ladies to find out, especially T-Baby, because Zen would often visit them, and they couldn't hold water when it came to Zen. Zen never visited Sundae to often because she was terrified of Bossy. So, Mario was going to reach out to her for help soon.

Mario created a happily ever after theme for him and Zen to renew their vows. They both were football fans; the house was divided between the San Francisco 49ers and the Green Bay Packers. If you were attending the ceremony for the bride, you would be in Green Bay Packers gear and 49ers gear for Mario. Mario wasn't too thrilled about the pinks and purple and the glitter and glam that Zen liked. He wanted this to be his vision; this was going to be their moment to embrace their inner love and affection and say I do once again amongst friends and family.

This was the reset button for the two. The turbulence and chaos were long gone. Love outweighed evil, and love is what they shared. No two people were happier together than Zen and Mario. They were made for each other, and nothing, no one, could break them apart.

CHAPTER 28

ZEN'S & MARIO'S HAPPILY EVER AFTER

The models Claudia, Isabella, and Olivia were designing team jersey dresses for the crew.

"Them jerseys cute and all, but I need something short, and with lace. I need to be revealing for my man." Raz spoke, giving the models a hard time. Zen's team of ladies would be wearing Green Bay gear, except Milly Mill, who was down with Mario and would be sporting 49ers gear. Whunda, the head Asian lady from the hair factory, was designing the men's gear for Mario, Zay, White Boy, Kash, Big Mike and Corrupt. Their shit was coming together, looking smooth.

Mario was racking his brain trying to make things right with planning the wedding renewal. He had been on the receiving end of Zen's attitude lately, and he had no idea why. Mario knew his wife well enough to know that she was holding something in.

"Bae, what's up? You alright? You have been moving funny lately," a concerned Mario asked softly.

"Stop asking me dumb ass questions, Mario. I'm fine; why the fuck wouldn't I be fine? Unless you did some fuckery to *make me* not-fine," Zen fussed.

Mario held his hands up in surrender. "I'm innocent, my love. We've been in a good place, Zen. I hope you're not revisiting our past. That would not be fair." Mario wanted to end that conversation quickly and love on his wife. Mario turned Zen's head and reached for a kiss, but Zen frowned and moved her head with attitude, so the kiss landed on her cheek. That was a major red flag and gave Mario clear confirmation something was wrong with his wife. Mario broke down and called Zen's crew. It was a must he figure out why Zen was switching up on him suddenly.

Lady J, Bleu and Raz meet up with Mario at his office. Mario immediately questioned them about Zen's odd behavior. He would have asked T-Baby and Star, but they were just as emotional as Zen these days.

"Bro, Zen has been a bit jumpy since we eliminated them Rastafarian bitches, Selena and Rainbow." Bleu filled Mario in on everything Selena said at the Lion's Den.

Mario's mind was racing; he knew Zen well enough to know that Selena's words reopened a lot of old wounds for her. Thinking quickly, he headed to Blackwell's barbershop in Easily on Cornerstone Road. Mario needed to speak with the old heads about this one, Mario received the best advice when he visited Blackwell's.

"Mr. Henry, I have five-hundred dollars for an exclusive cut and some old player advice." Mario requested while putting a large knot of twenties in Mr. Henry's hand. Mr. Henry was not about to turn that kind of money away; he escorted his unfinished customers out of the shop and locked the door. He smiled and shuffled over to the barber chair, dusting off the shaved hair, before instructing Mario to sit down, placing the barber cape around his neck.

"I take it you need the whole committee on this one, young blood." Mr. Henry looked at Mario from the rim of his glasses. Mario shook his head yes and sat in the chair for the next two hours receiving knowledge from the old heads. Mario was getting his finishing touches as the men continued to fill him in on the game that had kept them alive for so long.

"You've been running crazy behind that gal since y'all were kids." Mr. Henry chuckled as he wiped the around Mario's fresh line up with the alcohol wipes.

"Hell yeah." Mario agreed, reminiscing about the past with his wife. The hell was real with his and Zen's past. "That's why I gotta make this shindig outstanding. I must end all the negative bullshit from the past and present." Mario said with conviction. His wife was his number one priority and top focus.

"Then go get her, young blood. I've known Zen since before she was born. She comes from a long line of thorough women, so trust me, I know firsthand what you're dealing with." Mr. Henry schooled Mario.

Mario left the barbershop with a major play in mind. Mario sent a voice clip to Sundae to meet him at the bridal boutique. Sundae was close by, so she made it within minutes. Mario presented his courageous vision of his version of a fairytale wedding.

"I am not too crazy about going behind my girl's back because we are loyal to one another no matter what. But I see you're trying to get some major brownie points with the wife and stamp your player card off, so I'm all game." Sundae spat.

Mario was a Groomzilla; he barked out orders to the models to change the design. He knew Zen would not like those plan jane Green Bay Packer's jersey dresses. So, he brought the crew in to help him; he gave them enough information just to keep the ball rolling. Mario logged on to Zen's website and stole some ideas from her top ten weddings she has completed and won several advertisement articles in the bride's magazines.

Mario managed to flawlessly steal the wedding from Zen. Zen's wedding cake was large and extravagant, in the shape of a football field. There were pictures from when Mario and Zen first met, and all the memories in between; the pictures were printed on edible photos and displayed around the cake like a garland.

Mario rented out the Sterling Stadium as the Venue. The stadium was recently renovated with several amenities and added touches. Mario and Zen were big on family, so he wanted to make this a family affair. The stadium was a few blocks away from where they grew up, so it would be meaningful to them both. Mario thought of everything from signature team drinks to a kid-friendly area with a bouncy house and laser tag. He and Kash contacted the radio promoters and scheduled live entertainment. Kash had the gift of gab and was able to pull off the unthinkable. Mario and Zen's favorite rappers Eight-Ball and MJG, were booked to perform. The rappers' managers sent Kash an itinerary of the songs that will be performed and the length of stage time they will need.

This was going to be the event of the century. Not only was Zen worth it, but she deserved it. Zen's reputation as a party planner was top-notch, so Mario knew he must shine like a diamond. Zen must have rubbed off on her husband because Mario had become a perfectionist; he did an immaculate job for this to be his first rodeo. Mario was aiming to make Zen smile and blush like she did when they were kids. The thought made Mario's heart melt inside.

The crew assisted Mario with his plans; some nights, they would put in long hours critiquing every detail. That caused Mario to become secretive, but his actions raised a red flag with Zen. She questioned Mario about his whereabouts on several occasions. Mario seemed guilty about something in Zen's eyes, so she began to speculate. Zen's doubts were making her angry, and she was drowning her brain trying to find a conclusion.

"Where the fuck have you been, Mario?" Zen asked as Mario came creeping in after two AM. Mario was stuck, he could not tell Zen the truth and ruin the surprise, so he lied.

"Bae I was just out with Kash and White Boy at the new bar playing pool, I lost track of time." Mario put it on thick as possible, hoping Zen would by it. Mario knew Zen was becoming aggravated with his sneaking and lurking around. "Tubbie, you have nothing to worry about. I'm a one-woman man; come spread that ass over my face." Mario said as he tried to kiss his wife.

"Nigga just like that Sunshine Anderson song says, *I heard it all before.*" Zen walked off and slammed the bathroom door, then sits on the toilet and instantly began to cry.

Mario knew he and Zen could not get married again with this weirdness between them.

"Tubbie, I don't know what the problem is, but we need to fix it before it's too late. What did I do?" Mario pleaded through the bathroom door. Zen snatched the bathroom door open with tears streaming down her face.

"You're the fucking problem, Mario. What the fuck have you been doing out here in these streets?" Zen unloaded on him; she asked every question she could think of to address her insecurities.

"Zen, with everything we have been through, I will not lose you again. Even if you leave me, I'm still your husband. We go together real bad."

Zen displayed a small smile; she loved when Mario begged and fought for her love. They talked well into the morning, and Mario assured Zen she had nothing to be worried about when it came to him; he even offered to get a tattoo on his forehead that said ZEN.

"Nigga, you know I'll kill you, right?"

"Yes, Zeneta, I definitely know that," Mario responded. Zen lay across her husband's chest, laughing at her own statement.

"Zen, don't ever get it twisted; I'll fuck your ass up, too." Mario added.

"Nigga, bye." Zen said while placing Mario's hand on her pussy.

"Bend your ass over. I know what you want," Mario instructed his wife. Zen smacked her teeth but did as she was told. Mario tried his best to fuck some act right into his wife. The tension was still there, but they managed a truce. Mario was now more determined than ever to make his wife know she was the only one for him.

Going through old photos, Mario he came across Zen's high school yearbook. Flipping through the pages, he saw a page labeled the future. The page was covered with pictures of things Zen wanted; she wrote a letter to herself explaining everything she dreamed of. She designed a ring, and her design was very detailed. Mario took the information to Sahed, the jeweler, and he designed a beautiful Amethyst and diamond monster-size ring. Mario smiled and shook Sahed's hand repeatedly; he knew Zen was going to have an explosive reaction. Zen loved odd and over-the-top things, and this ring was definitely in that category. It looked like another win for Mario.

Mario was a bag of nerves leading up to the big day. He instructed T-Baby and Star to execute the first part of the plan.

"Some niggas just jumped me; I had to shake 'em. Tell Zen I need her to meet me at our kissing spot." Mario delivered a fake crisis.

Star was ready to ride herself, so that delayed Mario because he had to calm Star down. "

Trust me, baby girl. Your mom got this; just do that for me now, Star." Mario demanded. T-Baby and Star rushed to Zen's pool house and delivered the message, and boy did they add on the dramatics.

Mario displayed an edible spread of fruit, cookies, and other treats with THC-infused chocolate bars. Zen arrived in record time, she was breathing heavily, and her gun was cocked and ready to shoot.

"Mario, what's up? Are you okay?" Zen asked in a panic.

The sight of the flowers and edibles made her soften up. Zen immediately read the love-letter, recognizing Mario's handwriting.

Today is the day we start the rest of our life over with a reset button. Our first marriage was special, but we were young and didn't know shit about the quality of real love. But as we've grown older and wiser, love has conquered all. Our life is so meaningful together.

I was never able to give you your fairytale dream wedding, but today I will try.

Zen turned around, shocked, with her mouth open. Mario's back was turned so he would not see Zen.

"I don't want to look at you; I want to keep the tradition alive. But I know you are beautiful. I made sure Sundae took you to get the best hair and makeup money can buy. Please don't get mad; let me quarterback this thang and take charge for once. Let me give this day to you the way you deserve it." Mario handed Zen a gift bag as he left.

Zen reentered the car, and she displayed a glow so bright across her face. "Mommy, you're not mad at my pops, are you? Because he loves you, and you deserve everything coming your way." Star said.

"What do you know, Star? I won't tell your pops you told me, but please, baby girl. I'm extremely anxious."

"Just relax, mommy, inhale a few puffs of this strawberry Kush," Star said, passing Zen the pre-rolled blunt.

"Okay, take me to get dressed; I got a wedding to attend with my fine-ass husband." Zen was happier than a fat kid in a candy shop; she felt that teenage love feeling again. "I got you, mommy, but first let me grab some of them edibles and snacks pops got out here. I got the munchies."

Pound Puppy, Kash, White Boy and the ladies were moving full speed to get the stadium completed in time. Mario gave strict orders on how he wanted everything handled, he didn't want no substitution, and no one was to change anything. It was his way or no way.

Mario was dressed in an all-black San Francisco 49ers Polo tracksuit with matching custom Jordans. He purchased Zen a Green Bay Packers body suit with a long green lace train with matching Jordans. Zen bouquet was designed into a Parkers helmet with pom poms hanging from the handle. The bridal party would stand beside the couple in jersey dresses, Green Bay Packers for the brides' maids and 49ers tracksuits for the groomsmen and male ushers. Kash and White Boy were Mario's best men, and T-Baby and Sundae were Zen's maid of honor. Star was the junior bride, dressed identically to Zen. Team T-Shirts were provided for the guest; staff distributed them outside the stadium before the guests entered to be seated.

Zen was getting dressed at Sundae's shoe boutique. The ladies were excited and ready to rock their jerseys, gloating about the grand show Mario had put on. They were shocked he made it happen without them. Claudia and the other models did an amazing job with the wedding attire; they understood the assignment. Sundae ordered the crew lettermen jackets; they were black trimmed in Green Bay Packers colors with happily ever after on the back. White Boy did the same for his team. He wasn't leaving them out.

"OMG, this day could not get any better," Zen said as she fanned her face because she was tearing up. A knock on the door startled them.

"If Mario has one more gift, imma scream. We gotta get to the wedding." Raz sounded off. The ladies laughed hard at Raz; she was ready to show off her Green Bay Packers minidress.

"Your car is ready, ma'am." The driver announced. The ladies piled in the extended limo and headed to the stadium. The ladies were instructed to blindfold Zen and walk her to the fifty-yard line. Zen followed every instruction smiling hard while she took baby steps. Zen was ready to see what was waiting on her; she knew it was epic because Mario was on his grown-man shit.

Zen was not about to be outdone. While she was at the boutique, she placed a call to Grown man's Toy Box to have Mario's gift delivered. Zen was clueless about where to have the vehicle delivered; she knew the location was a secret, so T-Baby handled the details to the dealer. Zen purchased Mario an all-black Range Rover with chrome rims and fully loaded equipment inside. Whunda, her head Asian from the hair factory, packed up her equipment and met the dealer at the stadium. Whunda was instructed to embroider the seats with San Francisco 49ers logos and make the inside man-friendly. Zen wanted Mario to know this day was about him too. Zen was the perfect wife; she could not enjoy this day alone. She always thought of her husband.

Zen was glowing with love and excitement. When her blindfold was removed, Zen noticed the stadium was packed with guests wearing team shirts, and the staff was dressed in referee gear. It was the perfect replica of a real live game. Zen cried, ruining her makeup. Mario grabbed her and held her tight.

"Don't ever let no scumbag bitch discombobulate your trust and loyalty towards me. We are forever; I was a coward and a fool to jeopardize your love in the past. None of those low-budget dirty-skin thots ever meant shit to me; it was a quick fix and a cop-out on my end. It was never nothing you did; it was always me thinking like a boy instead of being a man. I was foolish and selfish and made some terrible corrupted decisions. Zen, you are my everything, and I love you with all my heart; it took you leaving me for those long dreadful years to wake me the fuck up. The drugs, the pills and the streets clouded my judgment, and I slipped on the realness and beauty of life, but never again, my love." Mario pleaded his love to Zen with tears streaming down his face.

When it was all said and done, Zen and Mario renewed their vows and remarried on the fifty-yard line with their friends and family to witness.

As Mario kissed the bride, the buzzer sounded off like it was kick-off time. The reception was epic; Eight Ball and MJG hit the stage and kicked it off with *You Don't want Drama*. That was the biggest event and party to ever go down in Sterling. The party lasted until 4 am; the city of Greenville and surrounding areas came out to show mad love to the hood legends. Mario and Zen were the OG couple respected by many and fucked with by none.

"You did it again, sis; you got your happily ever after with your Mario," Sundae said, holding onto Zen arm. She was drunk and was taken home by Nena.

Mario and Zen danced on the fifty-yard line until the sun came up.

"You did good, Mr. Vanhorn. I love you." Zen said, rubbing Mario's shoulders.

"I'm about to do even better." Mario handed Zen a 49ers minidress that Raz had custom for that purpose; she'd complained to Mario about the country jersey dresses the models were making. Raz had completed her own design, and Mario was impressed, so he placed an order for Zen. Mario undressed Zen and placed the dress on her.

"You gotta take one for the team, bae." Mario lay Zen down on the field and made love to his wife on the fifty-yard line while she wore a lace minidress with his favorite team.

ZEN'S AND MARIO'S HAPPILY EVER AFTER, AT IT'S BEST!

Made in United States
Orlando, FL
23 June 2023